Shadows
in the
Starlight

Tor Books by Elaine Cunningham

Shadows in the Darkness
Shadows in the Starlight

Shadows
in the
Starlight

ELAINE CUNNINGHAM

A TOM DOHERTY ASSOCIATES BOOK / NEW YORK

SHADOWS IN THE STARLIGHT

Copyright © 2006 by Elaine Cunningham and The Literary Agency East

This book is printed on acid-free paper.

A Tor Book
Published by Tom Doherty Associates, LLC
175 Fifth Avenue
New York, NY 10010

www.tor.com

Tor® is a registered trademark of Tom Doherty Associates, LLC.

Library of Congress Cataloging-in-Publication Data

Cunningham, Elaine, 1957–
    Shadows in the starlight / Elaine Cunningham.—1st ed.
        p.   cm.
    "A Tom Doherty Associates book."
    ISBN 0-765-30971-8
    EAN 978-0-765-30971-6
    1. Women private investigators—Rhode Island—Providence—Fiction.
    2. Providence (R.I.)—Fiction.   3. Missing persons—Fiction.
    4. Changelings—Fiction.   I. Title.

PS3553.U472S48   2006
813'.54—dc22

                                                                2005044639

Printed in the United States of America

0   9   8   7   6   5   4   3   2

For Susan,
with thanks for the long walks
and moral support

Shadows
in the
Starlight

Prelude

At this hour of the night, the East Side of Providence was about as quiet as city neighborhoods get. The people who could afford sedate charm and architectural interest were dozing in front of their high-definition televisions, while local newscasts alternated between self-promotion and breathless promises of news and weather reports to come.

An unexpected downpour, the last April shower of the year, had just swept through on its way northward. Sound traveled with uncanny clarity in the rain-washed air, and the quick, light slap of feet against wet pavement rippled through the silence like pebbles thrown into still water.

Two women ran full out along the deserted road, soaked to the skin by the sudden shower. Both were dark-haired and both ran with single-minded determination, but there the similarity ended. Kate Myers, the older of the two, was a tall, rangy woman with a long-legged, mile-eating stride. A serious runner since high school, she was built for speed and trained to win. She still ran every day, and she played soccer on the weekends with women half her age. Tonight she was running hard, yet her much shorter companion matched her pace with ease. Kate wasn't sure whether to be impressed or annoyed.

They rounded a corner at the edge of Swan Point Cemetery and began to run beside a stone wall, a staple of the New England landscape. This one, however, was built of improbably large rocks. Huge boulders perched here and there atop these walls, giving silent testament to the precarious nature of existence.

Kate glanced into the graveyard, a nervous habit she'd been trying without much success to break. Fog was starting to rise from the rain-soaked ground, only to be swept off by a quickening wind. This part of the cemetery was more horticultural park than resting place, but Kate could envision the swirl of earthbound clouds curling around nineteenth-century mausoleums and lending an illusion of flight to angel wings of immovable stone or bronze. It was that sort of night—one that H.P. Lovecraft, one of the more famous inhabitants of the cemetery, would no doubt find inspiring.

Kate had scant appreciation for the macabre, which, given her line of work, never failed to amuse people.

A soft, slightly husky alto chuckle snapped her attention back to the run, and she realized she'd picked up the pace considerably. Cheeks flaming, she dialed back her speed and glanced at her new running partner.

Gwen Gellman was at least a head shorter than Kate, and waif thin. Her slim legs were bared to the butt by skimpy purple running shorts, and a tiny black tank top contrasted with skin so pale it brought to mind fine porcelain. Kate guessed Gwen to be about a hundred pounds soaking wet, which she currently was, and though she wasn't more than a year or two younger than Kate, she didn't look a day over seventeen. Despite all this, words like "delicate" and "fragile" just didn't apply. Five kilometers of hard running, and the girl hadn't broken a sweat. If there were any justice in the world, all that let's-go-clubbing makeup rimming her eyes would be running down her face in dark rivulets. Her hair was as wet as Kate's, but instead of hanging limp and lank, the girl's short, thick locks reshaped themselves into glistening curls.

Kate could have forgiven Gwen for all that, had she not also been a former cop with all the annoying traits of that breed. She was relentless and cat-curious, with the usual arrogant disregard for her own safety. That last, Kate would never understand. She dealt with death every day, but she was in no hurry to experience it herself. But Gwen? Kate had yet to decide whether the girl was too stupid to recognize the danger she was putting herself in, or too driven to care.

They reached the end of the course and slowed to an easy trot. This was their third shared run in as many days, and they'd fallen into a pattern: meet at Brown Stadium, run a five-K loop through the quiet charm of Blackstone Boulevard, cool down on the way to Kate's house. Her neighborhood was a tangle of narrow side streets, with tall wooden houses painted in muted pastels and cars parked on both sides of the road. The only place to run was down the middle of the streets, but at this hour there was little competition from traffic.

Gwen waited until they'd slowed to a walk to bring up her personal crusade. "I hate to nag—"

"But in my case, you'll make an exception?"

Kate's sarcasm was answered by a quick, fleeting grin. "Hey, you asked for three days. Time's up. Did you find anything new?"

"Gwen, there isn't anything to find," she said patiently. "I reviewed all my notes and test results, and found nothing to indicate that Frank Cross's death was anything other than an accidental drowning. His blood-alcohol level was nearly four times the legal limit. I'm not surprised he fell off his boat. It's a wonder he managed to get as far as he did."

"Don't think that hasn't occurred to me," Gwen said darkly. "Any sign that the alcohol was forced into him? An IV track, maybe?"

"Nothing."

They walked several paces before Gwen spoke again. "What do you know about foie gras?"

Kate shot her a puzzled look. "Foie gras? It's a pâté made from duck or goose liver, usually served on crackers. I've never tried it, though I was tempted to after watching this old James Bond movie. Sean Connery sneaks some foie gras into a spa and feeds it to his physical therapist. Judging from her reaction, it qualifies as foreplay. Before I get too distracted by that line of thought, maybe you should tell me where this is going."

"Do you know how it's made?"

She ran an impatient hand through her wet hair. "With some sort of food processor, I'd imagine. Cooking doesn't interest me."

"Me either. But I dated a chef once, and he went on and on. Apparently the geese used for foie gras have to be fattened until their livers balloon up to seven or eight times the normal size. Since no animals except humans and lapdogs willingly fuck themselves up to that extent, people shove tubes down the birds' throats and force-feed them."

Kate grimaced. "That sounds like torture."

"You think? I'm guessing anything that extreme would leave forensic evidence, even after just one time."

"It would, yes. I wasn't specifically looking for . . . intrusion of that sort, but nothing I saw suggested that consuming half a bottle of Scotch was anything but voluntary."

"That's not what happened," Gwen said stubbornly. "There's got to be another explanation."

"And I'm sure you have several."

"I'm only interested in the one that's *true,* and so far we haven't found it," she said curtly. "Alcohol can be absorbed through the colon. Did you check . . ."

"For evidence of an eighty-proof enema? C'mon, Gwen."

"Did you?" she persisted.

Kate suppressed a sigh. "Not specifically, no. But the contents of his stomach helped establish time of death. There was enough alcohol present to explain his state. You were at his house—did you see anything to indicate a struggle?"

"No, but people have been known to clean up a crime scene. And maybe there wasn't much of a struggle. You said Frank had a cut on his head. They could have knocked him out."

"More likely he hit it when he fell. What about motive? Was anything taken from his house?"

Gwen took a moment to think that over. "The investigating officer didn't see any evidence of theft," she said carefully, "but that doesn't indicate absence of motive. Frank was a cop for over thirty years. If you do the job right, you can piss off a lot of people in three decades."

"Yes, I know."

Kate's voice was sharper than she'd intended. She softened her words with a faint smile before turning away to prop one foot on the third step of her front stairs. She took her time leaning into a hamstring stretch. When she could trust herself to speak without emotion, she said, "Give me a minute, and I'll drive you home. You shouldn't be running by yourself at this hour."

The girl flashed an angelic smile. "Like the man said, 'Yea, though I walk through the valley of the shadow of death, I shall fear no evil, because I'm the meanest motherfucker in the valley.' "

"Why do cops think you're invincible?" she snapped, hearing the bitterness in her voice but not particularly caring. "No job too sordid, no street too dangerous, no risk too stupid."

Gwen's smile broadened. "Don't hold back on my account. If that's how you feel about the job, I can see why you dumped Quaid." She cocked her head to one side and considered. "Well, plus the fact that he's about as interesting as white bread with mayo."

"Actually, I didn't mind that Gary Quaid was cautious and conservative."

"But . . ."

This wasn't a subject Kate liked to discuss, but she could see how it might work to her benefit tonight. She straightened up, put her other foot on the third step, and leaned back into the stretch, holding it while she gathered the composure needed to recite the grim facts of her girlhood.

"My father was a cop. He was killed on the job when I was still in high school, by a man he'd arrested years before. Knowing this, do you really think I'd skim over Frank Cross's autopsy? Take the easy explanation without a good, hard look at other possibilities?"

Gwen nodded slowly. "Point taken. Did they get the guy?"

That wasn't the response Kate would have expected from most people, but it seemed typical of Gwen. She'd met the former cop about a week ago, just after Gwen had fished the body of her mentor and best friend out of the Narragansett Bay. From day one, Gwen had wanted answers, not sympathy. No doubt she thought everyone processed grief in the same fashion.

"They got him," Kate said shortly. "But in Frank Cross's case, there's no one to 'get.' You've got to let it go, Gwen."

"Gee, Kate, you don't seem to be very big on closure. Didn't you give the same advice to Quaid when he was following up on the raid at Winston's?"

The memory was like an icy hand around Kate's throat. "You know about that? And about the . . . warning?"

"Yeah. So?"

Kate huffed in exasperation. "*So?* Someone broke into the morgue and mutilated the bodies of the two policemen killed in the raid. In my lab. Using my equipment."

"Seems to me you'd want to find whoever did that, if for no other reason than to keep your equipment clean."

Her gaze slid away. "The police are looking into it."

"Since when? Last I heard they were covering it up. Bad for morale, or some similar pile of bullshit."

"You'll have to take that up with the department." She straightened up. "It's getting late. If you're sure you don't want a ride . . ."

Gwen took the hint and trotted off. After a few paces she stopped and turned back. "One more thing—did you ask about the fingerprints found in Frank's house?"

"His prints were the only ones found on the glass of Scotch, but you knew that."

"What about the bottle?"

"Same thing."

Gwen's eyes narrowed. "Only Frank's prints," she repeated.

"On a bottle that's probably been handled by at least a dozen people between the distillery and the package store. That didn't set off any alarms?"

"What I meant was that his fingerprints were found on the bottle. I don't know how many *other* prints were found," Kate said hastily, "but I'll see what I can find out."

"Thanks. I wouldn't ask, but . . ."

She didn't elaborate, and didn't need to. Kate knew the story: Gwen had left the force nearly two years ago under a cloud and set up a small PI business. A few people on the inside were still willing to deal with her when no one else was looking, but the investigating officer assigned to Frank Cross's case was personally offended by any hint of tarnish on the badge, and he'd spitefully—and effectively—blocked Gwen's attempts to follow up on her mentor's death. That, apparently, was where Kate came in. A medical examiner known for her obsessive habits on and off the job, she could ask the occasional odd question without raising too many eyebrows.

She waved Gwen on her way and headed up the stairs. The screened porch on the front of her house was deeply shadowed. That was strange, considering how much attention Kate lavished on safety precautions these days.

Strange, too, that she hadn't noticed the darkness until now. But the nearest streetlamp was just across the narrow road, and the light outside the house was bright enough to distract the eye from the darkness within. Kate tested the porch door and found it securely locked. Most likely the lightbulbs had burned out, or perhaps she'd simply forgotten to turn on the light when she'd left. God knows she had enough on her mind to justify a lapse or two.

She let herself in and flipped the light switch. Faint, yellow light filled the small porch. She's just forgotten to turn on the porch light, something people did every day. *Most* people, that is. For Kate, it was the equivalent of a red-flag offense. When this was over, she was definitely going to take some of that vacation time she had piled up.

After securing the dead bolt on the porch entrance, she unlocked the front door. The heavy wooden door swung shut behind her as she stepped into the hall. Here, too, the lights were off, and she palmed the wall for the switch.

It felt slightly sticky. Kate regarded her hand, and her eyes widened.

Blood, so thick and dark it was nearly black, smeared her hand. Her eyes focused on the floor beneath her feet, and she noted that the sisal mat was sodden with blood.

The familiar smells of death hit her in a sudden rush. Panic struck, and she whirled toward the door—

And fell back, stumbling a little because she couldn't tear her horrified gaze from the door. Her throat worked as she fought back waves of bile. She desperately wanted to scream and run, but the nightmare quality of the ugly little tableau stole her ability to do either.

A neighbor's dog—a squat, ugly little mixed breed that looked like a cross between a Chihuahua and a footstool—had been duct-taped to the door. The little dog had been gutted, and above the killing slash was an elaborate design, carved into its broad, nearly hairless belly. Though somewhat obscured by blood, the design was plain enough: a circular, mazelike pattern that looked like a spiral and its mirror image.

The same design that had been cut into the bodies of detectives Tom Yoland and Carmine Moniz.

Kate lunged for the doorknob. The door opened only an inch or two before slamming shut. For a moment or two she tugged at the knob with both hands, then fresh horror swept over her in an icy wave when she realized what this meant:

Someone was in the porch, holding the door shut. *Someone was in her porch. Toying* with her. Taunting her.

For a moment, anger was stronger than fear, strong enough to clear Kate's thoughts and prompt her to action. She quickly flipped the lock and raced up the stairs, taking them two at a time.

Her bedroom was a minor fortress, with a solid wood door secured not only by dead bolts but with two long metal bars that slid into braces secured to wall studs on either side of the door. There was no way anyone could kick down that door, unless they planned to take most of the wall out with it.

She dashed into the room and slammed the door, sliding the various locks into place. A metal bat, a relic of her softball days, was propped against a potted plant by the door. Kate hefted it as she moved cautiously through the room, turning on lights, throwing open closet doors, checking under the bed. As soon as she was certain she was alone in the room, she picked up the bedside phone to call for help.

There was no dial tone. She slammed the receiver back into the cradle, picked it up, and listened again. A soft, faintly husky chuckle mocked her.

The receiver fell from her suddenly nerveless hands. The intruder was in the house. He'd left the line open, waiting for her to pick up the receiver.

She ran to the nearest window and fumbled with the lock. Alarms on the window were connected directly to the police station. Opening the window was as good as making a 911 call.

Her fingers felt thick and clumsy, frostbitten with fear. Finally she disengaged the locks and pushed at the window. It raised a fraction of an inch before it stopped dead. Kate peered out the window, and her heart sank as she noticed the heavy nails driven into the outer frames, holding the lower window sash shut. She checked the other windows, just to make sure, but as she expected, she was thoroughly trapped.

A sudden flare of light drew her eye to the lone tree in her narrow back garden. High in the branches, not more than twenty feet from her window, sat a shadowy figure, holding something that appeared to be a small torch.

An eternity passed as Kate stood frozen, staring into that grinning face. Then her tormenter dropped the torch. It fell into the bed of shredded garden mulch she'd had delivered last week but had never found time to spread.

The flame flickered and died. Thank God for tonight's rain shower, she thought fervently.

Even as the thought formed, a thin tendril of smoke began to rise from the pile of wood shavings, carrying an acrid chemical smell. Small, bright flames licked across the pile and slithered toward the house.

Kate sank down onto her bed and considered her options. She had a rope ladder in her closet, and if she had to, she could break one of the windows and climb out. But if she left the house by the bedroom window, the intruder would see her. Going down through the house didn't seem any safer. Her best bet was to stay where she was and hope the police response came in time.

If indeed the alarm had been triggered.

The jangle of the front doorbell brought her leaping to her feet. She was at the door, throwing aside the first dead bolt, when it occurred to her that the bell might not be a harbinger of rescue. For all she knew, it could be the intruder's ploy to get her out of her bedroom.

She peered out the side window, looking for any hint of the strobing light that might indicate a police response. Unfortunately, no light at all found its way into the narrow side yard.

A loud thump came from the floor below. Startled, Kate jumped back from the window. As she did, she realized the source of the noise—the back door had been forcibly opened. She heard the faint sound of footsteps, and a familiar voice called her name.

Weak with relief, Kate threw back the locks and cracked open the door. "Be careful," she yelled. "There was someone in the backyard. He was in the house, too."

"Stay where you are. I'll check it out."

Long minutes passed before she heard footsteps on the stairs. She peeked out again, then swung the door open wide.

"Thank God it's you! Did you see him?"

"No. The sick bastard is long gone. There's no one here but you and me."

Maybe it was her strained nerves, but that observation struck Kate as more ominous than comforting. Her eyes dropped to the gun in her rescuer's hand.

Of course there would be a gun. Who responded to an intruder alert unarmed?

On the other hand, who took time to add a silencer to their weapon?

Kate's gaze flashed up to that familiar face, and what she saw confirmed her fears. The first bullet tore through her shoulder, spinning her around and sending her pitching facedown onto the carpet. Oddly enough, she felt the impact of the floor before her mind registered the pain of the gunshot wound. Then the pain came in a screaming, blinding rush.

The second shot slammed into her, and the third. There might have been more, but Kate was beyond the point where such things mattered. Her entire world began and ended with the white-hot agony radiating from her chest into her useless, twitching limbs.

Dimly she was aware of a cool pressure at the base of her neck, and in some corner of her mind she understood what was about to happen.

A lifetime of fear and resentment fell away, and Kate welcomed Death with a gratitude so vast it bordered on affection.

One

A sudden gust of wind blew in from the ocean, carrying the tang of salt and the recent memory of winter's chill. It ruffled through the late-spring garden and swept across the balcony of a white clapboard house built by some prosperous, long-dead sea captain. The two men seated on the balcony broke off their argument and reached to steady their wineglasses. A silence fell between them, heavy with the windswept echoes of distant shores, distant times.

Ian Forest glanced at the sea, finding no pleasure in the spectacular view his perch afforded. The ocean reminded him of a spiteful ex-wife, endlessly reciting his secrets but reserving the right to keep a thousand of her own. He swept an impatient hand across his forehead to brush aside his windblown hair and wondered, not for the first time, why Salvadore Anselm kept a house on Martha's Vineyard. Both men had roots in island cultures, and to Ian, this scenic, tourist-infested hell was a reminder of the exile they shared.

Perhaps that explained why Salvadore called him here so frequently. Perhaps he chose this place because it gave their meetings an unspoken subtext: *Of course you will serve me, for what other choice remains to you?*

Ian stifled a sigh and turned his attention to his host, a lean, fit man of indeterminate age. Salvadore's face was unlined, but he projected an aura of experience and power that, along with his thick silver hair, tricked the eye into seeing a man in his mid fifties. His ethnicity was equally elusive, though few people moved past the Italianate name to ponder the slight tilt of his sapphire-blue eyes and the sharp, angular lines of his face. Salvadore's origins might not be betrayed by his face, but his character, more often than not, was written across it plainly enough. At the moment, his gem-colored eyes held a faint sheen of malice, and his decidedly unpleasant smile celebrated the dark joys of privilege and position.

"Shall we move on to the item of business?" he suggested.

Salvadore's voice—a silky baritone that retained an indefinable Old World accent—was a perfect match to his appearance. Their people aged slowly, but it had always struck Ian as odd that their speech patterns were likewise unaffected by the passage of time. Constant, conscious effort was required to keep from lapsing into their native tongue—or for that matter, into some older version of the languages spoken in their adopted homelands.

It suddenly occurred to Ian that their conversation had lapsed into the old language as it grew more heated. Salvadore's return to English decreed an end to their dispute. Ian acknowledged this with a slight nod that signified, if not defeat, at least recognition of battle deferred.

"I've decided to put the clubs under new management," Salvadore announced. "Tonight will be your last evening at Underhill, so enjoy it while you can."

Ian suppressed a wry smile. He'd spent years keeping the sleazy "gentlemen's clubs" profitable, but insinuating that he enjoyed watching young girls undress to bad music was deliberately insulting. So, for that matter, was the assumption that he might actually rise to snap at such tawdry bait.

Instead, he lifted his wineglass. "Here's to the new manager's success."

Salvadore's cool stare acknowledged the irony in Ian's toast, but he drank to it nonetheless. Among their kind, even the most superficial ritual words held power.

"We'll need you to begin your new assignment right away." Anselm paused, lifting one silver eyebrow in mocking inquiry. "Unless, of course, you intend to observe the ritual mourning for your liege lord?"

Long years of practice enabled Ian to keep his expression pleasantly neutral. In mourning? Not bloody likely. His only regret concerning Wallace Earl Edmonson's passing was that he hadn't had the pleasure of watching the bastard die.

No, make that *two* regrets: not knowing where the earl was buried made it impossible to spit on his grave.

"I can begin at once," Ian said mildly. "Be assured that Edmonson's passing will be marked with all due honor."

Salvadore responded with a knowing smile. "No doubt. And for your service, you've been granted a singular honor: you are entrusted with untangling the earl's affairs. Not the council's business," he cautioned. "He handled those matters admirably, but a few of his side projects were . . . somewhat questionable."

Ian had few illusions concerning the boundaries of "council business." The council would never openly admit to taking a monthly tithe of Edmonson's sex and drug trade, but what other reason could they possibly cite for their unquestioning support of the man, other than the substantial financial contributions his dubious activities made possible?

"Define 'side projects,' if you will."

Anselm's expression darkened at this breach of protocol. Their business was conducted under a strict code of law and tradition, with the understanding that vague definitions, subtle evasions, and a highly selective version of the truth would provide the necessary flexibility.

"You require specifics?" he demanded in a tone that mingled reproof with incredulity.

"I do, yes. Edmonson's life was long, eventful, and thoroughly misspent. Give me a place to start."

For a long moment, Salvadore sat in silence, his face eloquent with the battle between pragmatism and custom. "The alliance with Dennis Walsh," he said at last. "It seems unwise to involve the captain of a city's vice squad in our affairs. He's in a position to learn too much about us, and it seems likely to me that any man who can be bought by one person will eventually sell to another."

Ian rolled the stem of his wineglass between his fingers as he chose his next words. "We are in agreement concerning the man's character," he said carefully, "but I understand Edmonson's reasoning in this matter."

"And you concur?"

"No, but I'd prefer to address my concerns as a separate issue."

Salvadore shifted impatiently and glanced down at the antique sundial in the garden below. "Go on."

"Edmonson's recruitment of Captain Walsh was a response to changes in the structure of local law enforcement. When the city had separate divisions for drugs, gangs, and sex crimes, it was considerably easier to arrange for certain things to fall between the cracks. Unfortunately, it occurred to some enlightened official that crimes involving drugs, sex, and gangs were frequently related, and not infrequently committed by the same individuals. An experimental vice squad was put into place. When it started to prove too effective, Edmonson thought it necessary to subvert some of the top people."

"How?" Before Ian could respond, Salvadore grimaced and shook his head. "Never mind—I don't care to know. I find the appetites of such men . . . distasteful."

"But profitable."

Salvadore nodded, either missing the subtle rebuke or choosing to ignore it. He reached for a pottery decanter and refilled their wineglasses. They both sipped, letting the honey wine slip across their palates.

The mead was exceptional—light, fragrant, and surprisingly dry. Under the circumstances, however, Ian would have preferred a less civilized drink. The sordid matters under discussion were hard enough to swallow without providing so vivid a contrast.

Apparently Salvadore thought so, too, for he carefully placed his glass aside before continuing. "Very well, you've presented the logic behind Edmonson's decision. What is *your* opinion of this matter?"

"Our ties to Captain Walsh have become personal, and therefore dangerous," Ian said bluntly.

"Ah. You're speaking, of course, of our new foundling. How much of a problem is she likely to be?"

Ian glanced meaningfully toward the glass doors that led into the upper floor of Salvadore's house. In the room beyond was a wall safe, which held, among other treasures, a blue crystal that magnified the owner's innate ability to perceive things her eyes had never seen. Neither of them had any claim to the gem, but they were agreed on the folly of placing so powerful an inheritance in the hands of an untrained, untried changeling—especially one whose loyalties were far from certain.

Anselm conceded the point with a slight nod, "Your recommendation?"

"We could remove the source of her grievance."

Dark blue eyes flashed reprovingly to Ian's face. "Killing a high-ranking official might be an occasional necessity, but in this case, the benefit hardly justifies the risk."

The hum of an approaching powerboat caught Anselm's attention. His eyes focused on the driver, then took on a slightly malevolent gleam.

Ian followed the line of Anselm's gaze. A sleek white boat cut through the wind-ruffled water and pulled up to a skillful stop by the dock. The driver swung himself up onto the dock, moving with surprising grace for someone his size. He was not much above medium height—perhaps an inch or two short of six feet—but he was considerably broader and more muscular than either of the men observing him. His hair was nearly as dark as Ian's, and his sun-browned face proclaimed his Native American ancestry.

As if sensing the men's scrutiny, the newcomer looked up toward the balcony. He shielded his eyes against the sun with one hand and lifted the other in greeting.

Ian's jaw tightened in annoyance. He had not forgotten the beating he'd taken from those hands, or the way those kind brown eyes could turn as flat and focused as any attack dog's—an analogy, come to think of it, that lay entirely too close to the truth.

Understanding crashed over Ian, and he turned incredulous eyes to his host. "That man is an enforcer."

"So?"

"You assigned him to *befriend* Gwen. To watch her, yes, and to report back any difficulties she might be having, but surely with the goal of helping ease her way into her new life!"

Anselm's chuckle was as dry and cool as snakeskin. "It's not like you to be so naïve. Our new foundling—"

"*Gwen,*" Ian interjected. "Gwen Gellman is the name she knows and uses."

"Very well, *Gwen* is a potential problem. You know that as well as I do. You also know problems tend to take root and grow if not swiftly eliminated. As for *friends,* she has enough of those—too many, for that matter. She has no need of another, and certainly not a man like Jason Cross."

That struck Ian as the best opening he was likely to get to re-open their earlier discussion. "I couldn't agree more. The man you call Jason Cross—"

"*Enough.*" Anselm's open palm struck the table, and his tone rang with finality. "He has been thoroughly tested. For the last time, let it go."

Let it go? Ignore the fact that Edmonson's attack dog was trot-ting at Gwen's heels? For several days now, "Jason" had been posing as the estranged son of Gwen's mentor, a man recently murdered by Edmonson . . . or someone in his employ. Ian had his suspicions about that, but Anselm shrugged off his concerns. He was satisfied that Jason Cross had shifted his loyalty from Edmonson to the new regime. As far as he was concerned, there the matter ended.

Unfortunately, Gwen had accepted Jason for who he claimed to be. By all appearances, he'd already found a foothold in her life—a feat that Ian had been unable to duplicate.

So he swallowed his protests and watched in glum silence as Ja-son Cross loped up the wooden stairs to the balcony, making less noise than one might expect. Whatever he saw in Ian's face seemed to amuse him.

"Am I late?" he said casually.

"Your timing is admirable." Anselm sent his companion a sly, sidelong glance. "We were just discussing how best to clean up after your former master."

Jason's smile dimmed. "With all due respect, the Middle Ages ended about five hundred years ago. I don't appreciate being referred to as if I were—"

"A rottweiler?" supplied Ian helpfully.

"I was thinking more along the lines of 'slave' or 'serf,' but sure, that will do."

Anselm dismissed this exchange with an impatient wave of one hand. "I understand that your . . . father, the late Frank Cross, assisted Gwen with her investigations. Have you been able to replace him in this endeavor?"

"Not yet. In fact, I haven't suggested it to her."

"Really. What *have* you been doing?"

"Let's see," Jason began, "I've moved into my father's house, started a new job, set up local accounts, and taken care of a hundred little things that make an identity theft bulletproof."

Ian's eyes narrowed. "Such as making sure the real Jason Cross doesn't wander onstage?"

"That won't be a problem," the man said flatly. To Anselm he said, "Gwen trusted Frank Cross, and she's inclined to extend that trust his son. But how far would this impulse go, if right out of the box I started prying into her business?"

"A reasonable argument," Anselm allowed, "but the sooner you can start monitoring her investigations, the better."

"I'm on it." Jason smiled fleetingly. "I signed up for a couple of programming classes I could probably teach. Boring as hell, but it'll provide an opening."

"Why not simply present yourself as a computer expert?"

"Anything that's too convenient and coincidental is likely to raise questions in Gwen's mind, and I don't want to give her a reason to start looking into my background. It's better if she thinks I started playing around with Frank's equipment because it was there, and got interested in learning more."

Anselm conceded this with a shrug. "Is she likely to wonder why you're such a fast learner?"

"I doubt it. If anything, she'll wonder why anyone would want to bother. Another benefit of this approach is it allows me to screen information without raising suspicion. Since Gwen isn't expecting too much from me, she'll be more likely to assume that I'm passing along everything I know."

"I'll have to trust your judgment on this matter. When do you think you can start?"

"Soon, I think. I'm playing it by ear."

"Very well. Now, what progress on Captain Walsh?"

"Gwen knows that Walsh was hooked up with Edmonson, but she hasn't started focusing on that part of the puzzle. She's been obsessed with proving that Frank Cross's death wasn't a drunken accident."

Anselm's gaze flicked to Ian. "That could be a problem."

"I'll see to it."

"And you, Jason, will work with Gwen to discover and eliminate connections between Edmonson and Walsh."

A small, grim smile touched Jason's lips. "She's not going to cover for her ex-boss, I'll tell you that right now."

"Did I suggest that? Walsh has criminal associates. Such men live dangerous and uncertain lives."

"In other words, you want the middlemen eliminated before she's able to connect all the dots," he surmised.

"Aptly put."

"What about Walsh? Hands off?"

"For the time being. Focus on the girl, and keep her from inquiring too deeply into our affairs. We need to know what she knows, preferably *before* she knows it."

Jason let out an incredulous huff. "Right. Since Gwen's an easygoing gal without a shred of curiosity, that shouldn't be a problem. Anything else?"

"There are, in fact, two more things: You can spare me your sarcasm, and you can stay out of her bed."

The young man smirked and glanced at Ian. "I wonder where *this* is coming from."

"Wonder all you like, but do as you're told. Observe her closely, and keep us informed of anything unusual. Anything. Your reports will help us judge whether or not she's equal to the path ahead."

Hesitation flickered in Jason's eyes. "What happens if you decide she's not?"

Anselm's gaze dropped pointedly to Jason's hands, which were edged with calluses formed through many years of training in a killer's arts.

"You were not chosen for this task simply because of your computer skills."

"Wait a minute—didn't Edmonson get carted off because he killed a couple of you people? Isn't that against your laws?" he protested.

"Yes, but you are not, strictly speaking, one of 'our people.'"

Jason folded his arms and leaned back against the railing. His brown eyes took on a decidedly unfriendly gleam. "That's an interesting distinction."

"I'm so gratified to learn we're not boring you," Anselm said coldly. "That will be all."

For a moment Ian thought the young fool would attempt to argue, but he pushed himself away from the rail and stalked off, making no effort to hide his displeasure. It was not particularly judicious behavior, but Ian thought better of him for it.

But not well enough to trust him with Gwen's life.

As soon as Jason was out of hearing range, Ian tried one last time. "Is it really necessary to submit Gwen to such scrutiny?"

For a moment Anselm simply stared at him. "She is a changeling," he said, giving each word exaggerated emphasis to point out that he was stating the obvious.

"She is, yes, but the usual reasoning doesn't apply. There is no question about her bloodlines."

"Nevertheless, she has spent more than three decades denying what she is. Words have power, and denial can leave a taint not easily erased."

"She has come to accept that she is not human," Ian said quickly. "She knows she is a changeling."

"But does she understand what that means?"

Ian hesitated. In truth, Gwen was a long way from an understanding of her newfound heritage. The best he could offer was, "I heard her refer to herself as one of the Elders."

The older man responded with a derisive snort. "At the tender age of thirty-four? She's little more than a child. Teach her what she is, Ian, and quickly, before she's lost to us."

"She'll be fine," Ian assured him. "In fact, this surveillance strikes me as not only unnecessary, but risky."

That observation seemed to surprise Anselm. "Risky? How so?"

For a moment Ian considered giving his honest opinion: Edmonson had been a sadistic fool, and any human who willingly served him was likely to be every bit as twisted. But Anselm's icy gaze warned him not to revisit the Jason Cross argument.

"Relying on humans always holds risks," Ian pointed out, approaching the problem from a broader angle. "Those who perceive our true nature are usually outside the accepted parameters of normality—someone with a psychic gift, a great hunger for knowledge or power, even, occasionally, an unbalanced mind."

"Whatever the case, they are all tools," Anselm stated. "Of what consequence are a hammer's hopes and dreams, so long as it drives the nail?"

The edge in his voice spoke of flagging patience. He picked up his half-empty wineglass and shifted his gaze to the expanse of open sea.

Ian knew better than to ignore so pointed a dismissal. He rose and inclined his head in deference to Anselm's position, if not to his opinion.

For he was mistaken: Ian was certain of that. Anselm had warned Jason away from Gwen's bed, but that was a routine matter borne more of esthetics than necessity. Bedding humans was usually a harmless enough pastime. But during his long life, Ian had learned that bonds, true bonds, between elves and humans could be dangerous.

Sometimes, they could be deadly.

If Ian was right about Gwen, she might become very important to the exiled elves. They could not afford to lose her, as they had lost so many changelings before.

Two

Gwen Gellman walked swiftly through the dark basement, making her way toward the faint red glow of the exit sign. All of her senses were on alert, so she was already turning when she heard the first rubber-soled whisper of footsteps behind her.

The man was close, and moving in fast. His dark face was shadowed by a hooded sweatshirt, but the way he moved told Gwen he was young and reasonably athletic. And he was big—he probably had half a foot and a good sixty pounds on her.

He was there before she could complete the turn, plowing into her like a veteran linebacker. Gwen struggled for balance, but momentum and gravity swiftly decided the outcome. As he rode her to the floor, she threw her left arm straight out in front of her and curved her other arm up to shield her face.

They hit the floor with bone-jarring force. Gwen quickly shook off the impact and took stock of her situation: facedown, no weapons within reach, heavy son of a bitch sprawled on top of her. Not great.

She rolled toward her extended left arm, using her right arm to push their combined weight away from the floor.

For a moment Gwen thought she might roll him off her, but he quickly adjusted, moving with her so that she was still pinned beneath his body. Now they were face to face, with her right arm trapped between them. The wolfish grin on his face made it clear that he considered this situation an improvement.

His next logical move would be to seize her unfettered hand. Gwen offered a distraction: she wriggled her legs out from under his, so that her legs were spread wide and their lower bodies pressed intimately together.

That surprised him into immobility, if only for a moment. Gwen could almost hear the blood rushing from his brain as he started thinking with the other organ men used in decision-making processes. She wrapped her left leg around his right, pulling them even closer. At the same time she moved her trapped arm a little, so she could slide her palm up the side of his face—a movement that read more like a caress than an attack.

Before he could make sense of all this, Gwen slapped her left palm against the other side of his face and slid both thumbs into position over his eyelids. She pressed in, hard.

A startled curse escaped him, and he reared back—not much, but enough to create some space between them. Gwen seized his right arm with both hands. At the same time, she raised her opposite knee and planted her foot, then pushed her hips off the floor as hard and as high as she could.

The man lost his balance and started to fall forward. He tried to catch himself with his free hand, but Gwen was already rolling them both toward his trapped right arm and entangled right leg.

In less than a heartbeat, their positions were reversed. Gwen kept rolling and scrambled off him. She came up on one knee, pulled one fist up to shoulder height, and drove it down hard toward his groin.

She pulled up just short of her target, her knuckles brushing the rough fabric of his jeans. Holding that position, she glanced toward the shadowy form standing by the door.

"You can hit the lights now, Stan."

Long fluorescent bulbs flickered and hummed into life. Stan—a painfully thin man clad in a gray janitor's jumpsuit at least two sizes too big for him—yawned and picked up his broom. He drifted off, looking completely unfazed by the fight he'd just witnessed. Business as usual, where he'd come from.

Gwen rose to her feet and extended a hand to her "attacker." He gave it a light slap, turning her offer of assistance into a low five, then rose on his own and ambled toward a folding chair over by the watercooler.

She turned to the nine women who sat on a semicircle of mats on the floor of the church basement, their faces flushed and damp from the hour of rigorous exercise she'd put them through. They regarded her with wide, uncertain eyes. One woman looked to be minutes away from tears. Even though they all knew the demonstration was coming, it had hit them hard.

It was supposed to.

"Let's thank Officer O'Riley for his help," Gwen said. She began to clap, and the class joined in a short-lived, halfhearted bout of applause.

Damian O'Riley lifted one hand in acknowledgement, then went back to his usual demeanor: both hands stuck in the front pocket of his sweatshirt, long legs stretched out in front of him. In that pose, he looked like a bored high-school kid, not a city cop with a college degree and the tenacity of a pit bull.

It was a dichotomy Gwen could appreciate. She'd been the same kind of cop not too long ago, and even though she had a good ten years on Damian, she still looked like a teenager. Only recently had she started to figure out why. And tonight, for the first time, she'd have to explain to someone else a mystery she herself only dimly understood.

She forced that prospect into the back of her mind and focused on the seated women.

"Before the last class, all of you will participate in staged attacks. Not like that one, not at first," she added hastily, seeing panic flash across several faces. "We'll begin with familiar exercises, like breaking holds, only instead of working in pairs, you'll work with a male partner."

One hand went up uncertainly—a soft little hand belonging to a petite brunette in her mid thirties. In her pastel pink tee shirt and matching yoga pants, her shiny brown hair caught back in a neat ponytail, she looked like someone who'd gotten lost on her way to a Mary Kay Cosmetics home party. Gwen had a pretty good idea what was coming, and she stifled a sigh as she pointed to the woman.

"But some of the techniques we're learning are meant to . . . hurt people."

"You don't need to worry about that," Gwen said briskly. "All the men I know are used to taking abuse."

Damian let out an emphatic grunt. "She got *that* right."

This surprised a burst of laughter from the women, and some of the tension slipped from their faces. Gwen didn't necessarily consider that a good thing.

"You've got to forget all about your nice-girl upbringing. When your life's on the line, there's nothing wrong with inflicting a little pain, and there are a lot of good ways to do it. If you can't go for the groin, you can break his thumbs, crush his windpipe, or rip his ears off. That last thing is a lot easier to do than it sounds, by the way.

"But," she interjected, holding up a cautioning finger, "you can't *rely* on pain. Over sixty percent of sexual attackers are on some kind of intoxicant. That can take the edge off whatever you dish out."

"Now she tells me," Damian interjected.

Gwen waited for the collective chuckle to die down. "Your best bet is usually to make as much noise as you can, break free as fast as you can, and run like hell. But you won't always have that option. What Damian and I demonstrated here was pretty close to worst-case scenario: pinned, facedown, hands trapped."

"Why do we have to act out attacks?" another woman demanded, a shrill, you-can't-make-me edge to her voice. "As long as we learn the techniques, won't the training kick in when it needs to?"

"It might," Gwen allowed, "but one of the main reasons more women don't fight off attackers is that they're frozen with shock. The whole 'this can't be happening to me' thing. It's better to get past that emotional bullshit *now* than in some parking garage the next time you have to work late."

Several heads nodded, and the woman who'd spoken acknowledged the point with a grudging shrug.

"If this class is a statistical sample, some of you are here because you've learned it *can* happen to you. Some stats say one woman out of ten is sexually assaulted, some say one out of seven. Some go as high as one out of four."

"Twenty-five percent? That seems way too high," objected a reed-thin blonde who'd introduced herself earlier that evening as some sort of state bureaucrat. She hadn't had much to say since, but hey—the woman was in a position to know what lying bastards statistics could be.

Gwen nodded. "Yeah, but keep in mind that some women are raped more than once." Because a few of them looked skeptical, she added, "Sexual assault can happen to anyone, anywhere, but all of you in this class can take precautions that simply aren't available to some women. It's hard to stay out of a bad neighborhood if you live there. It's tough to avoid a rapist if he's your mother's boyfriend, or even a family member. When I was in juvenile hall, I knew girls who'd been raped three times or more, and one, an incest victim, who'd lost count before she was out of middle school."

Several jaws dropped, and they all stared at her with the glazed eyes of people who'd gone into information overload. Gwen wasn't sure if it was the concept of multiple assaults or her casual reference to her delinquent past that tipped the scales, but she figured it was time to call it a night.

A glance at the clock confirmed this. "That's all for this class. Next week we'll work with legal weapons anyone can carry: keys, key chains, flashlights, hiking sticks, and so on. We'll be working in pairs, so bring safety goggles to protect your eyes. You can pick some up at Home Depot. Bike helmets would be good, too. If that seems extreme to you, keep this in mind: The bad guys take their work seriously."

As the somber-faced women filed out, Gwen walked over to the young cop. He gathered his long legs under him and rose, pushing back the hood of his sweatshirt to reveal close-cropped hair he'd recently dyed a reddish brown. Gwen didn't particularly like this innovation, since the color didn't provide much contrast to the rich brown hue of his skin, but hey—it was his hair.

"That went well, you think?"

"If you meant to scare the shit out of everyone, I'd say yeah, it went great," Damian said dryly. "You think any of them will come back for the second class?"

Gwen shrugged. "If they're serious about staying alive, sure they will. I'm not getting paid to make them 'feel good about them-selves,' or whatever happy horseshit the community school had in mind when they named this class 'Self-Defense: Exercise and Em-powerment for Women.' Fucking morons."

"Damn, Gellman—aren't you the perky little cheerleader to-night." He grinned at her as he thrust his hands into his pockets and rocked back onto his heels. "Now, pay up."

"Yeah, yeah. You want some coffee or something? I'm buying."

"Forget it, white girl—you're not getting off that easy. The deal was quid pro quo: something for something. I let you kick my ass—"

"You *let* me?"

"Notice me ignoring that. Quid pro quo," he repeated. "One ass-kicking in exchange for a follow-up on that kidnapping case."

Not an appealing scenario, since "that kidnapping case" had changed Gwen's entire concept of reality, but Damian was one of the few people Gwen knew who might be able to hear the story without concluding that she should check herself into a rubber room.

"I'm going to pay up," she grumbled, "but I'm dangerously de-caffeinated and really, really hungry. You?"

"Missed supper," he said. "As usual. Yeah, I could eat."

The church janitor ambled back into the room and began to gather up the mats. Gwen had known the man for years: Stan Do-manski, an ex-junkie who owed his job, and probably his life, to Gwen's friend Sister Tamar. Despite this common touchstone, Gwen had yet to get more than a word or two out of him. True to form, he returned her thanks with a noncommittal grunt and hoisted a stack of mats, staggering a little under the load.

"Maybe we should help," Damian suggested, his gaze following the janitor's unsteady progress.

"I've offered. He took it as an insult." Even so, Gwen took her time heading for the exit and glanced back twice as she led the way up the back steps. But Stan seemed to be managing okay, and as soon as he dumped the mats into a bin, Gwen shouldered open the heavy door and stepped out into a damp spring evening.

A cold, soft mist was falling, and steam rose from the storm drains on the much-patched streets as Gwen and Damian walked to a nearby sports pub.

Damian followed her to a back table, his face dubious as he took in the scattering of patrons staring morosely at the grainy screen of the room's single wall-mounted television. "You sure about this?"

"What? Since I'm buying, you want to hold out for the Cheesecake Factory? This place isn't as bad as it looks."

It was, in fact, one of Gwen's favorite haunts in this part of town. The interior was about as glum as the weather, and the waitstaff were reliably surly. For some reason, the staff all seemed to be in the late stages of a Goth phase. Gwen figured they were offended by the white stripes on the referee shirts they were required to wear. But the food was cheap and reasonably good, and the cook thought "portion control" meant that you stopped piling food on the plates when it started to fall off.

Gwen raised her oversize coffee mug and waved it like a castaway signaling a passing ship. A waitress sporting bottle-black hair and multiple piercings came over with a full pot of coffee. She rolled her eyes when Gwen told her to leave the pot, but she set it down without argument and rattled off the night's specials—no small feat, considering the size of the silver stud in her tongue.

Gwen ordered a burger and fries and Damian said he'd have the same. As the waitress slumped away, Gwen poured coffee for them both and laced hers with five little tubs of cream and two sugars. She stirred it slowly, tasted it, and added another sugar. Achieving the proper balance was an important culinary ritual, also known as "stalling."

During these preparations, a young Black man called Damian's name and came over to the table. They touched fists and exchanged a little small talk, street-style, before the conversation turned to Gwen.

"This your lady, man?"

"She's a PI," Damian said quickly. "I like to pick up some extra work, off duty. Saving for a new car, you understand."

"Uh-huh. About damn time." He nodded amiably to Gwen and sauntered off.

An uncomfortable silence settled over the table. After a few moments, Gwen said, "That raises an interesting point."

"I'm sorry, okay?" Damian said quickly. "That was rude, me not introducing you and all. It's just that a lot of people I know don't exactly get behind the interracial thing."

"Yeah, I got that, but it doesn't qualify as an 'interesting point.' The thing is, you helped me with a case, and I usually pay people who do that. If this gets to be a habit, we need to work out rates and so forth."

The chagrin faded from Damian's face. "How about we just keep it off the books? I'll help out when you need me, and you return the favor."

"That's not going to get you a new car, but yeah, we could do that." Gwen leaned back in her seat. "You have a specific favor in mind?"

"Maybe. You do prenups?"

"Prenuptial investigations? Sure. Are you looking to get married?"

He sent her a look. "My sister Shawna is thinking about it. She's a few years older than me, has an MBA, works in a bank. Does real well for herself, except when it comes to men. She can't pick 'em worth a damn. This guy talks the talk, and he *looks* solid enough, but I get this weird feeling about him. It's not just because he's sniffing around my sister. It's a family thing, but not your *average* family thing. You see what I'm saying?"

Gwen nodded. According to Damian, his family tree included a voodoo priestess, a medium, a couple of professional psychics, and the occasional water witch. Dowsing—the ability to sense underground water with some sort of crooked stick—cropped up every generation or so. The practice of folk medicine was nearly a family-wide preoccupation. Damian was pretty open about all this, and he seemed to take it in stride. He shared Gwen's pragmatic view of such things: Like the man told Horatio, there were more things in heaven and earth, yadda yadda.

"Your sister didn't inherit any of the family talents, I take it?"

"Hell no. She doesn't believe in any of that shit. But a private eye, that sounds like something she could get behind. She likes this guy a lot, but you can tell she's holding back. My guess is she lost faith in her own judgment when her last fiancé took out three Visa cards in her name and maxed them out. I could probably talk her into meeting you."

Before Gwen could answer, a caressing wind swept over her—a psychic breeze that raised goose bumps on her arms and made the hair at the back of her neck rise. The tingling sensation swept down her body, setting nerve endings on edge and leaving her feeling as if she'd spent the past fifteen minutes engaged in innovative foreplay. She didn't need to turn around to know who was approaching.

A shadow fell across the table. Damian looked up, and his jaw dropped.

Figures, Gwen noted glumly. The young cop had known there was something weird about her the first time he set eyes on her. Naturally he'd pick up vibes from the Prince of Darkness.

Three

"Sit down, Ian," she said resignedly. "Stop staring, Damian, and for chrissake, shut your mouth. It makes you look like a goldfish. Or gay."

Damian shut his mouth with an audible click, but he continued to stare as the newcomer dropped gracefully into a chair.

Gwen had to admit that Ian Forest was worth staring at: hair that was black enough to pick up bluish highlights, eyes as large and blue as her own in a narrow, fine-boned face that brought to mind fallen angels and doomed poets.

Surprisingly, Ian was regarding Damian with equal intensity. "A magus," he murmured, not sounding entirely pleased by his conclusion.

The cop's eyes narrowed. "How's that again?"

"That's not an insult," Ian assured him. "Quite the contrary, in fact. The word refers to someone who sees more than meets the common eye. You probably know its plural form, magi."

"Three wise men. Gold, frankincense, and myrrh," Gwen elaborated. "Fancy bathrobes, camels, big-ass neon star overhead. Stop me when this starts sounding familiar."

Damian shot a quelling glance at her. "I *know* what the damn word means. I just never heard it used to start a conversation before."

"That is *not* what's happening here," she said fervently. "Ian has to rush off. Right now. No time to chat."

The newcomer ignored her and extended a hand to Damian. "Let's start with a more conventional opening gambit. Ian Forest. Gwen was briefly in my employ. And you are?"

"A little freaked out, but I'm adjusting." They shook, then settled back in their chairs and continued to eye each other.

Ian was the first to break the silence. "So, Officer O'Riley, what is your theory about our Gwen?"

The cop's eyes went wary, then turned flat and cool. "Since we're asking questions, I got a couple. First: any particular reason why you should know my name? Second: I should have a 'theory' about Gellman?"

"I would hope so, yes. But I'm answering your questions out of order, aren't I? In response to the first, you came to my attention when you started investigating a collection of DNA samples taken from people who attended a certain club the night it was raided. It was suggested to you that one of those samples was not human. If you are as intelligent as your college records suggest, you have eliminated enough possibilities to suspect that this sample was taken from Gwen. Assuming you are correct, what is she?"

Damian glanced at Gwen. When she shrugged, he said cautiously, "We were gonna talk about that later tonight."

"Is there any particular reason to wait?"

"Privacy?" Gwen suggested pointedly.

Ian studied her for a moment. "You have no idea what you're going to tell him, do you?"

"I'll figure it out as I go along," she muttered. "Not that this is any of your business."

"I beg to differ, but that's a discussion that *does* require privacy.

Since the topic is up for discussion, allow me to get the ball rolling."

Ian reached out and tucked a strand of Gwen's dark chestnut hair behind her ear. Instinctively she brushed it back. Her ears weren't her best feature, and her hair, although short, was always cut to hide the top half of them—

Suddenly she knew what explanation Ian was going to give. Incredible as it seemed, he was going to play the Elder Races card.

"Don't do it," she warned him.

"Oh, come now," Ian chided. "Young Damian here has seen you in the shower with your hair slicked back, so he knows what your ears look like."

Damian choked on his coffee and set the mug down hard enough to slosh some of the brew onto the table. "You got a peeper, Gellman? If he's stalking, say the word and I arrest his ass."

"Now, there's a thought," Gwen said wistfully. A few years back, Rhode Island's legislature had upgraded stalking from a misdemeanor to a felony, with first-time offenders facing sentences of up to five years, a fine of up to ten grand, or both.

Her sigh held genuine regret. Five years without Ian Forest hanging around sounded pretty damn good. "He's not exactly a stalker. He just . . . knows things."

"Yeah? You don't get that kind of info off the fucking Internet. I look hard enough, how much you want to bet we find out he bent *some* kind of law all to hell."

"Gwen recently turned thirty-four," Ian said, undeterred by the younger man's rant. "How old does she look to you?"

"Like there's a safe answer to *that* question," he sneered.

Ian smiled faintly. "I stand corrected. One final question: You fought Gwen tonight. How would you describe that experience?"

"Like trying to hold onto a hundred pounds of Siamese cat," Damian snapped. "If you got a point, make it."

"I think you know where this is going," Ian said softly. "Surely you remember a certain weekend in upstate New York during your sophomore year of college?"

Up to this point, Gwen had been watching this odd conversation like a spectator at a tennis match. Ian's last shot went right past her, but it was pretty obvious that it'd hit Damian right between the eyes. His face fell slack with astonishment, and his gaze shifted from Ian to Gwen and back. In the brief moment Damian's eyes met hers, Gwen read in them a welter of emotions: surprise, disbelief, speculation, denial.

"What's this about?" she demanded.

The young cop shifted uneasily in his chair. "It's not a big deal—at least apart from the issue of how the hell he *knows* this stuff. Thing is, back when I was in college, I was into fantasy books, online games—that sort of thing. I even went to a few fantasy conventions, but I usually ended up feeling like one dark sock in a washload of whitey-tighties. You don't meet up with a lot of brothers at the cons, I can tell you that. Shoot, there's probably more color at your basic Klan meeting, and—"

"This is fascinating," Gwen cut in. "In fact, I can hardly wait until we're both retired and have time to sit on a park bench and swap memories."

"Yeah." Damian blew out a sigh. "Short version: There was this LARP con—that's 'live action role-playing'—in upstate New York, and a friend of mine talked me into trying it out. Everybody played a character all weekend, ran around in costume."

A moment of silence passed before Ian asked, "And what were you?"

"Seems like you the man with all the answers tonight," Damian said coldly. "You want that put on the table, *you* say the word."

"Very well. Our young friend here was an elf. A *forest* elf, to be precise—a variety that apparently comes in green and brown camouflage."

Gwen shot a venomous look at Ian, then slapped both hands down on the table and leaned over them to glare at the young cop.

"Step into reality, fanboy," she snapped. "Elves don't exist, and even if they did, *I'm not a freaking elf!*"

"Did I *say* you were?" demanded Damian. He tossed his head toward Ian. "That's his story."

"I'm just trying to understand your point of view," Ian said smoothly. "Given your particular set of interests, I wondered if you might make that connection."

"Back in the day, I used to watch *Star Trek* reruns, too. Ooh, pointy ears! How 'bout that? Gellman's ears are just a little bit pointy, so maybe I should have pegged her for a Vulcan?"

Gwen threw up her hands in exasperation and prepared to launch into a tirade. While she was still drawing breath, Ian caught her eye and asked, "An unexpected conclusion, perhaps, but I doubt it's much stranger than those she grew up hearing."

It was a surprisingly shrewd comment, and it hit the mark hard enough to deflate Gwen's ire. Her hands dropped to the table, hard, as if weighed down by her childhood memories.

The anger faded from Damian's eyes as he took in her response. "Tell it," he said softly.

"Not much to tell," she said with a shrug. "I can't remember the first time I picked up a book or toy and knew who had held it last, or walked into a room and knew what had happened there last night. When you know things you shouldn't know, people assume you're lying, crazy, or a nasty little snoop. When I was nine, a foster family added a couple of new possibilities: I was either the devil's little mouthpiece, or I was an innocent victim of evil—sort of like Linda Blair in *The Exorcist,* I guess."

"No good options," Damian concluded. "So how did *you* explain what you could do?"

"An interesting question," Ian put in. "What about it, Gwen? Any 'forest folk' in your early experiences?"

She shrugged. "Santa's helpers, Keebler cookies. Nothing that rang any bells."

"In other words, since you didn't share Officer O'Riley's interests, you were never inclined to his . . . perspective."

"Hey, man, I *know* the difference between fantasy and real life!"

"Yet some might argue that you're unusually credulous. You accept as normal all manner of occult and psychic phenomena."

Gwen caught Damian's eye. "I didn't tell him."

"Never thought you did," the cop replied grimly. "All right, here's the thing, Mr. Forest: I don't waste time trying to convince myself that something didn't happen, just because it doesn't fit into the way things are *supposed* to happen."

"You accept alternative explanations," Ian suggested.

"Yeah, you could say that. We might not understand how and why something works, but that doesn't mean it *doesn't* work."

Ian smiled faintly. "An admirable sentiment, if somewhat difficult to parse."

By this point, Gwen was starting to understand what Ian was doing. Obviously he knew of Damian's slightly left-of-center childhood and the worldview that went with it, and wanted to find out just how far that credulity went. By mockingly pushing the pointy-eared E-word, he established the whole Elder Races thing as way, *way* outside the edges of the envelope.

Which, quite frankly, was exactly where Gwen preferred to leave it.

"So, what did I think I was?" she repeated thoughtfully. "Different, I guess. I never got much further than that, but it never occurred to me that I might not be human."

"Could be the lab tech made a mistake," Damian suggested. "Or maybe there are DNA variations among humans that we just haven't found out about yet."

His face grew more animated as he warmed to that idea. "Hey, why not? My mother keeps bird feeders out back, and the little brown birds that show up all look pretty much the same. With dogs, though, you get everything from the Saint Bernard to teacup poodles. Turns out the *birds* are different species, but the big-ass dog is the same species as the little white rat with the 'fro."

"Interesting point," Ian said. "So in your opinion, Gwen might be an as-yet undiscovered variety of human?"

"You got a better theory, Einstein?"

"It makes sense to me," Gwen said quickly. "In fact, it makes a *lot* of sense. If we're determined to slap a label on me, 'changeling' works as well as any. In my case, it's literally true—I was switched with another baby. My biological parents died before they could teach me how to deal with the psychic shit that comes with being . . . whatever."

The waitress clumped over with two orders of burgers and fries, effectively halting the conversation. Ian glanced at Gwen's meal, and his eyes widened with something that looked very much like horror.

"You want to order something?" asked the waitress, sounding more than a little put out by the idea.

"Nothing, thank you," Ian murmured, still staring at Gwen's plate.

A muffled ring came from the pocket of Damian's sweatshirt. He fished out his cell phone and glanced at the number, then promptly pushed back his chair and rose.

"I gotta take this." He glanced from Ian to Gwen. "You'll be okay?"

"Go," she told him as she reached for a French fry.

Ian seized her wrist before she got there. "No," he said adamantly.

Her eyes narrowed. "Why not? Do *changelings* have problems with high blood pressure?"

"No, but there is salt on those fried potatoes," he explained. "Quite a lot of it."

"Not enough, most likely." Gwen pulled her hand free and went for the salt shaker.

Ian snatched it away before she could reach it. "Do you eat like this frequently?"

"Constantly," she said. "I've got the metabolism of a fruit fly. I can eat anything I want and it doesn't bother me. I never get sick, never gain a pound, never had a zit in my life. In fact, the worse my diet gets, the better I feel."

His face cleared in understanding. "Better," he repeated. "By that I suppose you mean more 'normal.'"

Gwen thought that over. Come to think of it, whenever "freak week" rolled around—those occasional periods of heightened psychic sensitivity—she usually went straight for the salt-and-vinegar potato chips.

"Yeah. I guess."

"And you never wondered why?"

"Not really. Now that you mention it, I can see that maybe salt takes the edge off psychic ability. I mean, too much sugar makes it hard to concentrate, right?"

"True, but you're not taking it far enough. It didn't escape my notice how eagerly you latched onto young Damian's theory of variations within the species. He's wrong, you know. You are most decidedly *not* human. Your metabolism is different, as you've pointed out. Not just faster—*different*. So is your brain and body chemistry. It's time you faced facts, Gwen: you are precisely what I spent the past ten minutes convincing your friend that you are *not*."

Gwen suddenly realized that she'd been shaking her head throughout most of this litany. She stopped abruptly and sent him a narrow-eyed glare. "What I am *not* is stupid. You're so full of shit it's a wonder your eyes aren't brown."

"Would you care to test the truth of my claims?"

To her surprise, this notion held considerable appeal. Hell, she'd take just about any challenge that would prove Ian wrong and get him off her back, or better yet, out of her life.

"Maybe," she said cautiously.

"Repeat this: 'I will eat French fries no more. My oath on it, by moon and star, wind and word.'"

Gwen burst out laughing. She quickly caught herself and dialed it down to a grin. "That's got to be the most lame-ass incantation ever created."

"Nevertheless," Ian persisted.

Her smile faded, and she shook her head. "It sounds too much like a promise. I don't make them often, but once they're made, they're kept."

"An admirable philosophy, and not at all surprising under the circumstances. Just repeat the words, then, with the assumption that they are nothing more than—what was it? A 'lame-ass incantation'? Don't consider it a promise to me. I assure you, as far as I'm concerned you can eat as many of those culinary horrors as you're able to."

"Or how about this," she countered: "You hand over the salt, we forget this whole conversation ever happened, and everybody gets to live another day."

He smiled thinly. "As soon as you say the words, I'll leave."

"Oh. Well, in *that* case . . ."

She repeated the strange phrase, then glanced at Ian and lifted one eyebrow in inquiry. He swept a hand toward her plate, indicating that she should help herself.

Gwen picked up a particularly salty potato wedge and popped it into her mouth.

An acrid stench filled her nostrils—most likely because her tongue had inexplicably caught fire. Tears rolled down her cheeks, blinding her, and her throat closed so tightly she couldn't draw breath. She palmed the table for her napkin. Someone took her hand, turned it over, and slapped the napkin into it. She spat out the offending morsel. Instantly the burning sensation disappeared and the tension in her throat eased.

Gwen set down the crumpled napkin with shaking hands and backhanded tears from her eyes. "What the hell was that?"

"An oath," Ian told her. "The Elder Folk are bound by them. Once spoken, they are almost impossible to break."

They sat in silence for several moments as Gwen sorted through the implications. Since the Big Issue was too weird to handle, she focused her attention—and her ire—on the more manageable one.

"Listen, asshole, you said you wouldn't hold me to it! You said I could eat as many fries . . ."

Her voice trailed off as realization hit.

"As you were able to," Ian finished for her.

Gwen eyed the greasy, golden pile with longing. "What the hell am I supposed to do now?" she mourned. "I *live* on these things! Ah, son of a bitch!"

Ian rose, chuckling. "Call me, and soon. You have much to learn."

"Blow me," she invited coldly.

His eyebrows rose. "Apparently, you have more to learn than I thought."

With that parting salvo, he turned and wove through the gathering crowd. The evening mist had turned into a downpour, and people were pushing their way into the pub. Ian made his way through the standing-room-only crowd as easily as a fish passing through water. Openings just seemed to happen as he approached.

"You didn't have to wait for me," Damian said as dropped back into his chair.

Gwen snapped her gaze back to her companion's face. "I didn't. Talking to Ian made me lose my appetite."

"*There's* a first! You're not going to eat that?"

"Help yourself."

She barely had time to snatch up her burger before he took her plate and dumped its contents onto his own. She tried not to glare as he started to munch his way through the pile of fries.

"So, what's the story with that guy?"

"Pretty much what he said. I worked for him for a little while— long enough to figure out that whatever I am, he's one, too. But you already picked up on that."

Damian nodded, since his mouth was too full of fried potatoes to permit speech. He hastily chewed and swallowed. "So he's teaching you about that changeling stuff?"

"Something like that, yeah."

The cop considered this, then frowned. "I don't like it. I mean, I can see how you'd want to know about this shit. I just don't like this Forest guy."

"Who does? And to tell you the truth, I don't want to think about him right now." She reached for the ketchup and liberally anointed her burger. "You were asking about a prenup investigation for your sister?"

With obvious reluctance, Damian resigned himself to a change of subject. "Shawna's going to want details before she commits to the idea."

Gwen leaned back in her chair, relieved to be back on familiar, solid ground. "For some people, it's not much different from the credit checks her bank does every day. But if you're getting a bad feeling about this guy, your radar probably isn't picking up on his credit report. Personality glitches usually show up in how he relates to family and employees. I'll observe him, find ways to talk to people who know him. Ex-wives and old girlfriends are usually a good source of information."

"I'll bet. Problem is, Shawna's not about to listen to gossip. She likes *data*, you understand."

"And she'll get it. Tell your sister I confirm ID, check employment history, confirm school records, look into family history, and check for a police record."

"That last thing, I've already done."

"Yeah, I figured, but does *Shawna* know that?"

"Good point," he conceded. "Just so you know, she's also going to ask about your experience, maybe check some references."

"No problem. Not all precommitment checks are run on future spouses. One of my best clients is a corporate headhunter. She likes to run a thorough resume check before she recommends someone for a high-ticket job. Your sister can call her if she wants. I've also made 'discrete inquiries' for a university that wanted certain professors checked out before they got tenure—apparently it's pretty damn hard to get rid of them, afterward. I've even heard from a couple of local politicians who wanted me to scope out the opposition."

This earned her an incredulous frown. "You do that?"

"You're kidding, right? The only time I worked for a politician was when some guy hired me to look into his *own* past. He wanted to see what an opponent might be able to dig up. Basically, he wanted me to test the locks on the family skeleton closets."

He let out a long, low whistle. "Damn! I can't decide if that's really smart, or really sleazy. He win the election?"

"He decided not to run. Let's just say my report made for interesting reading." Gwen paused for a grim smile. "I might not vote, but I occasionally do my civic duty."

"Why settle for 'occasionally'? You were on the job," he pointed out, "and you could be again."

Gwen noted the fervor in his eyes and suppressed a sigh. Damian was gung-ho about clearing her name and getting her back on the force. She'd put him off for over a week, explaining that she needed time to get her head around recent events. Since "recent events" included the death of Gwen's first partner, Damian had made an attempt at patience. At the moment, however, he looked to be running about a quart low on that particular virtue.

"I've *got* a job," she told him. "Or maybe you forgot hiring me a few minutes back?"

Damian heaved a sigh. "Can you meet Shawna tomorrow morning before she goes to work? Say, eight-thirty, at that coffee shop down by the waterfront walk?"

"That'll work."

"One more thing." A flush crept up his cheeks, adding an interesting richness to the dark color of his skin—and cuing Gwen in on what was coming next. "My sister doesn't know that we . . ."

"Danced the horizontal tango?" she suggested helpfully. "Had carnal knowledge of each other? Got the sexual tension thing out of the way so we could get on with the process of establishing a working professional relationship?"

"Yeah, that. No offense, it's just that my family's kind of . . ."

He trailed off again, obviously expecting her to understand and fill in the rest.

But Gwen continued to regard him with wide eyes and a politely inquiring expression. She didn't have much use for social conventions of any sort, and saw no good reason to let him off the hook on this one—especially since this was the second time tonight the issue had come up.

"The thing is," he said hesitantly, "Shawna thinks—actually, most of my family thinks this way—that people should stay with their own kind."

"When you say 'own kind,' I assume you're talking about DNA?" Gwen inquired sweetly. "Can't bring a changeling home to Mama?"

Damian's face fell slack. After a moment he let out a rueful chuckle. "Puts an interesting new spin on that sort of thing, doesn't it?"

"I thought so." She leaned forward and whispered, "Oh, and Tyra Banks? Halle Berry? Beyonce? They're all changelings, too. Sorry if that puts a dent in your fantasy life."

His wry grin acknowledged the hit. "You just got to go for the takedown, don't you? It must have damn near killed you to pull up short on that groin punch tonight."

Gwen settled back in her seat. "It hurt," she admitted as she reached for her burger. "But strangely enough, I'm feeling much better now."

Four

"Holy shit," Damian said as he stared at the elaborate wrought-iron gate at the entrance to Sylvia Black's long gravel drive. His gaze flicked past it to the stately brick house, the sweeping hedge of white lilacs behind a sea of white tulips and irises. The rain had stopped, and a brisk wind was breaking up the clouds and sending the pieces skittering seaward. Dark cloud ribbons slid across a nearly full moon. Sylvia's white garden was luminous in the faint, dappled light.

"*This* is where you live?"

"Sort of. I have an apartment over the garage—that little building over there. I help with security."

"How'd you score this gig?" he demanded.

"It's a long story, and not really mine to tell. Let's just say that my landlady has a colorful past."

"Sounds like another tale for us to swap at the old cop's home. Before you go, I got something for you."

Damian leaned over and popped the glove compartment. He fished out a computer disc in a plain white paper sleeve and handed it to Gwen.

"Here's a copy of the files my friend recovered from your old hard drive. We've got to talk about this someday real soon."

"Sure."

"Soon," he emphasized. "I know there's a lot on your mind, but cases get colder as time goes by, not easier."

Gwen wanted to argue, but damn it, the kid was right. She slumped back into her seat. "I'm listening."

"Quick recap," he said. "Captain Walsh said you'd requested a personal leave, when he really assigned you to shadow Tiger Leone. The preliminary report you sent him before you went undercover was deleted, but not *gone,* you understand. When they tossed your old computer, I took it and had the hard drive stripped. The files on that disc prove you were doing exactly what you were told. Walsh is *owned.*"

Gwen brandished the disc. "It won't be enough."

"It will get people asking questions," he argued. "The rest will come out."

"Yeah, but after how many more people get fucked over? If you like your job, remember what happened to me and think long and hard before you take on Walsh."

Damian's face hardened. "You lost your job, sure, but two others died. Maybe three, if you count Frank Cross."

For a long moment Gwen stared at the young cop, too stunned to comment. She had good reason to know that Captain Dennis Walsh was a lying sack of shit, but a cop killer?

As far as she was concerned, Wallace Edmonson had killed Frank. Walsh was connected to Edmonson somehow, but she'd never considered the possibility that the captain was responsible for Frank's death, or for the two cops killed in the nightclub bust. She'd spent fifteen years as a cop, fifteen years taking part in something she considered flawed but basically decent. No matter how badly that had ended, a part of her didn't want to believe any cop, including Walsh, could be that twisted. Cop-killing police captains were movie monsters—celluloid nightmares about as likely as were-wolves and zombies.

On the other hand, the official ruling on Frank Cross's death was bullshit. Gwen would bet her life on that. Yet Frank's autopsy showed he was well over the legal limit, and Kate Myers, the medical examiner, had a sterling rep. When Gwen heard the results, she'd assumed that the killer had forced the alcohol into Frank somehow, but maybe the explanation was a lot simpler: Maybe Kate had lied.

She *had* been pretty nervous the first time Gwen talked to her, and totally freaked out by the B and E at the morgue that resulted in the mutilation of two dead cops. Since the pattern cut into their bodies was identical to the torture-tracks left by a trio of serial killers in Edmonson's employ, Gwen had figured the threads all tied together. But maybe Kate Myers was a loose thread, one left dangling when Edmonson disappeared.

And since the autopsy results and the fingerprint evidence were telling the same story, maybe someone in the police department was attached to Frank's death by yet another thread.

"If Walsh is dirty," she said slowly, "no one in vice is safe until this thing is over."

"There you go. Why do you think I keep trying to get you in on this?"

She conceded that with a curt nod. "I assume you've been doing more than just nagging me to get off my ass. Bring me up to speed."

"Now you're talking. That club that was raided? Winston's? Leone had two other clubs, and someone's still running them. I know for a fact they're still selling shit."

That didn't surprise Gwen. Tiger Leone had worked for Edmonson. Both men were gone, but that didn't mean the operations would automatically shut down.

"I went to one of the clubs, checked out the local talent," Damian went on. "You remember Jackie Teal?"

"One of Tiger Leone's girls. She snuck out the back the night Winston's was raided. Pretty girl—a Janet Jackson type."

"Right down to the malfunctioning wardrobe. Jackie's dancing at Extreme, a titty bar not far from the Foxy."

Something in his face set off warning bells in the back of Gwen's mind. "You wouldn't happen to know if she's doing any private dancing on the side?"

His gaze slid away. "I figured, hey—if I could get her alone and talking, maybe she'd say something I could use. A lap dance isn't my idea of a good time, you understand—too many rules, not enough hands."

"You're oversharing," Gwen advised. "Get to the point."

"Jackie offered me a hit of something new. It was like X, she said, only it started out mellow and worked up to wild."

Gwen sat bolt upright. "Please tell me you didn't buy some to test, not on your own time."

"How stupid do I look?" he said indignantly. "I told her I didn't have the money on me, but I could put some together. If this shit was as good as she said, I could maybe put a lot of money together. She promised to set me up with a guy who could get me all I wanted."

"A drug bust," she mused. "Not a bad way to jump-start an official investigation."

"That's my thinking."

"And if you can nail this dealer, maybe he'll give up someone a notch up the ladder. Keep at it long enough, you might eventually tie this to Walsh . . . *if* you're still around by the time the leads link up."

He shrugged. "So I'll work other angles, too, and come at it from every which way. You said Walsh was tied in with that attorney whose kid was snatched?"

"Ryan Cody, but that's a dead end. Walsh and Cody were only connected through a third man. He's gone."

As she spoke, Gwen had a sudden image of Ian Forest dragging Carl Jamison's body toward an ancient maple tree—and then simply vanishing. The police hadn't found a trace of the Jamison brothers or the homicidal bitch the two freaks shared. Ian was really, really good at making bodies disappear, and last time Gwen had seen Edmonson, Ian's men were taking him away. She was willing to bet Damian would find Hoffa before he found Edmonson.

Damian's eyes narrowed in speculation. "You know where this guy is, don't you?"

"Haven't got a clue." Since he still looked skeptical, she added, "You remember me telling you what Kate Myers said, about those three bodies that disappeared from the morgue thirty-some years back?"

"Sure."

"Two of them were my parents, the other was the kid they'd swapped me for." She sent him a warning frown to stave off sympathetic commentary and kept going. "I don't know much about . . . changelings, but apparently we keep a low profile. To the point where when one of us dies, the bodies don't get found."

Damian's eyes held a hundred questions, but he had the sense not to ask most of them. "So you're saying this Edmonson was one of you people?"

"As much as I hate to admit it, yeah, that's what I'm saying."

"And he's dead."

"I never saw a body, but yeah, that'd be my guess."

"No one's filed a missing-person?"

"Not going to happen."

"And if someone wonders where he went?"

"They'll find out someone using his passport took a one-way flight to Greece. I did some checking. Trust me, there's no finding this guy."

The cop blew out a long breath. "Okay, then I'll keep looking until I find a better lead."

It was on the tip of Gwen's tongue to remind him that *he* could disappear as easily as Jamison and Edmonson had. But why bother? He'd listen to her about as well as she'd listened to Frank's words of caution when *she* was a rookie. Of course, she'd had Frank looking out for her back then. Damian just had Quaid, and Gwen hadn't been too impressed with the way Quaid had watched *her* back. On top of that, there was the tie between Quaid and Kate Myers. If Kate was dirty, that increased the chances that Quaid was also tainted.

"What about your partner?" she asked. "What does Quaid say about this?"

"Not much. Be careful, watch your back. Keep me posted. Like that."

"Is he working with you?"

Before he could respond, the metallic purr of a high-ticket car caught his attention. The vehicle slowed and pulled off the road to park directly behind them. The headlights flared, brightly illuminating the interior of Damian's car.

Gwen's eyes had always adjusted quickly, so while Damian

blinked and cursed, she noted the silver gleam of a tidy little BMW sedan. Marcy Bartlett's car, though what Marcy was doing here at this time of night was anyone's guess. Gwen reached into the pocket of her battered leather jacket for her cell phone and switched it on. Sure enough, there were two messages from Marcy's number.

"What now?" Damian complained, reaching under the seat for his weapon. "Can't a man go off duty?"

She dropped a hand on his shoulder. "There's no problem. That's a friend of mine. She was probably just checking to see who was in the car. I'll call you tomorrow."

She got out of the car and slammed the door. The old hatchback took off, leaving Gwen standing in a small cloud of exhaust fumes.

Damn, he really did need a new car! Not that she could talk. Her aging Toyota was in the shop, and there it would stay until she came up with the ransom money to pay for a new transmission.

Gwen went over to Marcy's car and tapped on the driver's window. The door opened just enough to allow Marcy to slip out. She shut it quickly behind her.

Despite the late hour, Marcy was still in her lawyer clothes: a trim gray pantsuit, a silk blouse in royal blue, low-heeled black pumps, sapphire studs in her ears. But her usually sleek blond wedge was rumpled and her eye makeup thoroughly smeared. Either she'd been running her hands through her hair and rubbing her eyes—something she did only when her personal life went south—or she'd thrown her clothes back on after a quick tumble.

No doubt Trudy, Marcy's live-in gal pal, would assume the latter. Calling Trudy possessive was like calling George Dubya conservative—it was a good start.

"Don't you ever answer your phone?" Marcy demanded.

"Yeah, nice to see you, too. Who's in the car that you didn't want me to see?"

Marcy glanced over her shoulder at the idling BMW. "I've got a client for you. I wouldn't have brought him here before talking to you, but this is really important. I want you to promise me that you'll listen to him before you start cursing and throwing things."

A bizarre suspicion reared its head. Gwen folded her arms and studied her friend intently. "You jumped out of that car like a bat out of hell, and now the 'listen before you start throwing things' speech? I can only think of one person who'd need this much prep work, but your ex is the last person you'd bring here."

The expression on Marcy's face was all the answer Gwen needed.

"Goddammit, Marcy!" she exploded. "Hasn't Kyle Radcliff done enough damage? How long did it take you to get rid of his ass? How many times did he send you to a doctor before you got rid of him? I didn't risk my career kicking the shit out of him so we could get together later and talk about old times."

Marcy glanced back at the car. "Keep it down," she said urgently. "I had a hard enough time convincing Kyle to talk to you without reminding him of that scene."

"Give me a fucking break," Gwen retorted. "Face it, Marcy: Your bullshit meter shuts down the minute that guy starts talking. If he came to you with a problem and you ended up bringing him here, you can be damn sure that was his intention all along."

The lawyer thought this over, then shrugged. "Whatever his method or motivations, he's here. Look at it this way: he might be a complete bastard, but he pays his bills religiously. You said business was slow right now."

"Not *that* slow."

Marcy seized Gwen's shoulders with both hands, and the expression on her face forestalled Gwen's protests.

"I wouldn't ask you to do this if it wasn't important," she said with quiet intensity. "His son is missing."

Anger and indignation slowly slipped away. In Gwen's corner of the world, a missing kid trumped old grudges every time.

She hadn't heard that Kyle had remarried. He and Marcy had divorced about eight years ago. Factoring in wife-hunting and baby-making time, she figured Kyle's son would be very young. If he looked anything like his father, he'd be fair-haired and too damn cute for his own good.

And that was a big problem. Blond boys, aged four and under, were a favorite snatch. They were young enough to be attractive to adoptive parents trying to bypass the system's red tape, and old enough to be of interest to the worst class of pedophiles. Not that there was a *good* class of pedophiles, but there were maggots out there who'd buy a preschooler and call him a "throw-down piece." Same idea as an unregistered gun: use it and lose it.

Gwen took a steadying breath and stepped out of her friend's grasp. "How old is the kid?"

"Patrick just turned five. He and his mother have been gone nearly two days now."

The cold, sick feeling in the pit of Gwen's stomach disappeared, washed away by a sudden flood of exasperation.

"The mother's gone, too? Jesus wept, Marcy, why didn't you say so!"

"Kyle is just as worried about his wife as he is his son," she said defensively. When Gwen lifted an eyebrow in pointed challenge, she admitted, "All right! I focused on the kid because I knew it would get your attention."

"Let's review the facts, shall we? Kyle Radcliff has a history of spousal abuse. Wife number one divorces his ass. Good for you. Wife number two takes off with the kid. Good for her. I hope she *stays* missing."

"Talk to him," Marcy urged. "He's changed, Gwen, I swear it."

"Oh yeah—this is the very first time you've heard *that* story!"

"It's not Kyle's fault that Erin and Patrick are missing," Marcy went on doggedly. "He's frantic with worry. He loves Patrick. You know how much he wanted kids. Especially a son . . ."

Her voice caught, and her gray eyes were suddenly brighter than they should be.

Gwen, appalled and enlightened, bit back a heartfelt curse. So *that's* what was behind this little ambush! Kyle Radcliff, the schmuck, still knew how to push his ex-wife's buttons.

Marcy Bartlett was one of those rare people who were equally successful in love *and* war, which wasn't a bad description of her work as an assistant DA. Her cross-exam fell just short of vivisection. Professionally, she was amazing, and her personal game was just as tight. She was in a mostly happy relationship with a pretty and only moderately neurotic lit professor; she was on speaking terms with her family; she had good friends, a new condo, a great car, and a fat portfolio that had weathered the tech fallout.

Most people looking at the Marcy Bartlett package would find it hard to understand how she could have put up with Kyle Radcliff. But they'd married young, before Marcy had sorted out the lesbian thing. To complicate matters, she was only twenty-six when she'd been diagnosed with ovarian cancer. They'd caught it in time to save her life, but not her fertility. Unable to have children, ambiguous about her sexuality, Marcy had believed the verbal abuse Kyle dished out. Gwen had seen time and again how small a step it was from verbal abuse to the ER. Marcy had probably bought into the notion that she'd earned her "punishment" long before Kyle had landed the first blow.

Nearly ten years had passed since Gwen answered a neighbor's call regarding a domestic disturbance. She'd been stunned to learn that the victim was the tough young legal aide she'd run into at court two or three times. Gwen had decided that Radcliff had resisted arrest. Fortunately, Radcliff didn't want anyone to know he'd gotten his ass handed to him by a girl half his size. He didn't press charges, and better yet, he finally agreed to give Marcy a divorce and leave her alone.

The memory of his tenacity, even more than the pleading look in Marcy's eyes, convinced Gwen to hear what Radcliff had to say. All things considered, she'd rather have his attention focused on her than on Marcy.

"You go on home," she said at last. "The asshole can call a cab when we've finished talking."

Marcy gave her a quick hug and tapped on the window of the driver's door. The passenger door opened and a tall blond man climbed out.

Kyle Radcliff looked a lot older than he had the last time Gwen had seen him. There were a few fine lines around his concrete-colored eyes, and his hair was considerably thinner. As he rose from the car, she could see moonlight reflecting on scalp. But he was still fit, perfectly groomed, and wearing a couple thousand dollars worth of suit. Kyle was a corporate lawyer of some sort, and very successful at his job—which was another reason he'd finally agreed to a quick, no-fault divorce. Last Gwen heard, the man had some serious assets.

He strode around the car and extended his hand, as if she were another attorney who'd agreed to a consult.

"Thank you for seeing me," he said with polite insincerity.

Gwen just looked at his hand, and after a moment it dropped to his side. She turned her back on him and strode to the gate, punched the code into the security box. The iron gates swung inward.

They walked in silence to the garage. Gwen unlocked the small, first-floor room she used as an office, flipped on the light, and nodded toward one of the wingback chairs.

Kyle hitched up his sharply creased trousers and sat, cautiously, as if he suspected the chair was not only wired for high-voltage current but plugged into a faulty outlet.

Gwen settled down behind the table that served as a desk and folded her hands. "So, you have two missing persons."

He seemed relieved to be getting right to business. "My wife, Erin Westland, and our son, Patrick."

"You have pictures?"

Kyle reached into the inside pocket of his suit jacket and took out a wallet-size photo of a pretty young woman and a dark-haired, solemn-faced little boy.

A jolt of something very like recognition surged through Gwen as she studied the woman's face. The features were delicate, her mouth rosebud small, but her eyes were wide and very blue. The only time Gwen had seen eyes that big or that blue was when she looked in a mirror.

But there the similarity ended. This girl was a model of Barbie-doll femininity. Her makeup played up her pink-and-white coloring, and a soft blue sweater clung to impressive curves. Glossy, dark-brown hair fell in soft layers to her shoulders, framing a narrow, heart-shaped face. Her hair on the side nearest little Patrick was tucked behind one ear—an ear that, like Gwen's, was definitely not her best feature.

"How old is Erin?" Gwen asked.

A strange look slid across Kyle's face. "She was twenty-three when we met. That was about eight years ago."

"Really. For someone on the downhill side of thirty, she's holding up pretty well."

"Erin looked young for her age when we met," he said cautiously. "She hasn't changed much since."

"You ever wonder about that?"

He nodded. "Yes, but it didn't become an issue until things started going wrong."

Gwen put down the picture. "Let me guess," she said coldly: "Old habits die hard?"

"As usual, you'd be wrong. I never laid a hand on Erin. She never needed it," he added nastily.

"Don't go there," Gwen warned. "Just tell me your story, so we can get this over with."

Kyle took a deep breath and began to recite. "A couple of years ago, Erin starting having terrible nightmares. She couldn't sleep. Depression set in, and she was getting more and more withdrawn. She's an adopted child, and she became obsessed with finding her birth parents. She wouldn't let me help her—she said it was a personal thing, something she had to do alone. After a while her mood passed. She developed new interests, including a little business of her own. Then Sunday night, she and Patrick went out to pick up a pizza and never came back."

"Two days ago."

"If you're implying I should have come to you sooner, what would the point have been? You're not going to help me."

Ordinarily he would have been right. But three weeks ago she'd changed the name of her business to "Changeling Detective Agency." This was not only an acknowledgement of her identity, but a mission statement. There were other changelings out there, and Gwen intended to find them. It was that simple.

"I'd do it," she said curtly. "But first I want to know why you came to me. And don't try to sell me on 'Marcy talked me into it,' because we both know that's bullshit."

Kyle Radcliff was silent for several moments. "I saw you in the courthouse last week, when you came to testify in the Fergusson insurance case. You looked exactly the same as you did ten years ago. I don't know what that means, but I can't shake the feeling that it's important. That perhaps you and Erin are two of a kind—whatever that means. I thought it might give you an edge of some sort."

He shook his head and gave a short laugh, as if he'd just overheard his own words and couldn't believe his ears. "The bottom line, I suppose, is I'm desperate enough to try anything."

His litany sparked a connection Gwen hadn't yet made—a prospect that sent her heart racing at near-panic pace.

What if Erin Westland knew far more about a changeling's life than Gwen did? What if she had simply moved on, knowing she'd have to eventually? The thirtysomething mother in Kyle's picture looked like a teenager. Chances were she'd *still* look like that when her kid was in high school. Maybe she'd figured out what Gwen was just beginning to grasp: she was aging so slowly that she'd probably still look like jailbait in another five, ten, even twenty years.

She took a long, calming breath. "I'll need all the information you can give me," she said briskly. "Start with that new business you mentioned, and a list of Erin's friends. I'll also need her ID: driver's license, Social Security number, and so on."

Kyle's eyes narrowed. "You're a PI. Can't you get that information yourself?"

"Yeah, but why waste my time and your money, when you could just tell me?"

He hesitated. "To be honest, I don't have much information to give you."

"Sure you do. There are tax returns, a marriage license."

"Erin doesn't have an income, and we don't file a joint return. In fact, while I refer to Erin as my wife, we never actually married in a conventional sense."

"Oh, so *that's* why we never got a wedding invitation!" Gwen said. "Too bad—I'll bet Marcy and Trudy would have loved dancing with the bride."

She allowed herself a moment to enjoy the discomfiture in Kyle's eyes. A lot of guys might fantasize about watching their wives do another woman, but an ex-wife who'd sworn off men entirely? Not high on the list of macho turn-ons.

"What about Erin's bank accounts and credit cards?" she asked, getting back to business.

"I handle the family finances. Erin gets an allowance for personal expenses, and her credit cards are attached to my accounts."

Still the control freak, Gwen noted. "Okay. But you must have done some sort of cohabitation agreement—common-law prenuptial, or whatever the hell people do these days when they're shacking up long-term. If nothing else, you would have made damn sure she couldn't just take the kid and leave—"

Suddenly Gwen realized why he was here. In custody cases, the courts usually favored the mother. If the parents weren't married, the bias toward the female parent was that much stronger. If Kyle didn't have legal custody over the child, there was no reason why Erin Westland couldn't take her son and go whenever she pleased—

provided she could find a way out of the cushy cage Kyle had built around them.

The expression on Kyle's face confirmed her suspicions. Gwen lifted one eyebrow.

"I love Erin, and I love my son," he said. "I'll do whatever it takes to get them back."

"Yeah, you made that point by coming here. I'll find Erin. Whether or not she comes back is up to her."

"Fair enough."

For nearly half an hour, Gwen asked questions and jotted down information. The more interesting questions, however, were the ones she didn't ask aloud.

Was Erin Westland simply moving on? Or had she, too, recently found out a little more about herself than she could handle?

There was also the possibility that Erin was on the run. She'd been looking for her family. Assuming she found them, how did they respond to Erin's son, who was apparently a half-breed? Did they try to eliminate such children to keep the bloodlines "pure"?

Gwen wouldn't put it past them. Judging from what she'd seen so far, the "Elder Races" were a ruthless bunch. Ian Forest had hired her to investigate her own parents' deaths, in hope that she'd get their killer—her uncle, who at the time was looking for Gwen with murderous intent—to admit what he'd done. Apparently Edmonson had been eliminating family members so he could deploy some sort of magical trinket. It turned out he couldn't, but Gwen *could,* and therein lay Ian's logic. He figured Edmonson needed her, and needed to explain to her *why* she was needed. Ian had followed her around throughout and made damn sure Edmonson's words were witnessed.

Gwen didn't understand all the ramifications of this, but using the newbie changeling as a big, dumb tool? Yeah, she got that part. And the family treasure? Ian wanted to put the trinket "somewhere safe, until she was able to use it." Gwen figured she'd embrace *that* possibility the same day she took up celibacy.

There was one more possibility, and Gwen gave voice to it as soon as Kyle's store of information ran dry.

"Looking over the details on Erin, it occurs to me that someone made it pretty easy for her to disappear."

A red flush crept up Kyle's face.

"If I was going to hurt my family, why would I hire you to find them?"

"You'd be surprised what people hire me to do. But rest assured, that's one of the questions I'll be looking into," she told him. "If you can live with that, my retainer is fifteen thousand."

"Agreed."

Gwen took a copy of her standard agreement and several release-of-information forms from the file cabinet, filled in blanks, and handed them to Kyle to sign. He pulled his chair closer to her writing table and set to work without comment.

It was a good thing he didn't haggle about the price, Gwen noted. If Kyle was planning to set her up somehow, she'd need the bail money.

A month ago, that thought wouldn't have occurred to her. Kyle Radcliff wasn't stupid, but Gwen was pretty confident he couldn't pull off a complicated sting. But now, her pride still smarting from her unwitting part in Ian Forest's little game, she wasn't about to overlook any possibility.

Being paranoid sucked, but Gwen figured it was a lot better than being dead.

Five

Shawna O'Riley looked a lot like her brother, right down to the dark auburn hair. Gwen had no problem picking her out of the morning-glum crowd at Brewed Awakenings. It helped that Shawna dressed like a bank exec. She looked very polished and professional in a tailored navy coatdress trimmed with white, matching navy pumps, and artful makeup—which meant that she'd spent a lot of time to make it look like she wasn't wearing any makeup at all.

Gwen had taken the professional route herself this morning: a purple shirt with at least half the buttons done up, black pants, and boots with a stacked sole and chunky heel instead of her preferred stilettos. Her makeup wasn't nearly as subtle as Shawna's. Lots of black mascara and dusky eye shadow rimmed her eyes, a honey-beige foundation darkened her too-pale skin, and her full lips were the color of juicy plums. For her, it was a conservative look.

She pushed her way to Shawna's table and got the introduction thing out of the way. Her prospective client gave her the usual dubious once-over, but she was nicer about it than most. Most likely Damian had told her enough to take the edge off her surprise.

As Gwen sat down, she noted there were two cups of coffee on the table. Oh yeah—definitely nicer than most clients.

"Extra cream, extra sugar," Shawna said with a faint smile.

"Perfect," Gwen assured her. "Your brother doesn't miss many details, does he? Makes him a good cop."

"He speaks highly of you, too. It seemed important to him that you and I meet. To be frank, that's the only reason I'm here."

"Damian said you'd probably have reservations."

"Of course I do. If you love someone, you're supposed to trust him, not have him investigated."

"That's a good theory, but divorce statistics don't back it up. Taking a good, hard look at a prospective spouse is smart. You wouldn't give a loan to someone without checking his credit, right?"

"Of course not, but it's not the same thing."

"No, it isn't. Money is a lot less important."

Shawna smiled. "That's a good argument, but not the one I might have expected you to use on a banker."

"I didn't come here to make *any* argument, good or bad. If you don't want to do this, say the word and I'm gone."

The woman took a moment to think it over. She nodded toward Gwen's oversize cup. "Go ahead and drink that. It'll be cold before too much longer."

It wasn't the first time a client couldn't bring herself to say outright the words that would sic Gwen on a loved one. She took a sip of her coffee and nearly moaned when it hit her taste buds. If Ian Forest had made coffee off-limits instead of French fries, she would have had to kill him right then and there, and to hell with the witnesses.

She set the cup down with reluctance. "Tell me about your fiancé."

"He's not my fiancé, at least not yet," Shawna corrected, "but things are heading that way. Roy is a great guy. I couldn't begin to tell you why Damian has a problem with him."

"So you think Damian is overreacting?"

Shawna hesitated. "I want to say yes, but my brother's instincts are usually much better than mine. By the way, what did Damian tell you about Roy?"

"Nothing much. Tell me what *you* see."

The woman went into her spiel: Roy was smart, athletic, good-looking, responsible, a good conversationalist, and a decent dancer. He had a good education and a good job. They apparently had similar tastes, values, and political opinions.

Ooh, similar *political* opinions! How hot was that? To Gwen's way of thinking, this relationship was sounding about as interesting as fettuccine without Alfredo.

"But?" she asked when at last the litany ran down.

Shawna bit her lip, a gesture that mingled reflection and consternation. "If I had any worries at all, they wouldn't have to do with Roy."

Gwen steeled herself for a recitation of the usual feminine insecurities. It seemed that every woman she met, no matter how smart and successful and attractive, harbored a few self-doubts when it came to men.

"So what's the problem?"

"It might not actually be a problem. It's just that my family can be a little . . . eccentric. Roy's pretty conventional."

"Has he met any of your family?"

"Yes, but only my parents, Damian, and our three younger brothers. We had dinner together last weekend at a nice Italian place on Federal Hill. The boys were on their best behavior, and the evening went very well. But it's hard to get a feeling for how he'll react to my family in a gathering of only seven people."

Only seven people? That was an interesting perspective.

"So it's the extended family you're worried about," Gwen surmised. "How will Roy survive the wedding, much less holidays, family gatherings, and the occasional offer to read his fortune in chicken entrails?"

A strange look crossed Shawna's face, something that was equal parts chagrin and relief. "I take it Damian has told you about our colorful clan."

"A little. Nothing that would make any difference to me, if I were in Roy's shoes."

"That's what he says," Shawna agreed. "I've put out some hints about eccentric family members, and he just smiles and shrugs. The way Roy sees it, what we have is between him and me. No one else comes into it. It's just about us."

Gwen was starting to see where the problem might lie. "Five kids is a big family these days. How many siblings does Roy have?"

"None. His parents passed on a few years back. Roy is a few years older than I am," she explained. "Well, more than a few. He's in his late forties."

"I guess that's not too old to be starting a family. Assuming he wants kids, of course."

"Assuming *we* want children," Shawna corrected.

"No, you want kids, all right. Your face lights up when you talk about your family, even the weirder members."

Grief slid into Shawna's eyes, and was quickly veiled. "Roy knows himself well enough to realize there's no room in his life for children. He works long hours. He likes to sail or play golf on weekends, and he enjoys travel. He wants to marry a woman who's as serious about her career as he is about his. And he's realistic enough to know that people can't have it all. What's the sense of having children if you never see them?"

The argument sounded pretty well-rehearsed to Gwen. "And you're okay with that."

Shawna nodded. "Roy and I want most of the same things. I don't think it gets much better."

"You could be right. I don't have high expectations for relationships, myself."

"That's not what I meant!" she protested.

"No offense. What I'm saying is that most women take men way too seriously. It sounds to me like you're taking a realistic view to this monogamy thing, which means you're less likely to make a mistake than some starry-eyed romantic."

"I guess," she said hesitantly.

"One more question: What kind of things do you guys argue about?"

Shawna blinked. "Argue?"

Uh-oh. In Gwen's experience, that wasn't a good sign. No two people could rub together for any length of time without finding a few rough edges. The lack of any point of contention could mean that one person was deferring far too much, and that went nowhere good. It could also indicate the inability of one or both parties to confront problems. Or maybe there were deliberately hidden issues. Whatever the case, perfect harmony was a myth, and an insidious one at that.

And Shawna, judging by the expression on her face, had bought shares in that particular stock. "Why did you ask me that?"

"Answers can be surprisingly illuminating," Gwen said, keeping it cryptic. "So, I take a closer look at this guy, set your brother's mind at ease, and you're good to go."

"That sounds reasonable," she allowed. She was about to say

more, but her gaze settled on someone near the door, and a flash of panic shot through her eyes.

Gwen wasn't surprised to see a tall, well-dressed Black man approaching their table, coffee cup in hand.

"Shawna," he said, putting a bit of surprise into it. His gaze slipped to Gwen and back, and his eyebrows rose. "This is your breakfast meeting?"

"It's not like a *meeting* meeting," Gwen said, her voice pitched a few notes higher and several years younger than her usual husky alto tones. "It's more like, community-service time."

She stuck out her hand, keeping it a little stiff and awkward, as if business handshakes were new territory for her.

"GiGi Silver," she announced, giving one of her established teen personas. "I'm a junior at Mount Hope, and Ms. O'Riley agreed to help me with a school project. But you probably didn't hear about it. I sort of left it to the last minute," she confessed.

He took her hand briefly. "School project."

"Yeah! We have to research three different careers, and her brother—he's a cop, which is something I thought might be sort of interesting—told me to call his sister the banker and see if she could talk to me, and maybe let me follow her around for a few hours. You know—watch her at work, ask questions and stuff."

As Gwen hoped, Shawna picked up her cue. "Roy, maybe you could help out, too?"

A flicker of annoyance crossed his face, and he sent Gwen a smile that didn't quite reach his eyes. "I'd be glad to. Call my office, and my secretary can set something up."

"Great! Have you got, like, a business card?"

He fished out his wallet and handed her a card. His smile

changed when he turned it toward Shawna, turning warm and genuine. "Is dinner at nine still good for you?"

"Absolutely."

He actually blew her a kiss before wading off into the crowd.

Shawna heaved a relieved sigh. "That was quick thinking, girl. It was something, the way you changed the way you talked, even the way you moved. I swear you dropped ten years just like *that*," she marveled, snapping her fingers for emphasis.

"More like twenty," Gwen said. "I'm glad you're impressed, but like anything else, it comes with practice."

Enough practice, she added silently, to suspect that any meeting Roy's secretary set up would only be canceled later on. The man seemed to be genuinely into Shawna, but Gwen was willing to bet he didn't have a lot of time for anyone else.

"I don't expect to get much information from this career-day shtick, but it will give me a chance to observe Roy for a couple of hours, pick up some impressions."

"Pick up impressions," Shawna echoed, her expression suddenly more guarded. "Damian said your instincts are very good."

"Don't worry—I always back everything up with completely unspooky data. I'll get you a report within, say, two weeks?"

"That will be fine. What do I owe you?"

"Work that out with your brother. He helped me on a recent case, so this is me paying him back."

Shawna's eyebrows flew up. "Keeping it off the books?"

"Oddly enough, that's the term he used."

"I'm not surprised. Actually, I suppose I *am* a little surprised," she amended, "but that's because 'keeping it off the books' is what we call our in-family barter system."

"Oh."

Gwen couldn't think of anything to add to that. Family was a mystery to her. If she'd ventured onto O'Riley turf, it was entirely by accident.

After a moment Shawna glanced at her watch. "I've got to run, but I'll look forward to hearing from you."

"You go ahead." Gwen lifted her coffee cup. "I'm going to need a refill."

After her new client left, Gwen tossed back the cooling brew and went through line for a takeaway cup. She walked a couple of blocks down a side street to where she'd parked her car. Thanks to the check Kyle Radcliff had written her last night, she'd been able to pick up her Toyota first thing this morning.

The rusting blue antique didn't look any better than it had, but at least it didn't break down between the coffee shop and Gwen's apartment. She parked it in the garage next to Sylvia's black Mercedes sedan, turned off the car, and chugged her second cup of coffee while she listened to the engine sputter and wheeze into silence. Thus fortified, she marched into the office.

It was time to face her computer.

Brushing the dust off the laptop took longer than it should have. So did powering it up. The infernal machine seemed to be sulking about its long period of neglect. After too damn long, Gwen pulled up her list of bookmarked Web sites and got to work.

The information on Roy Williams's business card was enough to get her started. It didn't take long to find his home address, phone numbers, Social Security number, credit report, and over a dozen articles in local newspapers that mentioned his name. Apparently he sailed competitively, attended big-ticket charity events, and liked to hobnob with local politicians. A quick phone call to one of the few Providence cops who still spoke to her confirmed that Roy had no police record, other than a ticket for speeding four years back.

In fact, she couldn't find a single thing wrong with this guy.

Yet.

She sat up and stretched, catlike. The buzzer on her intercom sounded while she was still in midstretch.

"It's Jason Cross," announced the disembodied voice. "I was driving back from a computer class and got the impulse to stop by."

It occurred to Gwen that Jason had never been to her place. They'd gotten together several times since Frank's funeral, but she'd never invited him here. For that matter, she'd never told him where she lived. No mystery there—no doubt he'd found her address among his father's things.

"Come on up. My office is in the garage at the end of the drive."

She buzzed him through and watched as he drove up. He'd ditched the rental in favor of a used two-seater, and the day was warm enough to warrant putting the top down. His new ride gave her a chance to study him. She'd done quite a bit of that over the past week, but he still puzzled her.

For one thing, Jason Cross didn't look a thing like his father. Frank had always reminded Gwen of a Kodiak bear: big, blond, and powerful in a way that could be reassuring or intimidating, depending on which side of the law you happened to be standing. Apparently Jason took after his mother, whom Frank had described as small and dark, with more than a little Narragansett ancestry. Frank's features had been bluff and broad, but Jason had high cheekbones and a slight convex curve to his nose. His best feature was his eyes, which were a warm chocolate brown. Gwen had always appreciated Frank's edgy energy, but there was something to be said for the calm, kind, centered look in the younger man's dark-eyed gaze.

The problem was, she couldn't get *behind* those eyes. Reading people was a survival skill, one Gwen had learned early. For some reason, she couldn't begin to figure out what made Jason Cross tick.

"Door's open," she called in response to his knock.

Jason came in and gave her one of his peaceful smiles. "You look busy. Should I come back later?"

She pushed away from the table. "No, I'm glad you stopped by. I've been hooked up to this damn machine all morning. I can't believe you *pay* to play around with computers."

"I've got the equipment, so why not learn to use it?"

Gwen propped her feet up on the table. "That's pretty much what Frank said when the department issued computers. He figured what the hell—might as well do it right. Somewhere along the line he crossed over from hobby to obsession, but he had a good time with it."

"I can see why. The information on the Web is amazing. He bookmarked some really interesting stuff."

A wave of trepidation swept through Gwen. She'd carefully gone through Frank's files, deleting anything to do with his final case: the death of Gwen's parents and the key to her identity. But the disc Damian had given her last night was proof that computers didn't forget easily. How did Damian put it? Deleted, but not *gone*.

She reminded herself that Jason was a beginner, probably a long way from peeling secrets off a hard drive. Plus, why would he think to look? And even if he did, it wasn't as if she could do anything about it. Frank's stuff rightfully belonged to Jason.

An irrational surge of resentment followed that thought. Sure,

Jason was Frank's kid, but he was a stranger. She'd been the only family Frank had had for fifteen years.

It occurred to her that the silence had stretched for too long, and that Jason was watching her intently.

"Long morning," she said shortly, by way of explanation.

"Anything I can do to help?"

She shrugged and tapped her laptop with one boot-clad toe. "Not much more to do here. I've pulled together some basic info, but these days I outsource most of my electronic footwork."

His face brightened with interest. "Oh yeah? Who does that kind of work?"

"I use a public-information broker to collect info that's in the public domain. He's not cheap, but my time is put to better use gathering information in person."

"What about info that's *not* public domain?"

He sounded curious but not judgmental. This guy was definitely a computer natural—after a couple sessions, he was already developing a hacker's mentality.

"I've got contacts who can find anything."

"Legally?"

Another question that didn't come with moral baggage, she noted. Interesting. Most people had a truckload of it, even the ones who didn't let their moral codes interfere with their own behavior.

Jason cleared his throat. "I wasn't implying that you were doing anything illegal. Well, maybe I *was,* but I didn't mean to offend you."

"You didn't," she assured him. "My mind was wandering, that's all. The contacts I mentioned strive to be legally bulletproof. Part of the job—they're reporters for a tabloid."

He let out a long, low whistle. "You don't strike me as someone who'd be a fan of the tabloid press."

"Who said I was? My friend Sister Tamar—she's a nun, which you probably figured out from the name—claims there's a special layer of hell reserved for the people who publish that crap. But you've got to admit they're damned good at what they do."

His eyes twinkled. "Like the saying goes, 'It wouldn't be prudent to worship the devil, but we should at least respect his talents.'"

"There you go," Gwen said approvingly. "Who said that?"

"Mark Twain, I think. Or Oscar Wilde. It's usually one or the other." He settled one hip on the edge of her desk. "Do you have time to get some lunch?"

"I wish," she grumbled. "I've got another hour or so of work to do on another case, then I'll be heading down to Tiverton to talk to some people."

"You have a lot of irons in the fire."

"Yeah, well. Life is full of unanswered questions. So is death, for that matter."

Even to Gwen's ears, her words sounded bitter. A long moment of silence stretched between them.

"Gwen, let it go," he said gently.

She didn't have to ask what he meant. It wasn't the first time Jason had urged her to let the official story about his father's death stand: Frank Cross, a recovering alcoholic, fell off the wagon and into the Narragansett Bay.

End of story.

In a way, Gwen couldn't blame Jason. He never knew his father, and all he had to go on was what people had told him. Frank had been drinking pretty hard all during their partnership, and Gwen was willing to bet that Jason's mother had harbored some resentment.

Or maybe Jason was keeping it light because he was more interested in her than in restoring his father's reputation?

Nah, that didn't play. Jason treated her like a buddy. In the week since they'd met, he hadn't shown any inclination toward getting naked and sweaty.

And come to think of it, *what was up with that?* Just because a guy wanted to be friends with a woman, it didn't follow that he wasn't also interested in sleeping with her, if only just once. Since curiosity was one of Gwen's defining traits, this impulse had always struck her as not only natural but sensible.

"I've got to head down to Tiverton one of these days," Jason said. "Good place to get a kayak, I hear. You ever try that?"

"No. I went out clamming with Frank from time to time, but his rowboat is pretty much the limits of my ability."

"I'm glad you've been using it."

Gwen's only response was a curt nod. Since the funeral, she'd taken Frank's rowboat out several times, hoping this familiar activity would jump-start her capricious "gift" into doing something useful. But she hadn't been able to pick up any images or impressions, no glimpses of how he had died. When it really mattered, her visions deserted her.

"I've been thinking of selling the bigger boat," Jason said hesitantly. "What would you think about that?"

"Why should what I think matter?"

He shrugged. "You were Frank's family."

Gwen averted her gaze, not wanting Jason to see her response to that central truth. She swung her feet off her desk and rose, turning aside as she stretched.

"Listen, why don't you drive down to Tiverton with me? You're not working until tonight, right? I could swing by your place around noon to pick you up."

"She can take a hint!" he said cheerfully. "And since I also have that ability, I'll be leaving now. Noon works for me. I'll make a couple of subs to eat on the way."

She glanced over her shoulder at him. "You should make one for yourself, too."

"I've never seen anyone your size who could chow down like you do."

"What can I say? It's a gift."

His chuckle wafted back to her as the door swung shut. She watched his car pull away, then got out the notes she'd taken last night during her meeting with Kyle Radcliff.

Gwen found a Web site for Erin's place of business, a little shop in Tiverton called The Green Man. But when she started digging, she found that the shop was jointly owned by Alice Powers—the business partner—and Kyle Radcliff. Kyle Radcliff, not Erin Westland.

So much for "her own little business." Gwen wasn't too surprised; Kyle had always been a controlling bastard.

Come to think of it, he'd mentioned that Erin didn't have an income.

Nor did she have assets.

Her name wasn't on anything—not the mortgage on Kyle's house, not Kyle's bank accounts, not even the car she drove.

How much of that was Kyle's choice, Gwen wondered, and how much of it was Erin's? Was it possible that Kyle's desire to dominate and control harmonized with Erin's need to be invisible?

According to Kyle, Erin had been born in Mystic, Connecticut. Her birthday was in late March, so she'd recently turned thirty-one. But there was no birth record for anyone by that name in or around Mystic. No school records, no voter registration. A search for Social Security numbers yielded a few Erin Westlands, but none of them were from Connecticut. There wasn't much on Patrick, other than the SSI number. The kid wasn't in school yet, so he was too young to have left many electronic footprints.

Gwen shut down her computer and was on her way out the door when the phone rang. She lunged for it and hit the speaker button before the machine could pick up.

"Changeling Detective Agency."

"You busy tonight?" inquired Damian without preamble.

Gwen glanced at her watch. "No, but I'm busy now. Talk fast."

"I set up a meet for tonight. The dealer is expecting me to bring a girl with me. You want in, or should I bring another cop?"

"Yes to both. I want in, but you should still bring backup. When and where do I meet you?"

He gave her the name of a little park on the East Side, a common meeting place for drug deals despite its proximity to the police department.

"I can do that," Gwen said. "But with one slight change."

In a few words, she blocked out an alternate scenario. Damian heard her out, then chuckled appreciatively.

"Damn! I'm glad you're one of us. . . . So to speak."

Gwen's heart did a sudden free fall toward the pit of her stomach. "Geez, thanks for the reminder. I've gone all morning without once thinking about the whole not-human thing."

"Yeah? Sounds like your day's been more interesting than mine."

"That I doubt. I've been dragging my ass all over cyberspace."

"Don't let Forest hear you say that. He'd probably think you were spamming for a porn Web site—'Elves on the Internet,' or some damn thing."

Gwen supposed she should be pleased that Ian had accomplished his purpose so thoroughly, but she didn't want to hear the E-word from *any*one, even when it dripped with sarcasm.

"Ian likes to yank people's chains. Forget about him. Listen, I've got to run. I'll meet you at the park tonight."

"As far as our guy's concerned, you're there to sample a new party drug. Don't forget to dress the part."

She rolled her eyes. "And me with a closet full of plaid skirts and sensible shoes."

"Huh. Good point."

He hung up without saying good-bye, just like Quaid always did. Apparently he was picking up a few of his other partner's habits.

Gwen's grin faded abruptly. His *other* partner? Since when had she started regarding Damian O'Riley as *her* rookie trainee as well as Gary Quaid's?

Her gaze flicked to the disc Damian had given her last night. Some part of her hoped she could clear her name, settle the books, and go back to her old life. Maybe on some level she even believed it could happen. But c'mon—an elf on the Providence vice squad?

Wait a minute—a *what*?

For a moment Gwen stood frozen with shock. She slumped into one of the wingback chairs and dropped her head into her hands. It was a bit much, having *two* nasty little pieces of self-knowledge hit her in the last five minutes. The first was bad enough—what the hell business did *she* have training a rookie cop?—but the second was a full-fledged paradigm shift:

She believed Ian Forest. Down deep inside, she knew he was right about who and what she was.

And the funny thing was, Gwen suspected that she'd always known.

Six

As Gwen drove down the long gravel driveway, she noticed something sticking out of her mailbox.

The postal delivery wasn't due until afternoon, but a large manila envelope had been bent into an inverted U and slid partway into the mailbox, with at least a third of it exposed. Someone wanted to be sure to get her attention.

The vision hit her the moment her fingers touched the envelope. A lean, dark face, with cheekbones so sharp they cast shadows on the hollows below. Dark eyes studied her with a mixture of hunger and resentment, and the thoughts behind those eyes flooded her with numbing clarity. Wallace Earl Edmonson, her father's brother, had regarded her as both a necessity and a nuisance. He'd envied the "gift" she'd inherited, but he'd reconciled himself to using her as a tool and was eager to get on with it.

Edmonson's face dissolved, and the vision shifted into a smothering emotional cloud, a dark miasma of dread and death.

Gwen quickly released the envelope and drew in a long, shuddering breath. She reached into the pocket of her leather jacket for a pair of latex gloves and snapped them on, not so much to preserve fingerprints on the envelope—she doubted there would be any—as to mute the intense memories captured by whatever was in the envelope.

She tore it open and pulled out two photos. One was a black-and-white picture of Frank's fishing boat adrift on moonlit waters, just as it had looked the night he'd drowned. The picture was carefully composed and beautifully printed, mocking her grief with art.

Gwen quickly shuffled it behind the second photo, and her eyes widened.

The second picture was also black-and-white, but in this case a color shot would have looked much the same. A small, ornate silver handgun was displayed against black velvet. Gwen recognized the weapon immediately. Ian Forest had given it to her as a gift—and taken it from her hand the last time she'd faced down Edmonson.

The warning was unmistakable: Tie Frank's death to Edmonson, and we'll tie Edmonson's death to *you*.

Her lips firmed around a small, cynical smile. How stupid did Ian think she was? As warnings go, this one definitely lacked teeth. After all the trouble they'd gone through to make sure no one missed Edmonson? They weren't about to negate the effort by accusing her of his death. And even if they did, what use was a weapon if you couldn't produce a corpse? After her parents died in a car crash, their bodies had been stolen from the morgue to avoid close scrutiny. Gwen didn't know much about the Elder Folk, but one thing was very clear: when they died, they *disappeared*.

Her smirk faded as a new explanation occurred to her. They didn't need to tie her to Edmonson's death. Her fingerprints were on the silver gun. If she stepped out of line, someone would die. Almost certainly someone she knew. That she'd be blamed for it was beside the point.

Gwen carefully set the photos aside. Ian had it right—she *was* an idiot. He'd given her an unregistered gun, and she'd taken it. When he asked for it back, she'd handed it over without question. That wasn't like her, and the lapse bothered her almost as much as the threat.

She'd noticed that Ian was unusually persuasive, but it had never occurred to her that his particular "gift" might enable him to override people's normal reservations and inhibitions.

Muttering imprecations, she stripped off the gloves and dialed Ian's number on her cell phone. He answered after the first ring.

"Hello, Gwen. I'm glad you called."

For once his silky baritone had absolutely no effect on her libido. "Like I had a choice," she snarled. "Okay, you win. I won't challenge the official ruling on Frank's death. If you want, I'll take an oath on it, but first you have to give me back that little silver trinket and give me *your* oath that it won't be used on anyone else."

"That sounds reasonable. Shall I bring the item by your apartment?"

"I'll be out late tonight. But then, that won't be a problem for you, will it? You always seem to know where to find me. Damian had it right when he called you a stalker."

"Gwen—"

"Don't bother. Nothing you could say will change any of this. Overriding people's judgment, clouding their ability to make their own choices? In my book, that makes you no better than a rapist. Oh, and an extortionist. Let's not forget that."

A long silence followed. "In time, you'll understand why certain precautions were necessary."

She threw the cell phone into the passenger seat and yanked the gearshift into first. Gravel spit from her tires as she spun out of the drive. By the time she reached Jason's house in East Providence, her hands had stopped shaking.

Despite the bad start, the drive down to Tiverton ended up being surprisingly pleasant. Jason drove his car, vowing that that bottom was due to fall out of Gwen's any day now. That freed Gwen's hands to tackle the Italian subs Jason had put together for the trip. He had filled bakery-fresh torpedo rolls with spicy meats, provolone, onions, and hot peppers—enough good stuff to drown out the requisite lettuce and tomatoes. The car's top was down, the sun was warm, and jazz poured out of the sound system. By the time Gwen had worked her way through the second sub, she was feeling, for lack of a better term, almost human again.

They drove along the Sakonnet River in companionable silence, passing scene after scene ripped from the pages of the *Scenic New England* book on Marcy's coffee table. The whole town had an out-of-the-way feeling, and The Green Man, tucked as it was into a grove of beech and maple trees on a narrow side road, wasn't exactly designed to pull in drive-by customers.

Gwen got out of the car and studied the carved wooden sign over the door—a man's face surrounded by oak leaves, presiding over "The Green Man" carved in Celtic-style lettering. The sign looked handmade, artsy, and expensive. Apparently Kyle took his wife's hobbies seriously.

The setup was bigger than it looked at first glance. The storefront was narrow, but the main room was surprisingly long. The ceiling was opened to the rafters, giving the shop a lofty, spacious feel.

The Green Man looked and smelled like a cross between a health supplement shop, an old-fashioned country store, an herbalist's warehouse, and an English tearoom. In the main room, pretty oak shelves lined with rows of small boxes and pill bottles filled most of one wall. A long table held a couple of dozen small wooden barrels of dried herbs, each with its own scoop and small stack of prelabeled bags. Toward the back of the room, two newer wings jutted off to each side. On the left was cozy tearoom, on the right, a greenhouse.

A smiling, ash-blond woman wearing a small fortune in beige linen separates bustled over to greet them. Gwen figured her for another hobbyist, a woman who enjoyed playing at running a business but didn't need to depend on it for a living.

"Can I help you find something?" she asked, glancing from Gwen to Jason.

"Actually, I'm looking for some*one*. This is Erin Westland's shop?"

"That's right. I'm her partner, Alice Powers. Is there something I could help you with? Or are you a friend of hers?"

"I've never met her. My name is Gwen Gellman, and I'm a private investigator. I'm working for her husband, Kyle Radcliff. Erin hasn't been home since Sunday, and he hired me to find her."

The woman's eyes widened, and the hand she lifted to her throat was more than a little unsteady.

"Dear God. She's missing? Erin is missing?"

"I don't mean to be rude, but it seems like you would have noticed by now."

She gave a nervous titter. "You would think so, wouldn't you? But the shop doesn't really need more than one person here at a time. We take turns, so I didn't know—" Her voice trailed off, and she swayed on her low-heeled Italian shoes.

Jason took the woman's elbow and steered her toward the tearoom. "Let's all sit down."

She let him lead her to a chair, and sank gratefully into it. "Give me a minute to absorb this. I was just about to make a fresh pot before you came in. We have our own herbal blend here. It's very soothing, and I don't mind telling you that I could use a cup."

Gwen took the seat across from the woman. "Since you're here today, I'm guessing Tuesday is Erin's day."

"That's right. She works Tuesday and Thursday, from ten to five, as well as an occasional half day on Saturday."

"Would you have any way of knowing whether or not Erin came in yesterday?"

"Oh, I'm sure she didn't. We're not open Sunday and Monday, so there are usually quite a few messages on Tuesday morning. The messages were still there when I came in this morning, so clearly Erin didn't pick them up yesterday. Come to think of it, there were several calls from Kyle."

Either the woman was a complete flake, or Erin wasn't exactly the most reliable partner. "Is skipping work a pattern for her?"

"Not really, no. She takes a day off from time to time, but she calls to let me know, so I have the option of coming in or not. Our regular customers know that our hours are flexible, and they call before making the drive."

"When was the last time you heard from Erin?"

"Let's see," she mused. "Thursday? Yes, that sounds right. She called me about an order. We're running low on the chamomile citrus tea. And speaking of which, let me get that tea going. Would you like some lavender shortbread with it?"

"I'm sure she would," Jason told her, sending a small smile at Gwen. "Thank you, Mrs. Powers."

"Alice, please." She lifted one hand to smooth her hair, a movement contrived to show off a perfect pale-rose manicure and a couple of snazzy rings.

"Jason," he said, offering his hand.

An expression of mock exasperation crossed her face when she touched his hand. "Another man who thinks skin cream is only for women! We have a very nice lotion, all natural of course, with a lovely, woodsy scent. A very popular gift for men."

"I'll take a look at it afterwards," he assured her.

She beamed at him. Her smile broadened when he stood up with her. "How nice. You don't encounter many gentlemen these days." She gave Gwen an aren't-*you*-a-lucky-girl wink and headed to the little morning kitchen at the end of the tearoom.

"Suck up," Gwen murmured.

He smiled complacently. "What can I say? My momma raised me right."

Alice turned on the electric kettle and measured dried herbs into a plump white teapot, then piled a small silver tray with lightly golden wedges flecked with dried lavender. She brought the cookies to the table and returned for the tea things.

Gwen took an experimental nibble. The shortbread was rich and buttery, the lavender more ornamental than anything else. That was a relief. She'd expected it to taste more . . . purple. Maybe she'd try the tea after all.

After Alice finished the pouring, Gwen asked, "Would you object to me looking at the store's books?"

"Of course not! Anything I can do to help."

She got up and bustled off, returning in a few moments with a binder holding a computer printout.

"We have a very simple system. Neither of us are financial wizards, so this should be easy for anyone to follow. This is a copy. You can take it with you if you like."

After Alice settled back down, Gwen handed her a business card and a copy of the release form Kyle Radcliff had signed.

Alice flushed. "Oh my goodness. I didn't think to ask for your ID, or credentials, or anything. And here I am, just handing over the books."

"You're worried about your partner," Jason said soothingly. He lifted the small cup. "This is very good."

"It is, isn't it? That's our biggest seller. People come from all over southern New England for it, and you know how Rhode Islanders hate to drive any distance."

"I'm finding that out," he said with a grin. "If someone has to drive more than fifteen minutes to get to work, they start wondering whether they should move closer to the office or start looking for a new job. Around here, anything more than an hour away is a day trip."

She chuckled. "That's certainly true. And it's insidious! We moved here from Connecticut. My husband used to take the train into Manhattan every morning, but now he complains about driving from here to Providence."

The door chimes tinkled, and a trio of matrons walked into the store. Alice glanced over. "I've got to see to the customers. Please help yourself to more tea."

Gwen sipped hers while she looked through the records. "This is interesting. Erin takes a lot of days off. And even when she's here, the receipts on Tuesdays and Thursdays are significantly lower than on other days."

Jason poured himself a second cup. "Skimming, maybe?"

"I wouldn't be surprised. Hubby keeps a tight hold on the purse strings. This business is technically his. Well, more than technically,

I guess. His name is on the lease, and he wasn't kidding when he said Erin didn't have an income. This place isn't exactly turning a profit."

She glanced up at Jason and grinned. "I like it. Kyle pays the bills, Erin pockets the cash."

"You don't care much for the husband, I take it."

"Hell, no. He was married to a friend of mine." Gwen closed the book and pushed it aside. "I'm finished here. Is there anything you need to do around town? Want to stop at that kayak place by the bridge?"

He glanced out of the window. The sky was clouding over in one of those abrupt mood changes for which New England weather was famed.

"Another time, I think. Since the weather's turning, I think I'll head down to the library. I've been meaning to start some sort of volunteer work in the community. A lot of organizations post fliers on the library bulletin boards looking for volunteers."

"I can save you a trip. Monday nights I teach a class in self-defense for women. Interested in helping out?"

He nodded avidly. "I was thinking about doing some work with beach or wetlands maintenance, but that's good, too. How are you running the class?"

"Not much talk, demos as needed, lots of drills. I've had them practicing in pairs."

"But you want them to get used to employing these techniques against males. That's smart."

"Problem is, they're just starting out. And they're, you know, *girly*."

He grinned. "You say that like it's a bad thing. Tell you what:

Let's head back to Frank's place, and you show me the holds and escapes you'll be using."

She consulted her watch. "I've got a little time. Sure, let's do that."

An hour later, Gwen was in Jason's backyard, barefoot and disheveled, and grinning like a kid in a video arcade.

She circled, moving opposite Jason, her eyes on his. Usually she could tell what an opponent was going to do by watching his face. Most people telegraphed their intentions in a hundred little ways. But Jason was nearly impossible to read, and Gwen had ended up flat on the grass a dozen times.

He lunged for her, cat-quick. Gwen slapped away his hand and pivoted on her left foot, leaning away and snapping off a kick with her right foot.

She fully expected him to block. To her surprise, Jason grabbed her ankle and tugged in the direction she was already moving. The added momentum threw off her balance, and suddenly she was heading for the grass again. Twisting on the way down, she caught herself with both hands and kicked out with her free foot—

And met only air. Jason had already released her and moved aside.

She flopped down on the ground and immediately flipped onto her back, pulling her knees up to her chest. When Jason dove at her, she planted both feet on his torso and pushed out hard. He soared over her.

It was a near-perfect throw. It would have been perfect if Jason hadn't somehow managed to land on his feet rather than his back.

Gwen rolled up to a sitting position. Before she could scramble to her feet, Jason dropped to one knee and got her in a headlock, pulling her in tight against his chest.

Since she was several inches shorter than Jason, her butt fitted firmly against his lower body. To her surprise, he was very happy to have her there.

Normally this sort of thing didn't surprise her. The male psyche held few mysteries for Gwen. Men, in her observation, were driven primarily by a desire for sex and territory. Modern life lent a veneer of complication to these basis instincts, but most masculine responses boiled down to the three C's: curiosity, competition, and conquest. The thing was, Gwen had never picked up even a hint of sexual interest from Jason, not even during the physical contact of their mock sparring. But something was definitely happening now.

Jason splayed his hand on her stomach and pulled her closer still, making her aware that her tee shirt had ridden up, exposing everything that wasn't covered by her skimpy excuse for a bra. His hand suddenly felt very warm against her bare skin. A rush of pure, primal lust was coming off him in waves.

He relaxed his hold on her neck. Before Gwen could pull away, Jason turned her to face him so they knelt together, thigh to thigh. He buried both hands in her hair and tipped her head back for a kiss.

He lowered his head until they were nearly touching, until Gwen could see her face reflected in his chocolate-brown eyes.

Jason stopped suddenly, a breath away from her lips. Chagrin washed over his face. Apparently he'd glimpsed his reflection in her eyes, too, and didn't like what he saw.

Even before he released her, the palpable sense of desire switched off, as abruptly and completely as a door shutting between them. He eased away, then rose and put several paces between them, hands thrust in his pockets as if he didn't trust them to be out on their own recognizance.

"That wasn't planned," he said quietly, his back still to her. "In fact, I have no earthly notion why I just did that."

"You Tarzan, me Jane?" she suggested.

"That's not it." He turned to face her. "It's not my style to jump a woman just because she happens to be there and female. Especially not you."

Gwen rose to her feet. "Okay," she said cautiously. "But just out of curiosity, what did I do to rate 'especially'?"

"We're sort of like family, once removed. I'm not saying I look at you as a sister, but maybe—I don't know—a cousin or something."

"And as far as you're concerned, this isn't Appalachia."

"Not even close." He studied her face. "Are we on the same page with this?"

Gwen thought that over. "Being in a clinch felt a little strange to me, too. I don't know about the cousin thing, though. Never having had any family, I don't know how that works."

"Okay, scrap that analogy. You've got one that works better?"

"I'll give it some thought." She glanced at her watch. "Listen, I've got to go."

"Are you sure you're okay with this? You're not pissed off at me for grabbing you?"

He looked so contrite, even worried. Gwen sent him a reassuring smile. "We're okay. Listen, you want to take the boat out this weekend? We might as well take advantage of it before you sell it."

Jason greeted this suggestion with obvious relief. "Sure. How about Saturday morning?"

"Sounds good. You make the coffee, and I'll bring a dozen donuts."

"Make sure you bring something for me, too."

Gwen paused in the act of putting on her boots and shot a side-long glance at him. "Smart-ass."

He chuckled, obviously reassured by this exchange. Gwen waved good-bye and jogged to her car.

Rush-hour traffic clogged the streets as she drove toward Marcy's condo in downtown Providence. Impromptu visits weren't usually their style, but Gwen figured it couldn't hurt to check in. Marcy had been shaken by Kyle Radcliff's reappearance in her life, and Gwen wasn't about to see her friend lose hard-won ground.

She parked in the lot across from the condo and dashed across the street, dodging a small crowd of canvas-toting art students re-leased from late-afternoon classes. When the intercom hummed into life, she gave her name and grabbed the door when the buzzer sounded.

Trudy Wasserman met her at the door to the condo, a steaming mug in hand. She was wearing a sleeveless tunic of some silky fabric in swirling, watercolor shades of blue and green over black leggings—sort of an updated, upscale version of a tie-dye tee shirt. It suited Trudy, who was one of those people who definitely would have gone to Woodstock if she hadn't been in diapers at the time. She'd done something different to her sleek red hair, crimping it so that it fell nearly to her shoulder in a soft, wavy triangle. Her bangs were cut straight across. To Gwen, the look said Cleopatra with a henna rinse and a bad perm. Or maybe early Tina Turner.

"Marcy's not home," Trudy said without preamble.

Gwen rocked back on her heels, surprised by the edge in the woman's voice. Trudy had always been a little wary of Gwen. Every now and then a little jealousy showed through, but never had Trudy been so openly hostile.

"I'll come back another time," Gwen said.

Something flickered in Trudy's eyes, and the resentful expression dropped off her face. In fact, her whole demeanor changed so suddenly that Gwen could envision a switch being flipped.

"Don't go. I'm glad you're here, really. Please, come in." She seized Gwen's arm and all but dragged her into the room.

Gwen disengaged and took a step back. "Let me guess: you want know what's going on with Kyle Radcliff."

Her hostess blinked, clearly surprised by her own transparency. She quickly gathered her composure and sank gracefully into one of the white leather chairs, then took a sip from her mug before answering.

"Of course I'm concerned that Kyle has come back into Marcy's life. I don't trust him."

"Neither do I, but I'm a *private* investigator, as in, no, I'm not going to discuss the case with you."

"Did I ask you to?"

"I figured you'd get around it. Just like you pumped me for details about Jeff Monroe, not to mention Marcy's three assistants before Jeff."

Trudy set aside her mug with exaggerated care. "Marcy is the single most important thing in my life. Of course I'm interested in her job and the people she deals with on a day-to-day basis. It's only natural."

"I don't know about that. It's 'only natural' for people to keep having a life after they get a relationship. Not every aspect of Marcy's life revolves around you. Deal with it."

Trudy's gray eyes narrowed. "Really, Gwen, let me know what you really think."

"Okay, I think it's insulting that you expect me to talk about a friend behind her back. I think you need to get over yourself and get a life of your own. And I think I should leave right now and come back when Marcy's home."

"And *I* think you don't know the first thing about a real relationship," Trudy shot back. "Look at you—jumping into bed with anyone who catches your eye, never willing to commit. Your vocabulary includes every four-letter word but 'love.' You're—you're *as bad as a man!*"

In Trudy's lexicon, those were fighting words, but Gwen had to fight back a grin. "Yeah, I can be a real bastard."

The redhead threw up her hands in exasperation. "Is it any wonder people talk about you and Marcy? You're more of a man than that husband of hers ever was!"

"Yeah, but so are you," Gwen pointed out, "and you're the poster girl for lipstick lesbians."

Without warning, Trudy launched herself from the chair and came at Gwen, swinging a handful of manicure at her face. Gwen leaned out of reach, grabbed her wrist, and yanked it hard to one side. When Trudy spun away, Gwen planted one foot on the woman's rump and shoved her toward one of the sofas. She plunged forward and sprawled facedown on the white leather.

Trudy scrambled up and tensed for another spring, but something in Gwen's face froze her in place.

"You're just dying to haul off and punch me, aren't you?" she hissed. "You'd just love that, would you?"

"Now that you mention it," Gwen said dryly. "But this isn't about you and me, fingernails versus fists. Bottom line: Kyle Radcliff is a waste of skin. Marcy knows that. You've got nothing to worry about from him, and your only problems are the ones you're causing. Tell Marcy I was here, would you?"

She spun on her heel and left Trudy to fume and sputter. Enough time wasted—Damian was expecting to meet her at the park in less than an hour.

Suddenly, the prospect of a drug bust was actually sort of inviting. People were so much easier to deal with when you were allowed to kick their asses.

Seven

Later that evening, Gwen sauntered into the park on stiletto heels, one hand tucked in the back pocket of Damian's jeans. The dealer would assume that Damian had brought a girl along to help him test out the drug's supposed aphrodisiac effect, so she figured she should start acting the part. They'd come early to check out the area, but most likely their contact was doing the same thing.

After a quick stroll around the park they headed for the designated meeting spot—a bench tucked back among several old maples. Once they sat down, Gwen noticed that the trees blocked out the lamplight, leaving them in a deeply shadowed alcove. No passersby would see what happened in this place.

The minutes ticked by. Unseen cars swished past. A big man with sheepishly hunched shoulders skulked down the path behind a tiny dog, a toy breed of some sort with a prancing, mincing gait and a pink ribbon on its head. Gwen wondered if the sensitivity points the guy was racking up with his wife or girlfriend outweighed the humiliation of being seen walking the little mutt. Moments after the unmatched pair passed out of view, a shrill soprano yapping gave challenge to some passerby.

Damian nudged an elbow into her ribs, warning her to be alert.

She saw the man approaching before he did, and her heart began to race.

She leaned in as if to nip playfully at Damian's earlobe. "It's one of the blond kids who trashed the DNA lab," she whispered. "If he recognizes us, he'll run. Don't let him see your face until he's close enough for me to grab him."

"Why do you get to do the grabbing? Whose bust is this, anyway?" he whispered back. But he lifted a hand to play with her hair, shielding her face from view.

Gwen pulled her knees up so that her feet were braced against the edge of the bench. She nuzzled at Damian's neck and murmured, "Give me an ETA."

"Counting down: ten, nine, eight."

She completed the rest of the countdown silently, trusting Damian's ability to judge the timing of the blond man's approach. She didn't have much choice—the guy approached with ghostly silence. When she figured the moment was right, Gwen pushed off the bench with both feet, launching herself off into a flying tackle.

The blond guy went down with Gwen on top of him. Before he could move, she had her gun out of her thigh holster and pressed against his temple.

"Remember me?" she inquired sweetly. "And surely you recall my friend, Officer O'Riley?"

The young man's blue eyes darted toward Damian then returned to Gwen. "You're the police?"

He spoke softly, but his light tenor voice had a resonance that suggested a theatre background. His accent was more pronounced than Ian's, not to mention crisper and harder to place. The closest thing Gwen had ever heard was the accent of a short-term boyfriend, an Hungarian grad student whose English had a slight British flavor.

"Are you going to arrest me?" continued Gwen's captive.

"That's the plan, yeah."

"You can't do that," he stated, more calmly than most people could have managed under the circumstances. "Not if you expect to live until the next full moon."

"Don't be threatening her," Damian warned. "That's a real bad idea."

Gwen sent the cop a quelling glance. She slowly rose to her feet and stepped away, keeping her gun on the man.

"You know," she said conversationally, "not many people can pull off snooty when they're flat on their backs. I admire your style."

"And I your speed and agility. May I rise?"

"Do it slowly," she warned.

He got to his feet in a fluid sweep of motion that was absurdly graceful and impossibly slow: ballet played back half-speed.

"Damn," Damian muttered. "The man can *move*."

"As can you," the blond man told Gwen. "The first time I saw you, I knew what you were from the way you moved. Given your heritage, surely you know that turning me in to the authorities would mean a death sentence for me."

As much as she hated to admit it, there was a certain grim logic to that. It would be hard to keep a collective low profile if the police started taking too close a look at individuals. Most likely one of the Elder Folk who landed in jail had about the same life expectancy as a Mafia informer.

"I've heard that killing each other is a big no-no," Gwen said. "So the deal is, if you die because of me, I die, too?"

"You grasp the situation precisely."

"I grasp that it's supremely fucked up," Damian observed.

"This doesn't concern you," the blond man said coolly.

"Actually, I'd say it does." Gwen tipped her head toward Damian. "That guy isn't one of us. Even better, he doesn't answer to me. I'm not his boss, partner, wife, mother, or girlfriend. I am in no way responsible for what he does, nor do I direct his actions in any way. In fact, at the moment it's the other way around. This is his party, and I'm the tagalong."

The young cop knew a cue when he heard one. He pulled his gun and aimed it at the man's kneecap.

"You think?" he asked Gwen.

She shrugged. "Let's see what he's got to say first. Start with your name," she told him.

"Adrian," he offered. "When I'm required to offer a surname, I use Archer."

"Okay, Adrian Archer, what's your gig these days, now that Edmonson's gone?"

"Much the same as before. I do whatever the earl's business affairs require. At present I'm running the clubs until his heir steps forward to claim them."

Gwen suddenly had a bad feeling about this. "His heir?"

"The closest kin. In the earl's case," he said meaningfully, "his only kin."

"Oh, shit," she murmured.

Damian caught on fast. "Wait a damn minute," he demanded. "You're related to this Edmonson guy? And you just inherited a couple of high-ticket titty bars?"

"She will come into a considerable amount of property," Adrian responded. A tiny smile flickered at the corner of his lips. "Provided, of course, she meets the terms of inheritance."

"Gee, I can't wait to hear those," Gwen said with heavy sarcasm. "You guys have lawyers?"

"Of course. You would have been contacted once the official mourning period ended."

"Since I've shed all the tears I plan to, why don't you just give me the highlights."

He shook his head. "I am bound by certain oaths. I will turn the earl's affairs over to you, but several days remain to the mourning period."

Gwen thought this over. "I suppose you know where I live?"

"Of course."

"All right, then, we'll let you go if you give me your oath that when the mourning period ends, you'll contact me and lay out everything you know about the earl's drug business. Swear it by moon and star, wind and word."

Adrian looked at Gwen as if she'd finally said something interesting. "That is a most solemn oath."

"Yeah, it's a favorite of mine, too. Let's hear it."

When he said the words, Gwen returned her gun to its holster and gave him a curt nod. "See you around, Archer."

He touched two fingers to his forehead and melted off into the shadows.

An angry crashing erupted from a stand of bushes behind them. Gary Quaid came wading toward them, crumbled leaves in his brown hair and an angry scowl on his face.

"What the hell's wrong with you two? You're letting dealers walk now?"

"He'll be back," Gwen stated.

Quaid's eyes narrowed. "And you know this how?"

"Because I can't eat French fries anymore," Gwen told him. She shrugged at his puzzled frown. "Long story."

Quaid's breath hissed out in obvious exasperation. He sucked air in slowly, through clenched teeth, clearly fueling up for a major ass-chewing.

"Hold on," Damian told Quaid as he stepped between the former partners. "Before you two start throwing punches, there's something you need to see. We came out here for more than one reason. Follow me, and keep it quiet."

He took off without waiting for a response. Quaid glanced at Gwen. When she didn't offer any explanation, he shrugged and fell into step behind his rookie.

The three of them left the path and walked quietly to the other side of the park and around behind a thick stand of trees. Damian motioned for them to get down.

After a few minutes, three men slipped out of the shadows and off into the night.

When they were out of earshot, Damian said, "See that bench there, right by the trees? When I did the paperwork for this bust, that's the place I said we were supposed to meet the dealer. Anyone at the station could have read it. But I told you and the contact to come to another place, at a later time. Those guys have been waiting here for maybe an hour."

"It's a freaking ambush," Gwen summarized.

Quaid nodded slowly. "And the only way those guys would have known where to meet you is if someone in the vice squad told them. Smart move on your part."

His choice of words made Gwen wince. Quaid's chowder-thick Rhode Island accent left him severely R-impaired. Sentences such as "Smot move on yoah pot" were particularly painful.

On the other hand, Quaid's reaction answered an important question. He had no idea about the ambush. It wasn't absolute proof that he wasn't dirty, but at least he wasn't the one who'd betrayed his young partner.

"Switching the meeting place was Gellman's idea," Damian said. He sent her a wry grin. "I gotta tell you, I'm pretty fucking glad I ran the plan past her."

His voice came out a little shaky. Gwen slid an arm around the young cop's shoulders, but no reassuring words came to her mind.

"So what do we do now?" Damian demanded.

Quaid turned a cool, measuring stare toward Gwen. "We continue what Gellman started: figure out who's feeding info to Walsh."

"What do you—" Damian stopped short as understanding hit. "Damn, Gellman—you thought *Quaid* was the rat?"

"It's important to rule out possibilities," the cop said evenly. "In her shoes, I would have done the same thing."

They walked several blocks in somber silence, coming to Damian's car first. The rookie nodded good night and took off. Gwen batted away the resulting exhaust fumes and turned to face her former partner.

"Since we walked past your car on the last street, I figure you've got something to say to me."

Quaid folded his arms and returned her stare. "I saw Kate Myers last week. She said the two of you started running together."

Gwen frowned. Quaid had never been much for small talk, but that was abrupt even for him. "That's right. So?"

"If you don't mind me asking, how did that come about?"

She shrugged. "We both live on the East Side. We both run. It's convenient."

"But who initiated it?"

"Kate did," she said slowly. "What's this about?"

He thrust his hands into his pockets and stared moodily at the house across the street. "I started dating Kate shortly after you and I were partnered up. A week or two after I break up with Kate, I find out that you two are buddies? It doesn't play right."

"You think she might be keeping an eye on me?"

"It crossed my mind."

"For whom?"

"Well, that's the question, isn't it?"

Gwen thought this over. The most likely culprit would be Dennis Walsh, but it wouldn't be the first time Internal Affairs decided to observe a cop under investigation through an unconventional angle. After the raid on Winston's, IA had been all over her. It wasn't outside the realm of possibility that Kate Myers had been recruited to pick up secondhand info from Gwen's partner, then to observe Gwen herself.

Seriously sleazy, yes, but the Providence police force wasn't exactly a hotbed of trust and brotherly love. Like the time a small silver disk with flashing lights was found in an interrogation room, and the police department, assuming IA was checking on the cops, had an outside company evaluate the object. The hired geeks declared it a high-tech listening device. Local newscasts were all over that, and eventually it came out that the "high-tech device" had broken off a cheap piece of costume jewelry. An earring, to be precise. Gwen had laughed herself silly over that one. For starters, you'd think the thick shitheads at the station would think to ask why anyone would design a "secret device" to look like a tiny disco lamp.

It just went to show how paranoid cops in the post-Buddy era had become. The police force had often been described as Buddy Ciencia's private army, and the former mayor's ouster on corruption charges made a lot of government employees nervous. Gwen had experienced firsthand the let's-clean-house mentality that could transform accusation into nightmare and turn long-term friends and coworkers into cold-eyed strangers. Against that backdrop, Quaid's concerns didn't seem quite so outlandish.

"Did Kate ask a lot of questions about your work?" she asked.

"Some," Quaid admitted. "I didn't think much of it. Since she's an ME, some of her cases overlapped with mine."

"When Kate and I run, I'm the one asking questions, but I suppose that's another way of gathering info. Asking questions gives a pretty clear picture of what I know and where I'm thinking of heading. If someone wanted to find out my thoughts concerning Frank Cross's death, Kate would be the person to ask."

"There you go," he said glumly.

"I asked Kate to do Frank Cross's autopsy," she reminded him. "When it comes to coincidence, I'm as skeptical as the next guy, but that puts a dent in your 'let's keep an eye on Gellman' theory."

"Yeah, but did she bother to tell you that she was the only ME working that week? She would have done the autopsy regardless."

"Hmmm. Must have slipped her mind," Gwen murmured. "Interesting theory you've got going about your ex-girlfriend."

He shrugged. "You're not the only one crossing names off a list."

"You mind telling me why you thought to look at her? I mean, she's an ME. That's related to the job, sure, but a corpse-cutter playing Mata Hari?"

"She started pressuring me to back away from the investigation of that nightclub bust," Quaid said softly. "When I asked her where that was coming from, she tells me about what was done to Moniz and Yoland in the morgue. Says it was a warning to the cops to stay away. The weird thing was, no one else at the station said word one about it. I figured she was making it up."

"No, it happened," Gwen told him. "Teresa Moniz confirmed. She insisted on seeing her husband's body, and she made a sketch of the design cut into him."

Quaid looked genuinely shocked. "No way."

"In context, it made sense. The design was some sort of mystical symbol, and she's into that stuff. It's also the same markings we found on the women the Jamisons tortured and killed. When they weren't playing *those* games, the Jamisons dealt party drugs for the guy who owned Winston's. It all ties in."

The cop's brow furrowed. "But Tiger Leone died in the raid."

Since Gwen was the one who'd killed him, this wasn't exactly news. "Tiger wasn't the owner. The paperwork was set up to make it look that way. Tiger worked for a guy named Wallace Edmonson. Him, we won't find—he's in the wind. As of last week, he's out of the country. Last known destination, Athens."

Quaid took this in. "So Kate was telling the truth about what happened to those cops. About the warning."

"Yes," Gwen said slowly, "but come to think of it, maybe the warning wasn't directed at the police. Maybe the message was for *Kate*. That would explain why no one at the station heard about it. Both men were cremated, so there wouldn't be any buzz coming back from funeral directors. If Kate hadn't said anything to you, it would have stayed with her."

"What about Teresa Moniz?"

"Psychic. She's the real deal, so you can stop rolling your eyes.

I'm betting she got a feeling that something had happened. If she came down to the morgue and demanded to see her husband's body, there's not much Kate could do."

Quaid huffed out a long sigh and folded his arms. "For argument's sake, let's say you're right. That means Kate would be tied in with this Edmonson guy, right?" He shook his head in disbelief. "A drug dealer, a guy who owns sleazy clubs, and *Kate*? How the hell did *that* connection happen?"

"Edmonson was really good at roping people in. You said you've been talking to Kate. Did she by any chance know that we were coming out here tonight?"

"Not unless you told her," he said.

Gwen shook her head. "I haven't talked to her since Monday night. She knew I had a class on Tuesday, and I left a message on her machine telling her I couldn't run tonight."

A silence fell between them. "Can you look into possible ties between Kate and Edmonson?"

"First thing tomorrow," she assured him.

"Good. I'd love to be proven wrong on this."

"But you don't think you are."

Quaid shrugged. "Gut feeling."

"Yeah, but your gut's been wrong before," Gwen said lightly, hoping to tease some of the veiled sorrow from his eyes. "You thought I was one of the bad guys."

He turned to her, and his bleak expression didn't brighten in the slightest. "This Edmonson is in Athens, you say?"

"That's what his passport says. But by this time, I doubt you'd find him there."

The cop nodded slowly, never taking his eyes from her face. "Yeah, I doubt that, too."

A knot started to form in Gwen's throat. Had Damian passed along what she'd told him about Edmonson? Surely not—he couldn't let slip that Edmonson was dead without revealing what he knew of Gwen's odd heritage.

"You still don't trust me."

His smile was tight and humorless. "Let's just say I've noticed people you don't like tend to disappear. As far as I can tell, the Jamisons dropped off the face of the earth. Now you're telling me that Tiger Leone's boss is nowhere to be found. I've got to admit, I'm a little concerned."

Gwen let a beat or two pass before asking, "Is this your way of asking me if I like you?"

For several moments he simply stared. "Do you find this amusing?"

"No, but I *do* find it amusing that you're so worried about who's on my shit list," she snapped. "If you'd been paying attention, you might have noticed that my *friends* have more to worry about than my enemies. Tom Yoland died in the raid on Winston's. Frank Cross is dead. Someone tried to ambush Damian tonight. When I *start* liking you," she concluded grimly, "*that's* when you should worry."

CHAPTER

Eight

A tentative sunrise was experimenting with pastel pinks as Gwen jogged down Sylvia's long gravel drive. She let herself out through the pedestrian door beside the main gate and started down the road.

The door on a parked car swung open abruptly, swinging right into her path with a timing that was too perfect to be accidental. She leaped out of range and took a step forward. Pulling her gun from her thigh holster, she dropped to one knee, using the open door as a shield.

When no further attack was forthcoming, she slowly rose, holding her gun in front of her with both hands.

To her surprise, the driver was a fat man with a bad comb-over and a who-shot-the-sofa plaid sport coat. Dennis Walsh, captain of the vice squad and her former boss, slowly lifted his hands from the steering wheel and held them up, empty.

Gwen glanced at the passenger seat for a ready weapon, then into the backseat. Both empty.

She holstered her gun and sent a pointed glance at Sylvia's stately brick home. "I have *got* to get a better address. Any lowlife can wander into this neighborhood."

Walsh hauled himself out of the car and leaned his arms on the top edge of the open door. "It seems like you'd want people to find you, seeing that you're in business for yourself now.

"Business," he repeated emphatically, "in a residential area. We have zoning codes in this city, Gellman. You can't run a shop out of this place."

"Maybe not, but I *can* have a home office," Gwen countered. "I don't have a principal place of business. I'm like a consultant; I meet most of my clients off-site and do nearly all my work in the field."

"Yeah, but what address do you advertise?"

"You won't find me in the Yellow Pages. I work strictly on referrals."

"Smart," he approved. "I can see how you'd want to keep a low profile. This state has some pretty hefty fines for people like you, doing business without a PI license."

Gwen's laugh held more derision than humor. "People like me? Jesus, you're really fishing. I'm completely legal, Walsh. My bond is paid, and my license isn't up for renewal for another three months."

"And that's interesting, you having a PI license," he went on doggedly. "I thought one of the requirements was good moral character. Good moral conduct," he emphasized. "Maybe the IA couldn't prove it, but everyone in the department knows you were pretty friendly with a drug-dealing pimp. They sure as hell know the two cops who were looking into your little game ended up dead."

Gwen had taken two quick steps toward him before she realized she was in motion. She caught herself and clenched her fists at her side until her nails bit into her palms.

"You do not want to go down that road," she warned, "because you won't like where it's going to lead."

A mottled flush crept up Walsh's face. "Listen, Gellman, when you're not on the job, you can't see the whole picture. Look what happened when you butted in with the Cody girl."

"I didn't exactly crash the party. Meredith Cody's mother hired me to find her missing daughter, and with good reason. The girl had been gone for four days."

"And the kid would have been back at the end of those four days, if you hadn't started nosing around." The chief held up a hand to cut her off. "Ryan Cody filled me in on the details. After he brought me in, I insisted on it."

"Did he also mention that he was working for a sleaze peddler, and that his daughter was snatched to keep him in line? But you'd know all about that, wouldn't you? By that point you and Wallace Earl Edmonson were well acquainted, and I got the very distinct impression that you weren't very happy about that relationship."

His eyes narrowed. "Where is this going? All I know is Edmonson was Cody's lawyer."

"Edmonson owned Ryan Cody. I guess Cody figured it wouldn't be too good for his career if it got around that he gets off on kiddy porn. I'll bet a lot of people would love to hear what Edmonson's holding over *you*."

Walsh sent her a reptilian smile. "Don't take up poker, Gellman, because you can't bluff worth shit. If you had something, you would have put it on the table by now."

"I'm working my way around to it. Tiger Leone was also reporting to Edmonson."

"Yeah? That wasn't in the reports you filed after the bust."

"I didn't know about it at the time. Since then I've learned all kinds of interesting things."

"Like?"

Gwen suppressed a grim smile. Walsh usually wasn't so transparent. He stopped by to lean on her a bit, hoping a few threats might persuade her to back off. Barring that, he wanted info. Fine. She couldn't wait to see his reaction.

"Tiger Leone got a phone call the night Yoland and Moniz came to the club. An old friend, he said—someone who'd been busted by Yoland and Moniz. Someone who conveniently called when the cops were standing right there. That was Eddie Davis, wasn't it?"

Walsh shifted one plaid-covered shoulder. "Might have been. Him and Leone came up together."

"Davis got out just that day. You want to know why I know that? Because I'm looking into every case handled by Edmonson's pet lawyers. Ryan Cody, of Simmons, Fletcher, and Rye, handled Davis, and Edmonson handled him. I figure you assigned me to Tiger before Edmonson sucked you in. You couldn't pull me off the case or keep Yoland and Moniz from following their leads without raising questions, but you *could* set us up. You expected all three of us to die that night."

"That's bullshit."

"Maybe, but the truth frequently is."

He shrugged, proving he was still cop enough to concede her logic in this matter. "Even if that was true, you couldn't prove it and you'd sound crazy just saying it."

"It's amazing what people will believe. Like the IA buying your story about the Tiger Leone paperwork disappearing, along with the forms for the leave of absence I supposedly requested."

Walsh shrugged again. "One of those regrettable errors known to occur in busy offices."

Gwen leaned in close. "You're an idiot, Walsh, and what's worse, you're a fucking dinosaur. You know those little beige boxes sitting on all the detectives' desks? They're called 'computers.' Tenacious little bastards. Once they've got hold of some information, they hang onto it."

He had the sense to look wary. "What are you saying?"

"I sent you a preliminary report when you first assigned me to shadow Tiger Leone. It might have been deleted, but when my old computer was scrapped, the files were stripped off the hard drive."

For a long moment Wash stood very still. Then his eyes cleared, and a smile crept over his face. "Even if that's true, it doesn't mean a damn thing. That was just you covering your ass—"

He broke off and raked a scathing gaze over her outfit: good running shoes, a custom-made thigh holster with straps at the top and bottom to keep her gun from bouncing, and a black sports bra that matched her shorts.

"Covering your ass," he repeated, his gaze fixed pointedly on that portion of her anatomy, "and, as usual, not doing a very good job of it. You didn't send me this alleged report by e-mail, did you? If someone got into the guts of *my* computer, would they find a copy of that report?"

Gwen's stomach suddenly took a nose dive in the general direction of her Reeboks.

"There didn't seem to be a point," she said dully. "You never read e-mail. I printed a copy and put it under your door."

"Then there's no record you actually sent that report." Walsh winked at her. "Sometimes it pays to be a fucking dinosaur."

He swung his considerable bulk into the car and gunned the engine. As she watched him spin triumphantly off, Gwen thought about Ian's claim that she had some sort of ability to cause rain. Too bad that talent didn't extend to meteor showers. If ever a dinosaur deserved to have his ass bombed into fossil fuel, it was Walsh.

Two hours later, Gwen flicked on her computer and waited impatiently for the files she'd stolen from Ryan Cody's computer to upload. They formed the basis for a growing database into the activities of Simmons, Fletcher, and Rye, the law firm that Edmonson owned—

No, that *she* owned. She was, after all, Edmonson's heir.

This had possibilities. She quickly dialed Cody's private line. He picked up on the second ring.

"It's Gwen Gellman," she told him. "I'm looking for some information on Kate Myers. There might be a connection between her and Edmonson. She's not the drugs and dancing type, so I thought I'd start with his law firm."

The only sound for several moments was a faint static. "You were a police officer. I shouldn't have to remind you about client privilege."

"But you could confirm whether or not she was ever a client?"

"I suppose," he said cautiously.

"How long would that take?"

"About fifteen seconds. The law firm has a searchable database. Spell that last name?"

Gwen gave him the spelling and listened to the faint, rapid clatter of computer keys.

"Kate Myers wouldn't by any chance be related to Sergeant Brendan Myers, Providence city police?"

"Probably. She mentioned her father was a cop, killed in the line of duty."

"About twenty-five years ago, yes. His daughter Katherine received a full scholarship through college and medical school."

"From the law firm?"

"That's right. Over the years, Simmons, Fletcher, and Rye has assisted several promising students."

"Interesting. Survivor benefits to off-the-books employees? Or maybe an investment in the future?"

Cody sighed heavily. "I wouldn't be at all surprised. But since Myers's name only appears in the scholarship fund, I couldn't tell you what business Edmonson might have had with the sergeant or his daughter."

"You're being unusually candid. Thinking of moving on?"

"If I could, I'd quit tomorrow," he said bluntly. "You know I can't."

Gwen knew. Cody had been recruited by Simmons, Fletcher, and Rye because his personal flaws gave Edmonson a means of control. When that failed, Edmonson had Cody's fourteen-year-old daughter snatched to remind the attorney who held his leash.

"How is Meredith?"

"She's taking some time off from school. We felt she needed a change of scenery. Dianne took the children to visit friends."

In other words, his family was gone. "Your choice or hers?"

"Does it matter?"

As a matter of fact, it did. If Dianne Cody wanted to dump her husband because he was a sleaze, Gwen had no arguments. If the family was trying to put things back together, that was another story. Her gut told her Cody genuinely wanted change. He'd outgrown his hobby when he started realizing that the hot young things he'd been watching onstage were *kids,* not much older than his own daughter. To his credit, that had proved to be a major buzz kill. But when he tried to leave the corrupt law firm, his daughter paid the price for his rebellion. As long as Cody thought Edmonson had a hold over him, he wouldn't do anything that might put his family at risk again. Knowing that Edmonson was dead could make all the difference in the world to the Cody family.

On the other hand, Gwen had no reason to trust Ryan Cody. For now, a bit of cautious optimism was the best she could offer.

"I'm working on something that might have an impact on your career plans. If it pans out, I'll let you know."

Several beats of silence passed as he processed the possibilities. "If you require representation, I'd be happy to recommend another attorney," he said softly.

Another *criminal* attorney, Gwen noted, reading between the lines to the phishing expedition. Cody suspected that she was taking a less-than-legal approach to the problem of Edmonson, and his faintly eager tone suggested that he more than approved.

Gwen made some noncommittal noises and ended the call, glad she'd gone with her instincts about passing along information on Edmonson. Maybe Cody had changed his mind about kiddy porn, but he was still a sleaze.

Shortly after noon, Gwen walked up the stairs of a state-run nursing home, wearing a ball cap embossed with the name of a made-up florist and carrying a cheap floral arrangement she'd purchased at the nearest grocery store.

She stopped at the front desk, a battered wooden relic heaped with medical charts. A thin, tired-looking woman in an old-fashioned white uniform was working her way through the stack. Gwen got the nurse's attention and asked for Irma Williams.

The woman's ferret-eyed gaze took in the flowers. "Hmmph. About damn time, is all I got to say."

Gwen blinked in feigned surprise. "Delivery was guaranteed by end of the day. I'm actually a little earlier than I expected."

"Oh, I wasn't talking about you, honey. It's that son of Irma's. Son of a *bitch* is more like it, no reflection on poor Irma. Haven't seen him around here in maybe two, three years."

"Sorry to hear that."

"Be nice to your kids, I always say," the nurse went on. "Not that you're old enough to have kids just yet, and don't you be in any hurry. Just remember, someday those kids will decide where you end your days. Not that there's anything wrong with this place," she added hastily.

Gwen managed a smile. "I'll keep that in mind."

"No, you won't," the nurse retorted. "You kids all think you're immortal."

"Not me," Gwen said fervently. "What could be more depressing than knowing you were going to live forever?"

The nurse snorted in agreement and gestured toward her littered desk. "You might as well take those flowers right down to Irma. God knows there's no place to put them here."

Gwen got the room number and general directions, and set off down a series of halls floored in cracked, yellowed linoleum. The walls were long overdue for painting, and many of the rooms she passed were still the shade of institutional green that was considered soothing fifteen or twenty years back. The unsavory scent of lunch—liver and onions with a side of broccoli would be Gwen's guess—competed with a strong undercurrent of unwashed bodies and unchanged Depends.

Gwen couldn't help wondering what happened to her kind of people when they got old—or for that matter, *if* they got old. She couldn't see the Elder Races warehousing their oldest members. In her more facetious moments, Sister Tamar claimed the Canadian government could afford a uniform health-care system because they set their elderly adrift on ice floes. From what Gwen had seen of the Elder Races so far, she suspected they'd employ some similar method.

She found room 321 and tapped on the open door. A tiny woman with skin like thin, crumpled brown parchment was seated by the window. She regarded Gwen with bird-bright eyes.

"Yes, dear?"

"Are you Mrs. Williams?"

The woman looked puzzled for a moment. Her expression cleared and her eyes lit up. "Yes, that's me! Lord, I haven't heard that name in years. The people around here are 'Irma this, Irma that.' Talking to me like I was a child. I'm not, you know. I'm a married woman."

Gwen responded with a noncommittal hmm. "Where would you like me to put your flowers?"

Irma Williams flashed a radiant, toothless smile and held out her arms for the flowers. "Those would be from my Henry. He never forgets an anniversary. We've been married for some time, you know."

Thanks to the report Gwen had received that morning from her information broker, she knew that Henry had been Roy Williams's father. Roy had told Shawna O'Riley half the truth: his father was long dead. His mother was alive, but when her mind faltered under the weight of her years, she'd forgotten him and he'd apparently decided to return the favor.

She placed the flowers on the peeling windowsill, right next to Mrs. Williams.

"Enjoy them," she said as she backed out of the room. She swiftly retraced her steps down the depressing halls, knowing that she'd completed the job Damian had asked her to do: she'd found a reason for the vague unease the cop had felt around Roy Williams.

Gwen had a fairly good idea how Shawna O'Riley would react to this news. Knowing he'd warehoused his mother would be a deal-breaker.

She could picture Shawna's stunned indignation, but she couldn't understand it. Yes, Roy Williams had dumped his mother in a state-run home, to an unknown fate at the hands of strangers. That was no different from what had been done to her, and Gwen couldn't manage to summon the same level of indignation. What she had was questions. Lots of them.

She'd only recently learned that James and Ruby Avalon, not David and Regina Gellman, were her real parents.

When her parents died in a car crash, another baby girl had been strapped in Gwen's car seat—or whatever people used thirty-four years ago when they traveled with small children. They'd taken that little girl from her crib and left Gwen in her place. Apparently this was standard practice among her kind. What had prompted her parents to do this, and what did it say about them?

It wasn't a pretty picture from any angle. At the very least, James and Ruby Avalon had put another child at risk to save their own daughter's life. According to Edmonson, they had brutally slaughtered the girls' parents and left their own daughter, a changeling child, to be raised by the state.

And why were her parents running? What did they have that Wallace Edmonson wanted? Was it just the blue crystal he'd shown Gwen, or something more?

Over the years, Gwen had never given much thought to her family. During her childhood, practical matters—such as survival—had taken most of her focus, and she'd never seen much sense in dwelling on the past. But all of a sudden family was very, very important. There was no getting around it: to understand what she was, she had to know more about where she'd come from.

Even if—no, *especially* if—those answers were hard to face.

The scent of cinnamon greeted Gwen when she walked into The Green Man later that afternoon. Alice Powers hastened over, a steaming mug in hand.

"Any word of Erin?" she demanded before Gwen could speak.

"Nothing yet. In fact, I have a few more questions for you, if you don't mind."

"Of course not. Would you like some tea while we talk? It's the same kind you had the other day, only with a bit of cider and cinnamon added."

It sounded like one of the concoctions Trudy routinely made. She was always drinking some sort of green-smelling brew laced with juice and spices and god-only-knows what else. And she wasn't alone in this. You could actually buy the stuff in bottles at otherwise respectable coffeehouses.

"No, thanks. I'm a degenerate coffee fiend, myself."

Alice clicked her tongue reprovingly. "A good herbal tea is much healthier, not to mention far more soothing."

Who wanted soothing? Gwen was used to being tense and saw no reason to change.

On the other hand, Trudy would probably love this stuff, and considering their last exchange, perhaps a keep-the-peace offering was in order. Gwen picked up a box that had a label similar to the shop's sign. "Is this it?"

"Yes. Those are loose tea leaves. It also comes in a condensed syrup that's very convenient for making fruit-blend teas, warm or iced."

"I'll take one of each."

Alice's appraising gaze slid down Gwen, taking in her ancient leather jacket, the dozen or so cheap silver rings on her hands, and the boots from Payless, buy one pair get the second pair half-off.

"This particular tea isn't inexpensive."

What the hell, thought Gwen—it was on Kyle's dime. "In that case," she said dryly, "I'll take two of each."

The woman gave her an uncertain smile, but she rang up the sale and led Gwen into the tearoom. Alice sat down and pushed up the sleeves of her sweater in a getting-down-to-business gesture not usually associated with lavender cashmere.

"Now, what can I tell you?" she asked briskly.

"Anything you can think of. Any names Erin might have mentioned—friends, babysitters, her kid's friends, whatever. Any people who came here to see her recently."

Alice shrugged. "We're seldom in the shop on the same day. When we are together, Erin is pleasant, but very private. She really doesn't share much. Funny," she mused, "but I've never really noticed that before."

Apparently sharing wasn't something Erin did. Kyle gave her a generous household allowance, but he had no idea what she spent the money on. At Gwen's request, he'd sent a disc containing a record of their household bills, which he had scanned into a computer file and meticulously organized. Odd, that someone who was that particular about his finances would let huge chunks of cash go unaccounted for. Erin used one of Kyle's debit cards for mundane purchases—gas, groceries, clothing, and so on—but apparently she paid cash for anything that might leave a clue to her habits.

"Has she ever mentioned a favorite restaurant or shop? Or maybe where she gets her hair done?"

The older woman brightened up. "Yes! She had some very nice reddish highlights added about a month ago, and I asked her where she had them done. She mentioned a day spa in Newport: Esprit. It's down on Belleview Avenue, not far from the Tennis Hall of Fame."

In Gwen's opinion, that was a long way to drive to get a haircut. Usually when people went that far out of their way, they were going to a familiar salon or a longtime hairdresser.

That was good news. There seemed to be something about the fumes in those girly places that made women want to tell complete strangers about their lives. Maybe Erin had let something slip.

She thanked Alice and hit the road, heading back north to catch the bridge leading to the bay's biggest island. The drive to Newport was decidedly unscenic, winding as it did through streets lined with strip malls. Golden arches and similar signs hinted enticingly of off-limit French fries, breaking Gwen's heart every few blocks. It took her over a half hour to wind through this culinary purgatory to the island's southernmost town.

Apart from a couple of visits to the summer jazz festival, Gwen had never had much reason to visit Newport, but she figured Belleview Avenue couldn't be too hard to find. All the Gilded Era mansions were along this street—the "summer cottages" built by the Vanderbilts and their buddies back in the days before income tax and minimum-wage laws cut into a robber baron's profits.

After doing a few circles on narrow, one-way streets lined with historic clapboard houses and the occasional folksy tavern, Gwen found Belleview. She parked at the small, upscale strip mall and walked the rest of the way to the day spa, armed with Erin's photo.

Jason had scanned the photo Kyle had given Gwen into his computer and fooled around with it until he managed to crop little Patrick out of the picture and superimpose Erin's picture on a woody background. He'd made a good job of it. That was no major surprise to Gwen. Some people just had the knack—god knows Frank had taken to the computer like it was a new kind of donut.

Gwen showed the altered picture to the receptionist, a young woman with honey-blond hair gathered back into an artfully careless knot. The blonde pursed her lips and studied the photo.

"She looks familiar. Lisa? Take a look at this."

A thirtysomething woman with sleek black hair cut in an asymmetric wedge came over and glanced at the photo.

"Sure, that's Helene. Helene Tremaine. I've been doing her hair for years." Her eyes narrowed in sudden suspicion. "Why?"

Gwen gave a quick, fictitious explanation: she couldn't remember the name of the day spa Helene had recommended, only that it was on Belleview Avenue. She'd tried to call Helene to check, but she wasn't answering her phone.

Lisa cast a critical eye over Gwen's short hair, which had been styled only moments before by a brisk wind and a few impatient passes of Gwen's hands. "Unfortunately, I don't have any openings today."

"No problem—I'll call in later and make an appointment. What I was wondering is, can you tell me what sort of styling products Helene uses?"

"I could, but your hair is . . . a lot different from hers."

Gwen grinned. "That's more tactful than I would have been! I like the way hers looks—nice long layers, lots of shine—and I'm thinking of letting mine grow out. I know I've got a ways to go, but what can I do to help bridge the gap?"

The stylist explained in considerable detail the virtues of various bottles of overpriced hair goop. But where Erin/Helene was concerned, she sang pretty much the same song that Alice Powers had: the woman was pleasant, but didn't talk about herself very much.

"She's a very pretty woman," Lisa concluded, "but you shouldn't try to copy her look. For one thing, she's quite a bit older than you. In fact, her hairstyle is a little young for someone her age."

A jolt of surprise hit Gwen. She saw Lisa register the reaction, so she decided to hide it in plain sight. "Wow. I thought she was close to my age!"

The stylist smiled. "Now you're just being nice. I remember what it was like when I was a teenager. Anyone over thirty was ancient. Helene is a pretty woman and I can help her look her best, but she'll never look seventeen again. That's a nice photo, but it's years out-of-date."

That was interesting. The picture Kyle had given Gwen couldn't have been taken more than a few months ago. In it, Patrick had looked around four or five, and Erin looked like she was still in high school.

"How long have you been doing Helene's hair?"

Lisa pursed her lips and gazed toward the ceiling as she counted the years. "Twelve, maybe thirteen years? Maybe a little longer."

"Well, she looks great. I'll bet you have a lot of customer loyalty."

The stylist beamed. "Thanks. Helene's a pretty woman, but it's important to have your own identity."

Gwen didn't have to feign the rueful edge to her answering smile. Apparently "Helene" didn't share that opinion.

Well, this was just great. Kyle's runaway wife had multiple identities, one of which was established well before she'd met Kyle. Gwen had found missing persons who'd had more than one identity, but something told her that finding Erin Westland or Helene Tremaine or whoever the hell she was would be about as easy as herding cats.

Gwen stopped to restock her fridge on the way home: milk for coffee, rolls and meat for sandwiches, and lots of fruit. She was barely in the door of her office when the front-gate buzzer rang. Grumbling, she dumped the bags on her desk and stabbed the intercom button with her car key.

"Who is it?"

"Whoa! Snarl much?"

The light, humor-edged baritone was familiar, even through the crackle of the intercom. Plus, she only knew one guy whose syntax was influenced by *Buffy the Vampire Slayer*.

"Jeff?"

"She remembers me! Did you forget about our date, or are you just fashionably late?"

She glanced at the calendar and suppressed a groan. The appointment was clearly marked: "Jeff & Jazz, 7:00."

Jeff Monroe was Marcy's legal assistant, a pleasant-looking young man who shared Gwen's taste in music. Three or four times a year, they went up to Woonsocket, a mill town in northern Rhode Island and the home of Jimmy Chen's, the only Chinese restaurant in the state that featured live jazz. Tonight was supposed to be one of those nights. A few egg rolls, a little music, and a friendly tumble to round out the evening. She'd been looking forward to it.

"I forgot," she confessed. "It's just that this case I've been working—"

"Say no more. When you didn't show, I picked up some take-out. We can put on a CD while we eat. It's not the original plan, but it's close enough."

A smile played at the corners of Gwen's lips as she buzzed him in. Jeff was a good-natured guy, and easy to be around. His face was pleasant rather than handsome, he wore glasses to work, and he was thin enough and clean-cut enough to look sort of nebbishy in a white shirt and tie. Thanks to an addiction to racquetball, he looked a lot better when the business clothes came off. Nothing too exciting, but he was the kind of guy that went well with jazz and lo mein. He was definitely vanilla, but vanilla sex was a good flavor for a weeknight.

She reclaimed her bags and sprinted up the stairs. It took all of five minutes to put the groceries away, and she was finished by the time she heard his footsteps on the stairs.

Jeff had switched from office attire to his equally conservative casual look: khaki Dockers and a polo shirt. Tonight's polo shirt was pale yellow, and over it he wore a cotton sweater in forest green.

He greeted her with a quick kiss, then handed her a black leather CD case. While Gwen flipped through the CDs for something interesting, he made himself at home in her miniature kitchen. He quickly dished up two plates and brought them to the coffee table.

"The chicken Hunan is way too spicy," he warned. "Do you have anything cold to drink?"

Gwen glanced up from the stereo, CD in hand. "There's some herb-tea mix in that little bottle and some cranberry juice in the fridge. You can mix it if you want—there's a pitcher in the cabinet over the sink. Glasses, too."

Jeff stirred up the concoction and took an experimental sip. He made a "not bad" face and drained the glass. He refilled his and poured another for Gwen, and brought them over to the sofa.

A saxophone began a mournful exploration of lost love as Gwen settled down beside Jeff. She took a mouthful of the chicken—Jeff hadn't been exaggerating about the spices—and promptly reached for her fruit tea. Like Jeff, she drained the glass. It took that much just to put out the fire. He refilled her glass from the pitcher, and topped off his own.

As she took another sip, the flavor began to edge its way past her seared taste buds. It wasn't anything like the bottled blends Marcy and Trudy were always getting at Starbucks. Gwen couldn't figure out why anyone would enter that cathedral of caffeine without taking Mass, but the fruit tea there wasn't half bad. This stuff was so sweet and strong it was almost medicinal.

"Yikes! Didn't you add water?"

He took a considering sip. "I didn't know I was supposed to. Maybe it's a little strong, but I like the taste."

She set her glass aside and tucked into her pork fried rice and the lo mein, then went back to the kitchen for seconds on both. The Hunan chicken wasn't so bad once she stirred in extra white rice. Jeff, however, continued to eat the spicy stuff straight up, washing it down with the fruit tea.

"Good thing it's herbal," she observed as he poured his fourth glass. "If that was regular black tea, the caffeine would keep you up all night."

Jeff responded with a sidelong glance and a decidedly masculine chuckle. "I don't think I'm going to need caffeine for that."

It took Gwen a moment to catch the double entendre—she just didn't expect them from Jeff. But neither did she expect that predatory gleam in his eyes.

Or his impatience.

He took the plate from her hands and tossed it like a Frisbee in the general direction of the coffee table. Before she could comment, he pulled her into his lap so that she was facing him, her knees straddling his lap.

Their first kiss was Hunan-spiced, and from there things heated up fast. He devoured her, exploring with ravenous hands as they kissed. When they came up for air, Jeff pulled off his sweater and polo shirt in one quick, impatient motion, then reached for the top button on Gwen's shirt. His fingers fumbled in their hurry. Grimacing in annoyance, he took hold of her shirt with both hands. Buttons flew as he ripped it open.

"Why the rush?" Gwen's protest was slightly breathless, and more amused than annoyed. "What's another minute or two?"

"An eternity," he murmured, his breath whispering against her neck as he worked his way down.

She reached around to unclasp her bra, lest it meet a similar fate. Jeff tossed it aside, then cupped her bottom with both hands to raise her to nuzzling position. He teased her with his lips and tongue while his hands slid around to tug at the leather thongs fastening her lace-up jeans.

Several minutes passed in this fashion. He wasn't making much headway with her pants, but Gwen didn't mind. It slowed things down a bit, and besides, her boobs were definitely enjoying the attention.

Finally he gave up. A groan of frustration escaped him as he dropped his head to rest on her shoulder. "Ever think about wearing a skirt?"

She grinned. "I've been known to. Hang on."

Scooting off the sofa, she tugged the laces loose and shimmied out of her jeans. He was diving at her when her cell phone rang.

Gwen stepped nimbly beyond reach of his grasping hands and walked naked toward her kitchen.

"You're not going to answer that?" he asked, incredulous.

"I have to. I have several cases going. This could be important."

Damian's number flashed on the readout. She clicked on the phone. "What's up?"

"I just came from the Extreme. You know, the place where Jackie Teal was dancing? She was a no-show."

Guilt and concern hummed through his voice, but Gwen had no time for that right now. "Are you *insane?* You went to the club to see her after what happened last night?"

"Wanted to make sure she was okay, is all. When a cop turns up on the other end of a drug deal, people get unhappy, you know?"

"Only too well."

Jeff came up behind her and nuzzled at her neck. He'd shed the rest of his clothes, and it was obvious that the interruption hadn't seriously dampened his mood—Gwen felt the hard evidence of that pressed against her.

First Jason, now Jeff. What was going on with the men in her life?

Not that she was complaining. She reached over her shoulder with one hand and slid her fingers into his crisp, short brown hair.

"The guy from the park—he runs the club now," she reminded Damian. "You're lucky you were able to walk out of there."

"Let's hope Jackie was that lucky," he said grimly.

Jeff slipped both arms around her waist. His hands skimmed up to cup her breasts and he began to tease her with urgent, insistent fingers. Gwen's knees suddenly felt less stable, and she leaned back against his chest.

"I'll help you look into it," she told Damian.

"Tonight? Can you come down to the club?"

"No, she can't," Jeff said coldly.

Gwen stiffened in surprise. She turned in his arms and stepped away. Her hormones were still singing, but for a moment incredulity was stronger than lust.

"What the hell is wrong with you? Listening in to my phone calls? Telling my friends what I can and can't do?"

"Shit, you got company. Sorry about that. I'll call you tomorrow," Damian said hastily, and the line went abruptly silent.

An expression of contrition crossed Jeff's face. "I don't know what came over me. It's just the sight of you standing there naked, talking to another man, made me feel like a green-eyed monster."

Gwen switched off the phone and placed it on the counter. "No strings, no commitments, no possessive bullshit," she reminded him. "That's the deal, and you've always been okay with it."

"I still am. A momentary aberration, that's all."

He pulled her to him and lifted her in one quick movement, his hands on the back of her thighs. Gwen wrapped her arms around his neck and held his smoldering gaze as he lowered her, pushing into her in one slow, extravagant stroke.

Lust shimmered through her, chasing away her pique. Granted, jealousy could be a problem. There was no way in hell she'd put up with the crap Marcy took from Trudy, and she'd definitely have to do something about it.

But not right now.

She wrapped her legs around Jeff's hips as he carried her toward the bedroom, reveling in the sensations that coursed through her with each slow, languorous step.

By the time they got to the bed, the banked fire in Jeff's eyes had flamed into something approaching madness. They fell together onto the bed, rolling twice before they fell off the other side in a tangle of limbs and sheets.

Gwen had time for a small, breathless laugh before Jeff claimed her lips. Their fingers met and entwined, and he raised her hands over her head, pinioning her to the floor as they took each other in a ravenous frenzy.

Much later, Gwen crawled back onto the bed and flopped onto her back. Her limbs felt like pasta that had been boiled way the hell past al dente, and her ears were actually ringing.

"Where is Jeff," she demanded, "and what have you done with him?"

The only response was a faint groan from the tangle of bedclothes on the floor.

Gwen glanced at her watch and barely kept from echoing the sentiment. Dawn was less than an hour away—not much sense going to sleep now. She had an early appointment and a long drive to get there.

She dragged herself out of bed and stumbled for the bathroom. Ian Forest had told her that rain was restorative for her, which sounded as crazy as everything else she'd heard from him over the past several days.

This tidbit of information, however, wasn't hard for her to accept. Not that she was the type to dance in puddles and swing herself blithely around lampposts, but for as long as she could remember, she'd always liked rain, and she found that a shower was nearly as refreshing as sleep. It was the first positive aspect to this whole changeling business. As the steaming spray beat down on her, Gwen was almost willing to believe that there might be others.

All her life she'd had questions, but she'd grown up in a world where answers were in short supply. Raised by the state, alongside other kids who'd been abandoned, discarded, or just generally fucked with, she eventually stopped asking and put her energy into surviving.

Then she'd met a chain-smoking, foul-tempered nun, who was and remained the most inherently decent person Gwen had ever known. Sister Tamar had an Old Testament viewpoint when it came to evil, and her approach to helping the victims of evil had given shape and purpose to Gwen's personal brand of rage. Becoming a cop allowed her to give back or get even—her priorities varied according to circumstances. Finding lost kids had kept her from spinning offtrack after her career was pulled out from under her. And now she had a new shtick: seek out other changelings, help them find their place in the world. It was work worth doing, and she was uniquely suited for it.

Optimism was a new flavor. Gwen liked it more than she expected to. It was a nice balance to the voice in the back of her mind, the warning that no amount of good sex and falling water could silence:

Once she found these changelings, what awaited them? Induction into the hidden society of the Elder Folk, certainly, but what, ultimately, would be the price of admission?

Ten

Gwen found her way into downtown Plymouth without much problem. She drove along the harbor and pulled into the public parking lot around nine o'clock. She got out of the car and stretched, catlike, working away the stiffness that came of a two-hour drive.

Oddly enough, she'd never been to Plymouth before, even though she'd spent her entire life in southern New England. It was a nice place if you liked this sort of thing—a pretty seaside town with lots of old buildings and a couple of nifty historical landmarks.

Gwen watched as a school bus disgorged its cargo. A trio of frazzled-looking teachers tried without much success to interest their kids in the rock entombed in a miniature Grecian shrine. As far as Gwen could tell, Plymouth Rock looked pretty much like any other big hunk of stone. And the reproduction of the Mayflower docked nearby was *tiny*. No wonder so many of the pilgrims had died the first winter. It was a marvel any of them survived the sea crossing. Hell, if Gwen had been forced to live in such close quarters, she would have been responsible for most of the shipboard deaths.

Having gotten in touch with her national roots, Gwen left her car and walked up a side street, following the directions on the Yahoo! map Jason had printed out for her.

Jason Cross was really getting to know his way around cyber-space. He'd spent the previous afternoon helping her search for Helene Tremaine. Between the two of them, they'd pieced together a partial picture. Helene was born in 1944, which meant she would be in her late sixties. Assuming Helene and Erin were one and the same, that wasn't out of the realm of possibility, as long as Erin aged as slowly as, say, Ian Forest.

Of course, that was a rather large assumption. Helene's stylist had recognized Erin's picture, but she'd insisted that "Helene" looked considerably older than Gwen. The photo was recent, and it showed a girl who could have been in Gwen's high-school graduating class. The numbers didn't add up, so Gwen decided to come to Helene's hometown for a closer look.

The only member of the Tremaine family Jason could track down was an older brother, still living in the house he and Helene had grown up in. It had taken some talking to get the man to agree to a meeting.

Clyde Tremaine sat on the step of a small porch, a rickety affair fronting a tall, narrow house painted barn red. He was tall and rangy, with a craggy, pitted face. Rheumy eyes regarded Gwen with a sour expression.

"You're the girl who's asking about Helene?"

"That's right."

"Don't see why. She died in a car crash way back in '61."

That date seized Gwen's attention. After 1962, lists of Social Security numbers for the deceased became a lot easier to come by. Interesting coincidence?

She showed him the picture Kyle had given her. "Is this Helene?"

The old man patted his shirt pocket for glasses, slipped them on, and leaned in close.

"That's her," he said, his voice flat. "Pretty much as I remember her, too. She was seventeen when she died."

"What was your sister like?"

The lines on his face deepened in disapproval. "Let's just say she died the way she lived. She'd run off that night to meet some boy my parents said she couldn't see. The boy, or what was left of him, was with her when the car crashed—*my* car, by the way. She took *my car,* and when they found her, she was wearing my mother's necklace. That was Helene. She helped herself to any little thing she wanted."

"She wasn't adopted, by any chance?"

The man looked surprised, then thoughtful. "No, but come to think of it, I once heard my folks talk about some sort of confusion at the hospital, a possible switch. Me, I'd always thought it was wishful thinking on their part."

Gwen wasn't so sure about that. "I know this is a hard question to answer, especially so long after the accident, but do you think there's even a remote possibility that the girl who died was not your sister?"

He thought about that for quite a while. "You know," he confided, "down deep, I never really felt that Helene *was* my sister."

Gwen returned to her car and switched on her phone to check messages. The first one was from Quaid. She hit Return and waited through several rings.

"Did you find out anything about Kate?" he asked without preamble.

"Yeah. Apparently she went to college on full scholarship, courtesy of the law firm Edmonson controlled. Anything happening on your end?"

"I called her at work. She hasn't been in since Monday."

An icy shiver danced down Gwen's spine. Jackie Teal didn't show up for work after she set up the drug meet for Damian, and now Kate? Someone was very serious about keeping people from looking too closely into Edmonson's business.

"Has someone gone over to her house to check on her?"

"I called, but she's not answering the phone. She was off Tuesday and Wednesday, so she only missed one day of work. Enough to annoy people, but not enough to worry them."

"Maybe you could drive by and knock on the door?"

"I stopped by last night. No answer."

"Was her car parked on the street?"

"Not that I could see, but I don't know what she's driving. She was shopping for a car when we split up. Did she tell you what she bought?"

"It never came up." Gwen sighed in frustration. "Without a missing-person report, you can't check her place out, at least not officially. How are you with locks?"

"I'll pretend I didn't hear that."

"You do that. Maybe I'll swing by for a little girl talk later today."

"Let me know how it goes."

As usual, he hung up without saying good-bye. Gwen listened to the rest of her messages and headed toward the nearest restaurant to refuel.

After a quick breakfast and several cups of coffee, Gwen headed for the town library and asked to see the microfilm archives of the local papers. If there was some sort of scandal about a possible baby-switching, it might have been covered.

The hours rolled by more slowly than the miniature pages. Gwen finally found the article around two o'clock that afternoon.

There were a few follow-up articles, too. She was not entirely surprised to learn that the other baby's parents had dropped off the
face of the earth shortly after the birth, and the daughter had ended
up in a foster home. The little girl was one of the system's rare success stories—she'd been adopted.

After making a few phone calls and calling in a few favors,
Gwen tracked down the adoptive parents. John and Emily Meekins
had spent most of their married life in Dartmouth, Massachusetts.
John Meekins, a retired professor, still lived in Dartmouth. It was
more or less on the way back to Providence, so Gwen decided to
give it a shot.

Dr. Meekins was even less interested in Gwen's search than
Clyde Tremaine had been. She had to play the missing-child card to
convince him to give her five minutes.

They met on the college campus, by the history department
where, Gwen assumed, he used to teach. Certainly John Meekins
looked like a retired history professor, right down to the tweed
jacket with elbow patches. He was ancient, his body worn down to
a shadow and his voice to a whispery quaver, but once he started
talking it became plain that his mind was still very sharp.

"Vivian changed rather suddenly when she was seventeen," he
told Gwen. "Before then she was a sweet girl, a good student.
Seemingly overnight she was crazy about boys, and she started
drinking and staying out all hours of the night. She left home the
day she turned eighteen and that was the last we saw of her."

"Do you know where she went?"

"She moved to Providence. My wife tried to keep in touch, but
Vivian couldn't be bothered—not even when her mother was dying. I haven't heard from her since." He glanced up at Gwen, a mix-

ture of anger and resignation in his faded eyes. "I suppose you have news."

For a moment, Gwen debated how much to tell him. She settled on the truth—or at least, what she suspected was true. "I'm sorry, Dr. Meekins, but your daughter is dead."

He nodded, accepting validation of an opinion he'd held for a long time. "I suppose you have your reasons for asking about her, and I trust you won't mind if I don't care to listen to them. Vivian has been dead to me for a very long time."

The professor cocked his head as if listening to the echo of his own words. "I know how that must sound to you. You must think me sadly lacking in family feeling."

"Not really," Gwen said slowly. "I'm starting to understand just how complicated family ties can be."

Kate Myers's car was parked right outside the narrow two-story building. Gwen knew the gleaming black Passat was Kate's the minute she touched it—the mental image of Kate behind the wheel was so real that she could almost smell the woman's perfume.

She walked up the stairs to the screened-in porch and tried the doorbell. The deep, sonorous tolling was clearly audible, but it didn't raise a response. Gwen tried the door. It was securely locked.

No problem. She took her key-and-pick combo from her pocket and slipped it into the lock on the doorknob. The lock popped in about five seconds. The door bowed out a little when Gwen tugged on the handle, but it held secure. There was no other lock on the outside, so she figured it had a dead bolt, one that could only be locked from the inside. A little paranoid, maybe, but effective.

Gwen circled around the house. A pile of garden mulch was heaped against the foundation. It smelled a bit odd, so she crouched down for a closer look.

The shredded wood was sodden, even though the last rain had been four days ago. Some of the chips appeared to be blackened. She picked up one and sniffed. There was a faint smell of lighter fluid.

She rocked back on her heels and stood, her gaze sweeping the backyard. There was a flower bed with a few May-flowering tulips and a row of spent daffodils. A clump of lilac bushes, the purple buds still tight, grew by the back stairs. The yard was dominated by a single large tree. It grew close to the back fence, but its branches spanned half the yard and shaded the neighboring property, as well.

Gwen checked the back door. Someone had kicked it in, splintering the old wood around the various locks. Gwen glanced at the ruined door. A lock in the doorknob, two dead bolts, one with a chain. Kate was definitely security conscious. Much good it had done her. If someone was determined enough, no locks could provide much of a deterrent.

Gwen moved cautiously into the kitchen, called Kate's name. There was no response, but she hadn't gone more than a few steps when it hit her—the sickly sweet, coppery smell of death.

Two doors led out of the kitchen, one into a small dining room, the other into a central hall. Gwen headed down the hall. The front door drew her eye, though for no reason she could ascertain. She laid her palm against the door and was immediately flooded by sensations of mute terror and agonizing pain, and behind it, a simple, alien mind numbed with the astonishment of betrayal.

Gwen snatched her hand away and rubbed it on the leg of her jeans, as if doing so could erase the odd vision. She peered at the door but could see nothing to explain her reaction, other than a slight tackiness that felt like the residual gumminess a price sticker left on a hard surface.

The smell was stronger now, and definitely coming from upstairs. She climbed the stairs and stood at the bedroom door only long enough to identify the body.

The woman had been shot several times. One bullet had gone into the back of her head at close range, blowing off most of her face. Her hair was so thickly matted with dried black blood that it was impossible to tell what color it once had been. But it was Kate, all right—or at least, someone wearing the clothes she'd worn for their Monday-night workout.

Gwen headed outside and took several long, cleansing breaths before pulling her cell phone from her pocket. Quaid would be pissed at her for not calling him first, but the farther he stayed away from this case, the better off he'd be.

She dialed the station and asked for homicide. After passing along the basic details, she sat down on the front step to wait for the detective.

Her first instinct had been to make an anonymous call, but that struck her as too risky. Judging from Kate's clothing and the state of her body, she'd been dead since Monday night. That meant Gwen was one of the last people who'd seen her alive. If she was going to get pulled into this, there could be no question about where she stood.

Unfortunately, the responding officers were not inclined to think the best of her. Ben Cerulo and Kimberly Jackson had been partners for years, reaching back into the time before Frank's retirement. The four of them had gone out for a beer from time to time, or to shoot a game of pool . . . but Tom Yoland had been Kimberly's cousin, and she'd taken his death hard—and blamed Gwen for the mess that had caused it.

Her plain, much-freckled face was hard as she regarded her former colleague. "Let's hear your report," she said curtly.

Gwen went through the basic details, leaving out only her lock-picking activities and the strange, painful memories haunting the front door.

"The back door was open when you got here," Kimberly repeated.

"It was unlocked and slightly ajar," she confirmed. "That, plus that fact that Kate's car was here, seemed sufficient reason to check things out."

"Probable cause, yes, but that doesn't apply if you're not a cop."

"Like I told you, Kate and I started running together last week. She hasn't been answering her phone, she didn't show up for work. I came over to see if she was okay. That's what friends do."

"And you and Kate Myers were friends."

"Heading in that direction, yeah."

Kimberly sniffed. "Seems like you've been losing a lot of friends recently."

The snide, hateful tone in her voice snapped Gwen's patience. She rose and took one step forward, looking the taller woman hard in the eye. "True enough, but apparently not all of them were worth keeping."

A hand settled on her shoulder. Gwen spun toward Kimberly's partner, a ready snarl on her lips, and was stunned by what she saw in his eyes.

Compassion.

Ben Cerulo squeezed her shoulder and then released her. "You've had a tough time of it, Gellman. Go home, pour yourself a drink. We might have more questions later on, so stay in town, okay?"

Gwen nodded, not quite trusting herself to speak. Kimberly's hostility she could take and return in kind, but Ben's kindness simply undid her.

Sadly, she was cynical enough to wonder if he'd known it would, and had chosen his weapons accordingly.

Eleven

Shortly before closing time, Gwen walked into a pediatrician's office in East Greenwich, the pretty, rural, and mostly upscale community where Kyle Radcliff had lived with his family.

She went to the counter window and handed the receptionist a form letter Kyle had signed, requesting a copy of his son's medical records.

The woman glanced at it. "Where do you want these records sent?"

"Could I, like, wait for it? My dad wants a copy." Gwen rolled her eyes in silent commentary on incomprehensible adult demands.

The nurse smiled. "Usually Friday is our busiest day, but things are a little slow. Let me see what I can find for you."

She turned her chair to face the computer keyboard, and her fingers clicked busily for several moments. Her eyebrows drew together in a puzzled V.

"Are you sure you're in the right place, honey? We don't have any patient by the name of Patrick Radcliff."

Well, if Erin Westland went by more than one name, it was possible her kid had an alias or two. Gwen showed her the picture of Erin and Patrick.

"This is my brother. Maybe there's a problem with his records?" she suggested. "You're sure you haven't seen him here?"

A younger woman, a ponytailed nurse wearing a lavender smock covered with Scooby-Doo cartoons, noted the photo in the receptionist's hands and bent down for a closer look.

"I don't recognize the little boy, but the girl looks familiar. I'll get Jen—she'll know. She's been here forever."

Jen, it turned out, was an older woman with deep, parenthetical frown lines framing her mouth. These lines deepened when she glanced at the picture. She shoved it back across the counter at Gwen, her face stony.

"Wait, now I remember her," announced Scooby. "She was an office temp, but I don't think she lasted more than a day or two."

The reception's eyes widened. "Oh, *she's* the one who—"

She broke off abruptly and exchanged glances with the nurse. Jen marched off, her jaw set and shoulders rigid.

As Gwen reclaimed the photo, her mind was flooded by a sudden image of a short, balding man in a white medical coat, standing very close to the young woman seated on the examining table. The ring on his left hand was a match to the one Jen wore. His brown corduroy pants were in a puddle around his ankles, and a pair of slim, feminine legs wrapped around him.

Oops. That was more info on Erin Westland than Gwen wanted.

Gwen made a hasty retreat, leaving Nurse Scooby to deal with the metaphorical pile of shit she'd inadvertently stepped in.

Friday afternoon was a lousy time to be on I-95, but for once Gwen didn't mind the traffic. She had plenty to think about, starting with the question of who had died in Clyde Tremaine's car, all those years ago.

Had it really been Helene Tremaine, or did people see the mangled female body in her brother's car and make the logical assumption?

And what about Vivian Meekins? Her personality transformation had occurred right around the time of Helene's death.

Was it possible that Helene and Vivian had switched places when they were seventeen? Was the dead teenager in the car wreck Vivian, and did Helene take her place? Surely the Meekinses would have noticed if a different girl was living under their roof. Gwen could buy the theory of two teenaged girls who looked enough alike that a body, post car crash, could muddy the waters, but the girls would have to be damn near identical for Helene/Vivian to pull off a switch.

Or would they?

Two people had identified Erin Westland's picture as Helene Tremaine: Helene's brother and the stylist at Esprit. Clyde Tremaine said the picture looked like Helene had when she died, but the hairdresser thought that Helene was considerably older than seventeen. But Kyle Radcliff said the photo was recent. Comparing the perspectives of Kyle and Clyde, Erin/Helene looked exactly the same today as she had fifty years ago. According to Lisa the stylist, Helene was an older version of Erin.

There were two logical conclusions: either Erin and Helene were two different people, or they were two names for one person who could alter her appearance.

Well, make that *one* logical conclusion, and one conclusion that, though illogical, might be compatible with Gwen's broadening definition of reality.

If her theory was correct, the girl who died in the crash was in fact the *real* Helene, the daughter born to the Tremaines, switched in the hospital, and adopted by the Meekinses. The changeling child, a child of unknown heritage, grew up as Clyde's sister, and was now Kyle Radcliff's wife.

His runaway wife. It looked as if "Erin Westland" was well on her way to yet another identity. At least this time, no one had died to help smooth her path.

Was this common practice with the Elder Races? Did they routinely change their identities by arranging the death of a substitute? It appeared that they did, and in incredibly cold-blooded fashion. The amount of planning it would take to pull off the double switch—first as infants, then as teenagers—was mind-boggling.

The next question was whether or not Erin participated in Vivian's death, and to what extent. These questions were of more than academic interest to Gwen. It was always good to know whether you were tracking a scared rabbit or a cornered wolf.

Erin was no innocent. The visit to the pediatrician had proven that. Kyle's meticulous financial records showed a number of bills for Patrick's routine checkups, but the pediatrician had no record of the child. The only explanation was that Erin had finagled her way into the office as a temp and stayed long enough to steal a stack of blank bills.

That was definitely thinking ahead. It covered Erin's ass in case Kyle wondered about medical care for his kid, while neatly avoiding the possibility that a doctor might find some medical anomaly. And most likely, it wasn't as if the kid needed medical treatment. If he was anything like Gwen, he'd never been sick a day in his life, and any type of medicine would work its way out of his system fast enough to render inoculations a waste of time.

When Gwen got back to her office, she pulled up Kyle's file and studied the electronic copies. As she clicked her way through them, her eye fell on the numbers on the upper right corner. The invoice numbers didn't seem to be in any particular sequence, but the numbers were within a fairly limited range.

Curious, she printed out the receipts and arranged the bills according to number. The pattern that emerged brought a wry, almost admiring smile to her face.

When the receipts from Patrick's five years of checkups were put in numerical order, they were all sequential. Erin had put them out of order to make detection less likely.

Her own medical bills were more sporadic than her son's. She seemed to have a constitution similar to Gwen's. Her only medical expenses dated back to her pregnancy, and there weren't many of those, either. Apparently she'd opted for a midwife and a home birth.

Gwen glanced at the clock. It was well past seven. She'd have to wait until Monday morning to start checking out Erin's medical situation, which was fine with her. If Erin was willing to boink a balding pediatrician just to get her hands on a stack of blank invoices, God only knew what she'd do for a copy of her ultrasound.

Gwen trudged up the stairs to her apartment. Her bedroom door stood open, and the covers from her bed were still heaped on the floor after last night's marathon. She paused at the door and debated whether to remake the bed or just flop facedown on the mattress.

"Don't let me stop you," announced an amused male voice. "In fact, I may allow myself to be persuaded to join you."

Gwen jumped and whirled toward the sound. Ian Forest, damn his pointy little ears, was lounging on her sofa.

"Christ on stilts! Don't *do* that," she snapped. "What the fuck are you doing here? And come to think of it, why are your ears pointy all of a sudden?"

He came to his feet in a graceful, fluid movement. "Your perceptions have changed, that's all. People seldom notice ear shape unless the differences are extreme. A slight point toward the back of the ear is easily concealed and likely to go unnoticed. Only the jug-eared tend to draw attention."

"Like Ross Perot," she noted. "Or better yet, Prince Charles. That man could hang glide over half of Wales without equipment."

Ian's blue eyes widened in surprise, and he burst into genuine laughter.

It was, in Gwen's opinion, a big improvement from his superior, smirking humor. Against her better judgment, she felt pleased and even a little charmed.

She reminded herself that this was his gift—the ability to manipulate emotions. She remembered the too-young girls who danced at the club he managed. She reminded herself of the elaborate scheme he'd created to maneuver Edmonson out of power, using her as an unwitting tool. And finally, the reason why he was here. Ian Forost was a manipulator, a blackmailer, and quite possibly a murderer.

"Kate Myers and Jackie Teal," she said coldly. "Do you know anything about them?"

The amusement faded from his eyes. "The first name is familiar to me, but only because you two have been together several times of late. Why do you ask?"

"Kate is dead and Jackie's missing. She used to be one of Tiger Leone's girls. Lately she danced at the Extreme."

"I see," Ian mused. "That's one of Edmonson's establishments. I assume Kate Myers also had some connection with the earl?"

"He paid her way through college. I'm guessing she covered for him every now and then by fudging autopsy results."

Ian studied her. "You think those photos were a threat to frame you for murder. Edmonson's, perhaps even this Kate's."

"Wouldn't put it past you. Where's the gun?"

He reached into the inside pocket of his suit coat and drew out the small silver weapon. He placed it on the coffee table, which was still littered with the remnants of last evening's takeout.

"I know this is difficult for you, Gwen," he said softly. "Your friend's honor is important to you, and that's as it should be. But you must understand that your first loyalty is to your own kind. Looking too closely into Frank Cross's death would draw too much attention to us. We can ill afford that kind of scrutiny."

"You have my oath," she snapped. "Now let me hear you say that you had nothing to do with Kate's death and Jackie's disappearance."

"Easily done. I brought no harm to either of these women. This I swear."

Gwen felt some of the tension between her shoulders seep away. "Since you're here, you might as well make yourself useful and answer a few questions. You said I have two Qualities—"

"Three, actually. The ability to remember things you haven't seen, an affinity for rain, and one that is as yet undiscovered."

Okay, that wasn't *too* disconcerting.

"Three, then," Gwen said, adding this new revelation to her growing list of Things to Deal With. "What I need to know is, can some of you guys—"

"Some of *us*," Ian interjected patiently.

"Would you stop with the interrupting?" she snapped. "Okay, can some of *us* change how we look?"

The supercilious little smile was back. "I assure you, Gwen, the apparent change in the shape of my ears is nothing more than selective observation on your part."

"Hate to be the one to break the news, buddy, but it's not all about you. I need to know if this is something one of us can do."

His smile broadened. *"Ahhh,* finally she says 'us.' We're making progress."

"Ahhh. Blow me." Gwen took a deep, steadying breath. "I used to go out with a guy who was into Arthurian stuff, and he nagged me until I read this book he was crazy about. *Mists of Avalon.* I wanted to bitch-slap most of the characters—"

"Your namesake in particular, no doubt."

"Didn't we talk about this interrupting? But yeah, you're right. The book made Gwenevere out to be a spineless simp. But the thing is, some of the magic in that book sort of . . . made sense to me."

"I can see where this is going. You're speaking of the glamour cast by the priestesses of Avalon."

"Well, yeah."

He leaned against the wall and crossed his arms. "The writer wasn't far off. The ability to cast a glamour was one of the Old Gifts. There have been several attempts to revive it, but too often that gift conflicts with another Quality. And sometimes, it's the sole Quality the bearer possesses."

"If you have to be a one-trick pony, that's one hell of a trick. There actually were people who could change what they looked like?"

"Beauty is in the eye of the beholder," Ian said, "and perception is a powerful thing."

Gwen bit back the impulse to comment on his sudden penchant for clichés. "So, they didn't actually change how they looked, but how people perceived them."

"That's correct."

"How?"

Ian lifted one eyebrow. "You're asking for a scientific explanation?"

"Give it your best shot."

"All right, then. The mind functions on a sort of electrochemical energy. When that chemistry is altered, the mind can be persuaded to change how it interprets the data collected by the senses. Excessive alcohol, psychotropic drugs, even pheromones can influence perceptions."

"Maybe pheromones can influence more than perception," Gwen mused. "Not long ago a friend of mine gave me this article about prayer and healing. There was this study done on people who believe in that sort of thing. Apparently they give off this pheromone when they pray. Other people pick up on it without consciously noticing it. If someone sick is in range, so to speak, prayer might actually speed up the healing process through a sort of chemical jump start."

"An interesting point," Ian said. "Humans draw lines between magic, religion, and the natural powers of the mind, but those boundaries keep shifting. According to this study you mentioned, it would follow that people who have exceptionally strong and varied pheromones could alter the perceptions—and, as you have observed, perhaps even the physical realities—of the people around them."

"And we have stronger and more varied pheromones."

"Surely you've noticed that your arousal is highly contagious. Men respond to your sexuality because they perceive it physically. Chemistry, in your case, is quite literal."

"And here I thought it was my ladylike charm," Gwen said

dryly. "So it could be done. Changing appearances, that is—making people see you differently."

"Theoretically, it's possible that this Quality might still exist," he specified, "but it's unlikely. In fact, we no longer breed for that gift."

For a long moment, Gwen simply stood and stared. "You did say 'breed,' didn't you?"

He nodded. "That will no doubt offend your human-instilled sensibilities, but consider the situation: each of us has three Qualities, all of which ebb and flow in certain predictable patterns. It's vital that these qualities be compatible."

There was probably some sense in what he said, but Gwen was too tired to care.

"Okay, I've officially gone into information overload. Why don't you let yourself out the same way you got in—whatever the hell that was—and we'll talk about this in, oh, another month or so."

Ian held his ground. "Don't let it wait, Gwen. If you have any reason to believe this particular Quality is surfacing in you, you must let me know at once. Me," he emphasized, "and no other."

His tone was serious, almost ominous. Gwen shrugged and headed for the shower. "I suppose my life depends on it," she tossed back.

"For once," he said somberly, "you are most definitely right."

Twelve

The disturbing conversation with Ian echoed through Gwen's thoughts as she drove to Sister Tamar's safe house. Saturday night was their pizza-and-poker night, weather permitting and if no major crisis contravened. Missing a night's sleep simply didn't qualify as an excuse.

The safe house was a sprawling old Victorian located a few blocks from Providence College. The proximity to the school allowed the dozen or so young female residents to come and go without much comment, and the old-fashioned iron fence around the property was easily dismissed as the remnant of the original owner's pretensions.

Few people noticed the state-of-the-art security system, the bulletproof windows, the guard dog. The latter, an English sheepdog, was certainly visible from the street, but he looked more like an affable pet than a trained assassin. Gwen noticed it was hard for people to take any long-haired dog seriously. Dobermans, pit bulls, German shepherds, rottweilers—those clean-cut guys got all the press.

The nun's dogs tended to be as unconventional as their mistress. All dogs were pack animals, and any creature with functioning brain cells recognized Sister Tamar as the resident alpha bitch. If her life was all about serving and protecting, who were they to do otherwise?

The sheepdog's MO was to gamble over, his tongue lolling in a goofy canine grin and his killer eyes shielded by long, shaggy fur. He looked like an oversize stuffed toy, but he could take several chunks out of an intruder before the guy realized that Fluffy liked to play rough.

Gwen parked on the street and walked over to the intercom. Because she knew where to look for it, she glanced toward the camera in the old beech tree just inside the fence long enough to let it get a good shot of her face. The gate buzzed, and she walked through, making sure it clicked shut behind her.

The sheepdog greeted Gwen with a little woof, then followed her through the small yard and around to the back door like a shaggy, four-legged shadow.

Sister Tamar had a small apartment on the first floor, three rooms that she kept fiercely tidy and sparsely furnished. Her only luxury was a collection of high-quality ionic filters, all of which were kept running constantly.

The reason for this hit Gwen as walked in. Tamar was sitting at her small table, feet propped up on a second chair. As usual, she was smoking like a bad chimney.

Gwen grimaced and swatted at a plume of menthol-scented smoke. "I thought you were going to give up the habit."

The nun glanced pointedly down at her skinny, jean-clad legs and bare, bunion-lumpy feet. "'Give up the habit?' Since when did you start talking in bad puns?"

"Seriously. Those things will kill you."

Tamar sucked at her cigarette and blew out a leisurely cloud. "Never happen. Not in this business."

"What? Brides of Christ have a special dispensation against cancer?"

"No, but I figure I'll be shot by someone's irate husband, knifed by someone's pimp, or run over by someone's stalker first. Something with a little drama and pizzazz."

She had a point. Gwen had never been optimistic about her own life expectancy, either.

Until recently, that is.

The nun's gaze sharpened. "Why so glum?"

"Maybe I don't like the idea of outliving you," Gwen said. And because that was too close to the truth, she added, "Besides, who would take care of your girls?"

Tamar glared, then ground out her cigarette in a deeply stained ashtray someone had bought in Niagra Falls circa 1964.

"Not bad," she said grudgingly. "When results count, go straight for the guilt button. Where'd you learn that trick?"

"Well, my best friend grew up Irish Catholic . . ."

One corner of Tamar's lips twitched. "Shut up and deal the cards."

They played a few hands of Texas Hold 'Em, but neither of them had much luck concentrating. The pizza was more successful; between the two of them, they demolished a deep-dish pizza piled with extra cheese, Canadian bacon, green peppers, onions, and pineapple.

"You're playing worse than usual tonight," Tamar pointed out as she snagged the last slice. "Something on your mind?"

"A lot of things," Gwen admitted. "But there's one thing in particular I did want to discuss with you. I haven't made any progress finding Irena's friends. If you think she's up to it, I'd like to talk to her."

Tamar looked dubious, and Gwen could see why. It had only been a week or so since the teenage girl had escaped from enforced prostitution and made her way into the nun's care.

"She doesn't speak much English, and you don't speak Russian or Polish. Unless you plan to get out the hand puppets, I'm not sure what you think talking to Irena is going to accomplish."

"It's hard to explain," Gwen said. That, she added silently, just might be the largest understatement in the history of Rhode Island. How could she tell Sister Tamar there was a chance that she might pick up a mental image from Irena, something that might help her find the pimp who'd imprisoned Irena and two other girls?

Even if pragmatic Tamar bought into the whole psychic thing, recent events had added a whole new layer of weird. Gwen's psychic flashes, which had always been capricious, had recently become even more problematic. A few days ago, she'd had several vivid, hologram-type visions that anyone could see. It hadn't happened since her showdown with Meredith Cody's kidnappers, but the risk was there.

Still, when you considered the two girls still in the pimp's hands, the biggest risk was doing nothing at all.

Since Tamar was obviously waiting for an explanation, Gwen shrugged and said, "It's a long shot, but I'd like to try."

The nun rose and brushed crumbs off her gray sweatshirt. "I'll ask Irena if she'll talk to you. She's come a long way this week, so I think she might be ready. She has a hard time formulating her thoughts in English, but she should be able to understand you if you speak slowly. If you like, I can stay and translate."

"No, I think we'll be fine." If things went wrong, Gwen thought grimly, the fewer witnesses, the better.

Several minutes later Tamar was back with a blond girl who

looked to be about sixteen. Irena was too pale and thin to be pretty, and her narrow face was nearly overwhelmed by a large nose. She glanced at Gwen and said sometime to Tamar in either Polish or Russian, something that made the nun snort with laughter.

"Do I want to know?" Gwen asked.

"Probably not. I've explained to her that you find people, and that if she answers your questions, you might be able to help Marina and Anya."

Gwen smiled reassuringly at the teenager. "Tell her I think she's very brave."

Tamar's translation brought a faint smile to the girl's face. Even so, her gaze followed the nun as she left the room and closed the door behind her. She turned back to Gwen, her eyes wary.

"I need you to picture the man who kept you, Marina, and Anya in that house."

The girl frowned and pantomimed drawing. "Make picture?"

"No. Make picture here," Gwen replied, tapping her head.

Irena nodded and closed her eyes. Her desire to help her friends must have been strong, because the picture that flooded Gwen's mind was vivid and immediate.

A piercing shriek shattered Gwen's concentration. She opened her eyes—

And saw her vision reproduced in translucent colors and startling precision. The ghostly form of a burly Latino was right there in the room with them.

Irena scrambled away from the apparition, screaming something in Russian.

The door flew open hard, slamming into the wall hard enough to send a thin crack snaking up the old plaster. Tamar rushed in, wrath in her eyes and a small bottle in one hand. Without a moment's hesitation, she pummeled the vision with holy water and colorful curses. The situation might have been darkly amusing if it wasn't for Irena's terror.

Gwen doubted the holy water had much effect, but her own guilt appeared to be a real vision-quencher. The apparition faded quickly. While Tamar soothed the sobbing child, Gwen called the last doctor in New England who made house calls—most likely because he'd been one of Tamar's pupils back in the day, and still had a lively fear of her.

It took more than an hour to restore order. Finally Irena went off to bed, taking with her Tamar's favorite dog, a gaunt greyhound the nun had rescued from his "retirement." The girls seemed to find comfort in the ugly guard dog. The beast might not be able to race anymore, but he sure as hell remembered how to bite.

When Tamar and Gwen were finally alone, the nun took a bottle of brandy from the kitchen cupboard and poured generous three-finger portions into two glasses. Gwen tossed hers back and waited for the nun to catch up.

Tamar took a sip and sank into her chair, holding her glass in both hands.

"Ugly son of a bitch, wasn't he?" she murmured. "I'd always had my doubts about the whole 'fallen angel of light' crap, but the devil looks like some guy who pumps gas in Cranston."

"I don't think that was a demonic visitation," Gwen said hesitantly. "In fact, I'm sure it wasn't. Tamar, I've got a confession."

"Do I look like a fucking priest?" the nun snapped. "Besides, no sensible person expects devils to look like Clark Gable. Evil works best when it's mundane and banal and *normal*. That way, it can sneak up and bite you in the ass. Every one of the men who tormented Irena is a devil, and how many of them do you think are sexy, Hollywood vampire types?"

"Not too many of them were transparent, either."

The nun dismissed this with an impatient gesture that sent the contents of her glass sloshing onto the table. "That . . . *thing* we saw. Is that the man who has Irena's friends?"

"Yeah."

Tamar nodded—a single, decisive inclination of her head, then she tossed off the rest of her drink and reached for the bottle. "Well, go find him."

Gwen stared at her. "Just like that. You don't want to know what happened in here?"

Tamar poured herself another drink and regarded the smoky gold contents for a long time. Her thin shoulders rose and fell. "I used to demand explanations. Mostly about the sort of things you'd expect a young religious to contemplate: the paradox of an all-powerful God and a profoundly imperfect world, the nature of good and evil. In my business, answers are in short supply, so I stopped asking certain questions a long, long time ago."

"Yet you never left the order."

The nun laughed shortly. "I didn't have a crisis of faith, kid. To the contrary. Enlightenment isn't guaranteed. Useful work is. I just figured out I have all the answers I need to do the work that's in front of me."

"Must be nice," Gwen murmured.

"So you don't have all the answers yet. Keep at it. You'll find this bastard."

"I plan to." Gwen took a long, settling breath. "Actually, I was talking in a more general sense."

Tamar's shrewd eyes studied Gwen's face. "Looks like we need to have a long talk . . . in a more general sense. But another time," she concluded briskly. She held up the bottle. "You've got work, and I've got some serious drinking to do."

Gwen dialed Ian Forest's number while she was driving home.

"So you decided not to wait a month before contacting me," Ian said by way of greeting. "I'm glad you changed your mind."

"Yeah, hello. You know those visions I told you about? The hologram things? Well, they're back."

"What did you expect?"

"That's why I'm calling you! You're the guy with all the answers."

"I consider that admission a true sign of progress on your part."

"Whatever. Can we get back to the home-movie thing? I've got to get a handle on this before someone drowns me in holy water."

For a long moment, the only response was the static on Gwen's cell phone.

"I'm sure there's a story there," Ian said in a slightly bemused voice, "but it will have to wait for another time. I prefer to speak of this in person."

"Like anyone who overheard us would believe any of this," she scoffed.

"You might be surprised who listens to conversations, and why. Shall we meet in Sylvia's moon garden in, say, ten minutes?"

Gwen's eyes narrowed. "How come you're so close? You're not still following me, are you?"

"Not as such. It just so happens that I can walk from my home to yours in that length of time."

"Great," she muttered. "Ring the intercom at the gate. I'll buzz you in."

"That won't be necessary. Meet me by the old maple tree in ten minutes."

"Make it fifteen. I'm still driving."

She shut off her phone and tossed it onto the passenger seat. The lights in Sylvia's house were on, but that was because they were on a timer. Gwen's landlady wasn't home and wouldn't be for another week or more. A bad shock had sent her to the hospital. After her release, she'd decided to take a cruise. The first one had gone so well she signed on for another. Most likely she'd found an elderly admirer or two.

Or maybe she needed time away from the weirdness that Gwen had brought into her life.

And that was something to think about. Gwen gazed wistfully at the calm, green haven behind the black iron fence. She liked living here, but doing so was putting Sylvia at risk. She really needed to find a different place.

Gwen pulled into the drive and stopped her car by Sylvia's garden. This chapter of her life was drawing to a close, but for tonight she would enjoy the heady sweetness of lilac, the luminous glow of the white flowers.

Ian emerged from the deep shadows under the maple and came to stand at her side. He observed the garden for a long, contemplative moment. A cloud drifted lazily over the moon, dimming the wattage coming from the flowers.

He glanced at Gwen. "Tell me this: what is the moon phase?"

"What phase?" Gwen huffed in exasperation. "Adolescent? Premenopausal? How the hell should I know?"

"It's one of the things you must know," he said adamantly.

"You're obviously manifesting your moon-cycle Quality in the waning phase. This is not a common pattern, but it does occur."

"How about repeating that in English?" she demanded. "Preferably as it's spoken in the twenty-first century?"

"Very well. Each of us is capable of learning a number of . . . unusual skills, but we're born with certain gifts, also known as Qualities. These abilities are closely tied to the cycles of the year and the position of the moon and the stars. Your ability to Remember—to powerfully envision things you yourself have never seen—is apparently tied to your moon phase."

"So I'm . . . what? Like some kind of werewolf?" Gwen demanded.

Ian chuckled. "Hardly. Our cycles are far more subtle and complex. Your ability to Remember wanes and waxes with the moon. You can call storms. That Quality is tied to the turning of the year, so it's very powerful right now."

"Beltane," Gwen murmured, naming the old Celtic holiday that fell on the last day of April.

"That's right," he said, sounding pleased. "It remains to be seen whether your third Quality will manifest at the corners of the year—summer and winter solstice, spring and autumn equinox—or on the dancing days: Beltane, Samhaim, Lammas, and Imbolic."

"I've heard those names."

"No doubt. Some of the Old Ways have modern counterparts in this or that bit of folklore or religion. Once you understand the pattern, you'll be able to chart your path, and make decisions based on the ebb and flow of your abilities."

Gwen thought this over. "Okay, what happens when all three lines intersect?"

"That depends, of course, on what these Qualities might be."

"And if they don't get along with each other? Or maybe they work well together, but *too* well?"

Ian suddenly appeared to be very interested in the flight pattern of a moon-white moth.

"Well?"

He sighed and turned to face her. "You needn't worry about that. Your parents' bloodlines were carefully matched."

Gwen suddenly understood the resigned expression on Ian's face. The outburst he clearly expected from her simmered just under the surface, but she feel too numbed by informational overload to get at it.

The Elder Races had bloodlines, like stallions and champion dogs, carefully matched to produce the right kind and balance of abilities.

She shook her head in utter bemusement. "As God is my witness, I don't know what to say."

Ian's lips twitched. "If that is so, then ignorance truly is bliss."

Gwen's cell phone chirped. She glanced at the screen. The number took her back—it was the number for Tiger Leone's cell phone. She glanced at Ian. "I need to take this."

He swept one hand out, palm up, in an elegant "by all means" gesture.

"I'm a private investigator," she reminded him. "Notice the emphasis on *private*."

He nodded and headed for the maple tree. "We've just begun," he warned her. "I'll meet you again, soon."

She waved him away and walked toward her car. "Gellman," she said curtly.

There was a lot of background noise—voices and music—and it

took her a few moments to place the voice: Adrian, the blond kid who'd sworn to help her figure out Edmonson's drug business.

"Where are you?" she shouted into the phone.

"Do you know Extreme, the dance club?"

"I know where it is."

"Come down. I have things to show you."

She clicked off her cell and jogged up to her apartment to get her gun out of the gun safe. Adrian might be oath-bound, but she wouldn't put any bets on his buddies.

Thirteen

Music thumped and throbbed, binding the gyrating crowd like a collective heartbeat. A slim Black girl swayed lazily onstage, one hand moving slowly across her body in a languorous caress. With some relief, Gwen recognized Jackie Teal. She was barely dancing, and seemed almost unaware of the crowd. Gwen averted her eyes from what appeared to be an intensely private moment.

She caught sight of Adrian's pale blond hair in the crowd. She pushed her way over to him and used his earlobe as a handle to pull his ear low enough to shout into it. "What's so important that I had to come to North Providence at this godforsaken hour?"

Adrian pulled away and tipped his head in the direction of a nearby door. Gwen followed him to it, then up a small flight of stairs to a small, glassed-in room overlooking the club. Soundproofed, too. The relative silence washed over Gwen in blissful waves.

"So, why am I here?" she repeated.

He gestured to the smoked window. "I thought you would want to see the clubs. Since you are the earl's only heir, you should start learning about his affairs."

"Why? I want to shut them down, not improve operations."

"You might want to reserve judgment until you know all the facts. Look at that dancer."

Her gaze flicked back to Jackie. "Yeah, I noticed her. Kind of risky, putting someone who's under the influence onstage."

"If she were arrested tonight, she would be released within the hour. There are no intoxicants in her system."

Gwen raised an eyebrow. "Then whatever she's taking has one hell of a placebo effect."

For no reason that she could fathom, that seemed to amuse him. Before he could speak, sirens wailed outside, slicing though the din.

Adrian took her arm and led her to a wall panel. He rapped on it sharply, and it swung open. "You have contacts in the police department. Ask them tomorrow what happened here, and you will begin to understand. Now go."

He gave her a shove that sent her reeling into the darkness. She caught her balance against a rough concrete wall, then looked around to get her bearings.

She was in a narrow stairwell, built into what appeared to be a double wall. The narrow alley was open at the top, and faint city light filtered down.

Gwen walked down the stairs and through a narrow door. She emerged into a basement stairwell in the alley behind the club. She waited until the noise died down, then clicked on her phone and dialed Damian's number.

His sleepy voice came online, grunting something that might have been "hello."

"There's a drug bust going down at the Extreme. I need to know everything you can tell me about it. But be careful—Jackie Teal was picked up. You might not want her to recognize you."

"She's okay?"

He put enough into that question to pique Gwen's interest. "You sure you didn't play?"

"With a drug-dealing stripper? What are you smoking? The drug business coming out of that titty bar is our best link to Walsh. If Leone's people get shut down, *we* get shut down. And it's not like we've got a lot of time. Quaid and me got ourselves on Walsh's shit list, remember? Or maybe I should say *hit list.*"

"I hate to interrupt someone who's got a good rant going, but listen up. Jackie was on some sort of horny high. I've seen her dance before, and trust me—she doesn't have that much juice. Adrian assures me she won't be held for illegals. You and Quaid need to follow the evidence every step of the way. If you can catch someone fixing things for Jackie—"

"We're that much closer to nailing Walsh," he finished. "I'm on it."

The dial tone hummed. Gwen clicked off her phone and listened to the clamor in front of the club. Jackie's shrill protests rose above the murmur as she was taken away.

Gwen quietly climbed the stairs and edged around the building. Four black-and-whites blocked the street, red lights strobing into the night. A dozen or so cops, both uniformed and plainclothes, hustled dancers and partygoers into cars.

A faint smile curved Gwen's lips. For once, departmental politics would actually accomplish something worthwhile. A lot of people in the law-enforcement establishment hadn't been wildly enthusiastic about the vice squad. This wouldn't be the first time a street cop called for backup without referring a case to Walsh's department. With this many people involved, it would be harder for Walsh to lay claim to his territory.

A profound sense of relief washed over her, easing some of the tension that had kept her moving for too many hours. Suddenly Gwen's eyelids felt incredibly heavy, and the prospect of crawling into bed had never been so appealing. She slipped down a side street to the nearly deserted parking lot where she'd left her Toyota.

To her relief, everything was quiet at Sylvia's house. No handsome but irritating visitors lurked in the shadows of Gwen's apartment. She stumbled into her bedroom and fell facedown on the bed, not even bothering to kick off her boots.

But sleep proved elusive. After a few minutes of tossing and turning, Gwen decided she might as well get some work done.

She grabbed a quick shower and dressed in jeans and a black tee shirt, then padded downstairs to her office to type up her report to Shawna O'Riley.

Gwen's four-fingered technique wasn't designed for speed. She worked carefully, listing the steps she'd taken and the information she'd uncovered. Roy Williams was a solid citizen with a good job, money in the bank, a good portfolio, no police record, and no interesting vices. He wasn't cheating on Shawna, he didn't fudge his tax returns. He'd lied about one thing, but it was a doozy.

Somehow Gwen doubted there would be a wedding invitation in her mailbox any time soon.

She completed the report and sent it to Shawna as an e-mail attachment. Her phone rang while the file was still uploading, and Quaid's number floated onto the tiny screen.

Gwen took a deep breath and clicked on the phone. "Listen, about Kate: I couldn't call you in on the murder of an ex-girlfriend."

"You did the right thing."

That wasn't what she'd expected to hear. "Do they have any leads yet?"

"They think they do," he said heavily.

Gwen blinked. "Does that mean what it sounds like?"

"Unfortunately. When I stopped by Kate's house the other

night, one of the neighbors saw me. She just can't remember exactly when that was."

"They can't charge you on something like that."

"It gets better. They found the murder weapon in the lilac bush behind Kate's house. No prints—it was wiped clean—but it turns out the gun was taken from the weapons locker over at vice. Naturally they like a cop for it."

"And because you and Kate have history . . ."

"You got it."

"Jesus, Quaid! What can I do to help?"

"Keep an eye on O'Riley," he said softly.

Gwen sat bolt upright. "What aren't you telling me?"

"I'm in holding now. They made the arrest late last night. I was arraigned in night court. Bail was set at two hundred thousand."

"That's ridiculous!" she sputtered. "No cop has that kind of money. Not an honest one, anyway."

"Yeah. Kinda like the Monty Python witch hunt, isn't it? Throw the witch in water. If she floats, she's guilty. Burn her. If she drowns, she's innocent but dead."

The analogy came too close for comfort. A convicted vice cop wouldn't be very popular with the other inmates.

"Have you tried a bond?"

"The union rep wouldn't even make the calls. He figures at this hour, on a Saturday, there wasn't much point."

"If and when the lazy bastard calls, tell him your new lawyer and your bond money are on their way."

"Gellman—"

"Don't start with me. The lawyer and the bond agent owe me. And if you skip out, I'll hunt you down and take out your kneecaps with a crowbar."

"Jesus, you say that like you're hoping I'll skip. Who'd you have in mind for a lawyer?"

"Ryan Cody."

He whistled, long and low. "Talk about the devil's advocate. That'll get their attention."

"That's the idea."

"Problem is, with the clients Cody represents, hiring him is second cousin to an admission of guilt."

"Let's hope you stay alive long enough to worry about it."

Gwen hung up before he could embarass them both by thanking her. She dialed Ryan Cody's home number, letting the phone ring until Cody picked up.

Gwen quickly described the situation. "I need you to call around right away and assure everyone that Quaid is your client and that he'll make bail."

"Will he?"

Amazing how the mention of money brought Cody wide awake. "Write a check on Simmons, Fletcher, and Rye. I'll meet you afterward at the breakfast place in Barrington—that little diner on Old Country?"

"I know where it is."

"Good. I'll bring enough cash to cover the bail and your fee."

A long silence followed. "You can put that kind of cash together in an hour?"

"Sure, but you might have to pick up breakfast."

She hung up and dialed Ian Forest. "I need a quarter of a million, in cash. How much do you think I could get on eBay for that big blue gem of mine?"

"That's nothing to joke about. When do you need the money?"

"Forty-five minutes?"

"I'll be there in thirty."

He made it in about twenty-five and handed her a small back-pack of the sort middle-school kids carried.

Gwen unzipped the bag and peered inside. Fat stacks of twen-ties filled the backpack. She shook her head in astonishment and closed the bag. "I'll make sure you get it back."

"No need. The money is yours—or will be, as soon as Edmon-son's estate is settled. Since that task has fallen to me, you can con-sider this an advance. Do with it as you like."

She shouldered the bag. What she'd *like* to do is shove it up the ass of every pervert who put the money in Edmonson's pocket. Keeping Quaid out of jail was not quite as noble, but it'd have to do.

Later that morning, Gwen headed over to Jason's bungalow. He met her at the door, grinning when he noted the size of the bakery box she carried.

"That should do for both of us. I've already made coffee. Give me a minute to put it in some travel cups. We can take it out on the boat, if you want."

She nodded and followed him to the kitchen. While Jason fixed the coffee, she gazed over the backyard to the river. A light wind ruffled the water into a shimmering silver blue, and the boat an-chored a few feet offshore bobbed invitingly. It was one of those spring mornings that made everything look bright and fresh. And speaking of which, Gwen noted that Jason had made some repairs to the small dock. As they approached, she was glad to note that Frank's old rowboat was reassuringly unchanged.

She got into the backseat and took the oars. Jason deftly untied the mooring rope and hopped in.

"You want me to row?"

"Kind of hard to do from where you're sitting."

He shrugged and settled down in the front seat. Gwen rowed out to the fishing boat. She pulled up to the float that marked the second anchor line and tied the rowboat, then scrambled up into the boat.

To her surprise, the temperamental motor turned over for Jason at the first try. Most likely he had tinkered with that, as well.

"What's wrong?" he asked her.

Gwen smoothed the frown from her face. "Caffeine deprivation. Hand me one of those cups."

Jason didn't look convinced, but he refrained from further questions. He steered the boat down the river and into the bay. The wind was brisk enough to entice early morning sailors, and he moved among the slower crafts with ease and skill.

"I forgot to ask you if you could drive this thing," Gwen said, "but you've sort of covered that. Where'd you learn?"

"My stepfather liked to fish. Hunting, too. He took me out quite a bit. Growing up in Florida, you can do both year round. In fact, I spent a lot of summers working as a guide down in Big Cypress, the Seminole reservation." He grinned. "You look appalled. Are you one of those people who frown on hunting?"

"Hell, no. I'd whack a cow any day, if that was the only way to get a burger. It seems to me that if you're going to eat meat, it's more honest to kill your own."

"So . . ."

"It's just that I've never met a real country boy before. Won't you miss all that, if you settle down here?"

He sent her a quizzical look. "If? I'm pretty settled already."

"You're really diving into the computer stuff. Thinking of changing careers?"

"What, and give up the lucrative lifestyle of a martial-arts instructor and occasional carpenter?"

Gwen grinned. "You don't seem to care much about lifestyle. Except for the car. That's a sweet little ride."

"It's a Miata," he told her. "They're about the same price as an econobox, and a lot more fun. You can get some great deals on used cars. If you want, I'll help you look around."

"Why not? I've got nothing better to do than go car shopping."

Her sarcasm prompted a quick smile. "I can see that. You must have searched high and low for that heap of blue scrap metal."

"It runs. Most of the time."

She helped herself to a cinnamon donut. "So, you still up for that self-defense class Tuesday night?"

"I'll be there. I've been meaning to ask how you got started teaching."

She swallowed a sugary mouthful and chased it with a gulp of coffee. "It's a community school. Several classes are held in a local church. A friend of mine goes there. She heard about the program and talked me into doing a self-defense class."

"Do you like teaching?"

Gwen shrugged. "None of the women are all that serious about it. I'm guessing none of them have had to be."

"Not like you."

She sent him a quick, sidelong look. "I was a cop, for chrissakes."

"But you started learning martial arts when you were, what? Around twelve?"

"You've got a good memory. Yeah. I was small for my age and I got beat up a lot."

He shook his head. "Somehow I have a hard time seeing you as anyone's victim, no matter what your age and size."

"Who said I was a victim? I said I got beat up a lot. The other people didn't walk away without a scratch." And some of them, Gwen added silently, didn't walk away at all.

Jason throttled down and settled the boat into a more leisurely pace. "I've been meaning to ask how you're doing. You know, with Frank gone."

Gwen's throat tightened. "I miss him. Other than that, I don't know what to tell you."

"So you're content to let the official version of his death stand?"

"Actually, I'm a long fucking ways away from 'content,' but it's out of my hands. The man who killed Frank—or at least, the guy who was responsible for it—is dead."

"The guy who ordered the Cody girl's kidnapping."

"That's right."

"Aren't the police still looking for the kidnappers?" he asked cautiously.

Gwen met his tentative gaze squarely. "They'll stop eventually."

He gave that some thought, then nodded slowly. "I can live with that."

It suddenly occurred to Gwen what he thought she was telling him. "You think I killed those guys!"

He studied her face for a moment before answering. "You never told the police Frank's laptop was missing. When you gave it to me, I figured that was your way of letting me know the score had been settled."

"And you were okay with that."

"It's one solution. In fact, I can't think of a better one."

"Some people could. Most of my former colleagues, for example."

"I'm not going to run to the police, Gwen," he told her. "You seem surprised by my attitude. Keep in mind that I grew up as a citizen of the Seminole Nation. I never went out of my way to break American laws, but I didn't hold them in high regard, either. My mother's influence, in part."

"Cops' ex-spouses are seldom crazy about the system," she admitted.

"Add to that the fact that I'm a Southerner and a male. Our motto is 'Deal with it.' To be honest, I'm glad Edmonson is dead."

Gwen jolted in surprise, sending coffee sloshing onto the deck. Her hands were shaking as she put down the cup. "Edmonson?"

Something flickered in his eyes. "You mentioned him when you told me about Meredith Cody's kidnapping. I put the pieces together from what you said and figured he was the guy in charge. Was I wrong?"

She didn't remember mentioning Edmonson's name, but Jason's explanation was plausible. With all she'd had on her mind, it was no surprise she'd let something slip.

The conversation switched to general topics: movies, music, the Red Sox. Gwen liked football and couldn't give a rat's ass about the Bambino and his curse, but it turned out that Jason was a lifelong Sox fan, and still damn near giddy over the 2004 World Series. Morning ran into afternoon, and they docked at the Wharf Tavern in Warwick for a bowl of chowder.

Her first creamy spoonful triggered a memory, and a profound sense of loss. She swallowed hard, forcing the soup past the lump in her throat.

"You look sad," Jason observed.

She shrugged. "Frank used to make chowder about once a week. It was sort of a tradition."

"Sorry I missed it."

"Me, too."

She would have said more, but suddenly yawning seemed much more imperative.

She noticed Jason's stare and stopped in mid yawn. "Sorry."

"When was the last time you slept?" he demanded.

"What day is this?"

"Very amusing. I'm serious."

"And you think I'm not? I don't sleep a lot. Sometimes I go a night or two without bothering to sleep, but it catches up with me eventually."

"Apparently." He nodded to her chowder. "Eat up, then I'll take you home. You're going to fall face-first into that bowl."

Because Gwen couldn't argue with that assessment, she finished up her soup and didn't complain when Jason drove the boat back to Riverside at a less-than-leisurely pace. But she put her foot down when he tried convincing her to let him drive her back to her apartment.

She made her way home and headed for the bed. No need to set an alarm—she always woke up the moment the sun hit her.

Cycles of nature, she thought as she drifted off to sleep. Maybe Ian was on to something.

First thing Monday morning, Gwen went to the office of the obstetrician Erin Westland had seen when she was pregnant with Patrick. Thanks to yet another form Kyle had signed, she was given access to Erin's chart.

It wasn't strictly legal, but fortunately for Gwen, the medical profession was still sorting through the do's and don'ts of the Privacy of Information legislation. Medical-office workers spent a lot of time shuffling papers. Handing them something that looked official was like ringing a bell around Pavlov's dogs: they automatically went with familiar patterns.

According to the records, Erin had come in only once, just to get a referral for a sonogram. She preferred a home delivery, so the doctor had referred her to a midwife.

Gwen went back to her car and fired up her cell phone. After a few calls, she tracked down the midwife, who'd apparently taken up organic vegetable gardening in Vermont. She introduced herself and explained briefly why she was calling.

"I remember Erin very well," the woman said. "It's hardly something I'm likely to forget."

"Why's that?"

"For one thing, the baby was born very late."

"Is that really so unusual, especially for first babies?"

"I'm not talking about a few days, or even a week or two," the midwife said.

Gwen took a moment to absorb that. "Was the baby normal?"

"Yes, he appeared to be fine, if somewhat small. Erin had a remarkably easy delivery, considering that it was her first child."

"What about Erin's ultrasound? Did that show anything strange?"

"I didn't actually see the ultrasound, but I received a report. Apparently the baby was developing normally. The test showed a fetus in the sixth week of development."

"You say that as if it's a problem."

"Well, the dates just don't add up, not on either end. Patrick was born more than nine months after that ultrasound was taken. And the date on the test report was nearly two months after Erin's appointment with her obstetrician."

"So when you do the math, it turns out that Erin wasn't pregnant when she went to her doctor."

"Yet her pregnancy was confirmed by physical exam. The doctor estimated that she was nearly two months along."

"Don't they usually do blood tests to confirm?"

"Erin said she had a phobia about needles. That's why she insisted on a home birth. The idea of giving birth in a hospital terrified her."

Smart girl, Gwen noted. Most likely members of the Elder Races who checked into hospitals met the same fate as those who ended up in jail. Keeping a low profile was very high on the priority list.

"Was there anything else unusual about Erin's pregnancy?"

"You'd think that would be enough," the midwife said, "but actually, there was. The report noted that although the the fetal development was normal, there was some concern about the mother. It showed what appeared to be three ovaries, raising questions about the possibility of a tumor. The report strongly advised that she have another test."

"Did Erin follow up?"

"She told me she did, and that everything was fine."

"You don't sound convinced," Gwen observed.

The midwife was silent for several moments. "I asked questions. After all, I was responsible for two lives. After a while, I stopped asking."

The tone of her voice suggested that lack of interest was not the reason she stopped seeking answers.

"What happened?" Gwen asked softly.

"A lot of things. Harassment. Hang-up phone calls late at night, slashed tires. Nothing I could trace to Erin—not that I thought there was any connection. Then my dog was killed. Hannah, a beautiful golden retriever. She was pregnant at the time. She was left by my door. Her belly was slit open, the puppies left to die."

"And you think Erin had something to do with this?"

"Hannah always barked when Erin came in for her checkups and prenatal classes. She was a lovely dog, very friendly, but she didn't like Erin at all."

Gwen heard the faint sigh of a long, steadying breath as the woman prepared to spill the rest.

"One night Hannah set up an awful racket. She was outside— she had a doghouse in the yard. I went downstairs and looked around, but there was no sign of any intruder. Hannah calmed down, or so I thought at the time, and I went back to bed. The next morning I . . . found Hannah. I was terribly shaken, but I had several appointments that afternoon. One of them was with Erin. When I went to get her chart out, I found that all of my notes were missing."

"So you think Erin was responsible?"

"I know she was." The woman's voice broke, and she cleared her throat. "She didn't say anything, but the look in her eye when she came in that day was . . . like nothing I've ever seen before. Malevolence came off her in waves."

"I'm surprised you kept her as a patient."

"Oh, I tried to drop her, but she let me know in no uncertain terms that wouldn't be a good idea."

Gwen thought this over. It didn't seem very smart to piss off the person who'd have your life and that of your unborn child in her hands—unless you had some sort of guarantee.

"What else did she do?"

"Again, nothing I could trace to her. I received some pictures in the mail—pictures of Hannah, after . . ." Again she broke off and cleared her throat. "And in the same envelope, a picture of my daughter. She's going to college in North Carolina. The picture was taken in her dorm room, while she was asleep. There was a newspaper lying on her quilt, showing the date, and her alarm clock was placed beside it."

"The picture was taken around the same time that Hannah died," Gwen concluded.

"Yes."

Well, that message was clear enough.

"Your name won't come into this investigation," Gwen assured her.

"It doesn't matter." The dullness of old grief colored the woman's voice. "I really don't care what happens to me, and my daughter's dead."

"I'm sorry," Gwen murmured. "Was it—"

"Erin Westland? No. Oddly enough, I think that would have been easier for me to deal with. Sometimes it helps to have someone to hate. My daughter died in childbirth, in a hospital. She went that route on my advice because she was having mild symptoms of preeclampsia. The doctors did nothing wrong. But Sarah had a congenital heart problem, something we'd never picked up. It was asymptomatic until the strain of childbirth . . ." Her voice trailed off.

"I'm sorry," Gwen repeated. "Thank you for taking the time to talk to me. It has been a big help."

She ended the call and drove in silence, thinking through this new information.

The most logical conclusion was that Elder Folk had longer

pregnancies, with the extra time most likely in the early stages. Women who walked around with a bump for a year or so would draw attention, but who the heck could tell if a woman was six weeks pregnant? If Erin was figuring this out as she went along, it was possible that she'd been to more than one doctor, and had had more than one ultrasound taken.

Thanks to the whole Privacy of Information thing, getting that information wouldn't be easy. Gwen was lucky to have gotten as far as she had with signed releases from Erin's "husband." It was definitely time to bring in a heavy hitter.

She pulled into the parking lot of a fast-food joint and dialed Harley Faden. His voice-mail announcement told her to leave a message. She followed the drill and hung up.

Her cell phone rang almost immediately. "This is Harley," announced a nasal tenor voice. "What have you got for me?"

"No story. Sorry about that. I'm working on a case. Thanks for calling back so soon."

"You don't need to thank me," he said. "You need to pay me. The clock starts now."

"I need you to check on some medical records for me. One person with at least three names: Erin Westland, Vivian Meekins, Helene Tremaine. There might be more."

"I'm getting it down," Harley murmured. "What else?"

"She'd have to go to someone specializing in obstetrics and gynecology to get referrals for ultrasounds. Several of them. I need those tests. The actual films, if you can get them, not just the reports."

"You don't like to make things easy, do you?"

"What fun would that be? Here's something that might help: this woman might have three ovaries rather than two."

"Cool. How many tits?"

"Standard issue, as far as I know."

"Just checking. These tests—what's the time frame?"

Gwen considered this. Patrick Radcliff was born about six years ago. "Go back eight years," she suggested, "and cover a period of at least two years."

"Wait a minute—one woman, two years, three egg crates, multiple names, and a photo album of ultrasounds? What's going on here?"

"This woman gets pregnant a lot," Gwen said blandly. "She's supplying a lab doing illegal stem-cell research. One of the researchers is knocking up the volunteers himself, and selling the videos as Internet porn. You think there might be a story in that?"

His moan sounded faintly orgasmic. "Damn it, Gwen, it's not nice to tease."

Fourteen

On her way through the East Side, Gwen stopped at an art-supply store near the school of design and picked up a roll of white paper and several drawing pencils. She tossed her purchases into her car and called Damian about last night's bust.

"Got anything for me?"

"Not a damn thing," he grumbled. "Archer told it straight; Jackie Teal was clean."

"You followed the evidence?"

"I met the beat cops at the station, followed our girl through the whole routine. Stuck to her like a tick. I took her over to the lab myself, stood right there while they ran a tox screen. That came up negative for all known illegals. You sure she was using?"

"I'd put good money on it." Gwen hesitated. "You talk to Quaid since then?"

"Hell, no. It was past midnight by the time they were finished."

"You should call him."

"Tried to. He's not answering his cell."

"Then call his home number. If he doesn't answer that, stop by his place."

A couple beats went by as Damian took this in. "What's going on, Gellman?"

"It's not my place to tell you. Quaid's okay, or was when I talked to him last night.

"I'm on it. Anything else?"

"How are your art skills?"

"Not worth a steaming purple crap. Why?"

"I need you to help me do a drawing of someone."

"Huh. Something tells me you don't want to sit down with a sketch artist."

"Good call. I'm heading to my apartment. How soon can you be over?"

"Give me an hour. I'll talk to Quaid, come right over."

"Thanks. I'll leave the gate open. Park by the garage, and come right upstairs."

She drove home and set to work, cutting long sheets of the paper and taping them to her bedroom wall. She was just finishing up when she heard footsteps on the stairs.

Damian ambled in and regarded her handiwork. "I'm tempted to make some comment about needing to see the big picture."

"Fortunately, you're man enough to resist temptation."

"Not that I've noticed. Okay, what now?"

"Watch. And try not to talk too much. It's hard to hold onto the image if I get distracted."

Gwen took a deep breath and called to mind the man she'd pulled from Irena's memory. The translucent image began to take shape as Gwen projected it powerfully onto the papered wall.

"Holy shit," Damian murmured. To Gwen's relief, he sounded impressed, not freaked out. "I get it. It's like one of those lame light projectors teachers used back in the day."

"Less taking, more drawing."

He picked up a pencil and started to trace the image. By the time the vision faded, he had a reasonably good sketch. He stepped back, pursed his lips, and considered.

"Not exactly wallet-size."

"I know a RISD student who can scale it down for me."

"Sounds like a plan. In the meanwhile, I'll take a look at the books, see if I can find this guy's mug shot."

"Are you sure that's a good idea? Showing up on the weekend is the sort of thing that'll put you on Walsh's radar."

His face hardened. "Do you want to catch this guy, or not?"

"But Quaid—"

"He'd be there, too, if he could. So would you, if you were still on the job."

Since Gwen couldn't argue with that, she gave Damian a see-you-later wave and reached for her cell phone. She'd switched it off to avoid interruption. During that brief blackout, she'd missed three calls, all from the same number.

Harley Faden answered on the first ring.

"Where the hell have you *been*?" he demanded "And I'm not talking about your physical location. I don't know what parts of cyberspace you visited, but something really big and ugly followed you home."

"What the hell are you talking about?"

"I found those sonograms for you, and tried to send you a scanned copy. No can do—there's spyware on your computer, and fairly sophisticated stuff. When I send you something, it tries to follow the path back to me. Wait a minute."

Gwen heard a brief clicking of keys, and he let out a low whistle. "It did better than just try—it got past my first firewall. Hang on."

This time the clatter of his keyboard went on for several moments.

"Ha! Got the little bastard nailed down—nope, there it goes. Holy shit, Gwen! Seriously, where have you been recently?"

"Online? Nowhere exotic."

"Well, whatever you've been doing has attracted some high-powered attention."

Gwen thought back to Winston's, and the pictures taken of everyone who came to the club. Someone had used those pictures to identify and locate everyone who'd been there the night of the raid. Yeah, someone on the sidelines of her game definitely had some megageeks on the payroll. It was disturbing to know that these guys were still working even though Edmonson was out of the picture.

"Got any advice?" she asked.

"Give me your address. Real world, not e-mail. I'll come right over with a software program that'll hunt down and kill most spyware. Once your system is clean, we can go over my reports."

She gave him the address and hung up, then carefully took down the life-size sketch and rolled it up. She left a message on the phone machine of the art student who did an occasional odd job for her, telling him to pick up the scroll at the gate and have the eight-by-ten version back as soon as he could possibly swing it.

She left the scroll where she'd said it would be and opened the gate for Harley's little red two-seater.

Harley was one of those people whose voice didn't match the visual. His nasal, slightly whiny voice suggested a geek stereotype—a scrawny, twentysomething, low-budget Bill Gates. In the flesh, he resembled an out-of-shape lineman, from the big cubic-zirconium studs in his ears to the flabby remnants of once-heroic biceps to the belly that hung over his belt and stretched the faded Patriots jersey to the limits of the fabric's tensile strength. His head was bald, his black beard was sprinkled with gray, and rumor had it he'd worked in military intelligence toward the end of Vietnam.

Apart from the inherent oxymoron in "military intelligence," Gwen was willing to buy that. Harley definitely knew his shit. The fact that he was also a church-lady gossip with less moral backbone than your average squid made tabloid reporting a natural career choice.

She hopped into his car and rode up to the garage with him. He inserted a disc into her laptop's drive and tapped a few keys. While his spyware hunted down invaders on Gwen's computer, he spread a series of seven fuzzy black-and-white pictures on the desk.

"These are the sonograms for Erin Westland, Helene Tremaine, and Vivian Meekins. These were taken over a period of three years, but they're all the same person."

Gwen squinted at the blur, trying to make sense of it. "How can you tell?"

"How can you miss it? Look here; see these three small blobs, with the tubes running down from them? Those are the ovary triplets. Same in all seven ultrasounds."

"So they're the same person."

"I'll go you one better," said Harley. He gathered up the photos, fanned them like a deck of cards, and brandished them with a read-'em-and-weep flourish. "These are all the same pregnancy."

"How can you tell?"

"What's the first thing new parents look for?"

"How the hell should I know?" A terrible thought occurred to her. "Sweet Jesus! Don't tell me *you've* reproduced."

"Ha. Much laughter on my part. C'mon—ten fingers and ten toes? It's a cultural cliché, chickie. If you look very, very closely, you'll see that this little dude has an extra digit. Check the piggies on this shot—it's the one with the best angle."

Gwen took one of the pictures and studied the blurred squiggle that looked more like a chicken embryo than a future child. Sure enough, there was an extra tiny stub on one of the little feet.

Erin Westland had been pregnant for almost four years. Which meant, among other things, that Kyle Radcliff was not Patrick's father.

An hour later, Gwen was sitting in Kyle's downtown office and none too happy about being there. Sure, he was a son of a bitch, but she wouldn't wish the news she carried on any living soul.

"Did you find them?" he demanded.

"I've learned a few things," she said cautiously, "but mostly everything I've found just leads to more questions."

"Great. That's just great." He slumped into his chair and gave her a resigned look. "What do you need to know?"

Gwen settled down in one of the wing chairs opposite his desk. "For starters, does Patrick have an extra toe on one foot?"

He looked startled. "No. He was perfectly normal. In fact, he was a beautiful baby."

"Were you right there in the room when he was born?"

He shook his head. "I know that's the fashion these days, but neither Erin nor I wanted that. As I've said before, she was very private about certain things. She just wanted the midwife, no one else."

Gwen made a mental note to place another call to Vermont and steeled herself for the hard part.

"Tell me about Erin's sex life. Leave out the boring parts, which would be anything including you."

He let out a short bitter laugh. "So, you did manage to find out a thing or two about Erin."

"You knew she was fooling around?"

"She was a slut," he said flatly. A bitter smile stretched his lips. "Well, what do you know. I finally figured out what you two have in common."

Gwen folded her arms. "Real nice. You're talking about the mother of your child, right?"

"As far as I know," he said glumly.

"You have any reason to doubt paternity?"

"I always assumed Patrick was my son, even though he looks so much like Erin. Now I'm not so sure."

"When did you find out she was involved with other men?"

His jaw clenched so hard that a muscle twitched alongside his mouth. "Yesterday," he admitted.

"I'm going to need a name." Something flickered in his eyes that prompted her to add, "Or a list."

"I can do better than that. I can get you pictures."

He reached into his desk drawer and pulled out a manila envelope, which he threw into Gwen's lap.

She slid out a sheaf of eight-by-ten prints and began to leaf through them. The pictures caught Erin in a wide variety of compromising positions—the girl was nothing if not flexible—with several attractive partners. Gwen shuffled through them until one caught her attention. He was young, blond, and very familiar.

Gwen knew this man—or more accurately, this *changeling*—as Adrian Archer.

Fifteen

The rest of the weekend passed quickly. Gwen left a message at Extreme for Adrian Archer, making it plain he needed to call her immediately. She called Jason and left a message warning him about the spyware that had shown up on her computer and letting him know there was a good chance his system had also been infected.

She stuffed three twenties into an envelope to mail to the artist who'd scaled down the sketch. It was a quick job, but he'd faithfully translated the big sketch, and even added some depth and shadow without changing the subject's appearance. Gwen fed the original into her scanner and sent a copy to Tamar. By sunset, the nun's contacts would have it all over the streets.

After a brief hesitation, she dialed Ian's number. She had a lot of balls in the air right now, but Ian was right—she needed to explore and master her "Qualities" as soon as possible.

For the first time she was actually looking forward to it. After all, look at how successful she'd been with Irena. Granted, she'd scared the crap out of the poor kid, but the end result was a damn good lead on the girl's former captor and her friends' current location.

Ian answered on the first ring. "Ready to resume the lesson?"

"As a matter of fact, that's why I called. Can you come over again tonight?"

"Let's see—moonrise is around seven tonight. I can meet you in the same place, shortly before."

"I'll be there."

She hung up and dialed Marcy's work number. Jeff Monroe answered with a crisp, "District attorney's office, Ms. Barlett's line."

"Hey, there. Is your boss around?"

"Gwen," he said, suddenly sounding much more tentative. "I've been meaning to call you."

Her brow furrowed. "Problem?"

"I'm . . . not sure."

"Just spit it out," she said impatiently.

"Not easily done during work hours," he said softly. "And speaking of which, I was late to work the night after our date. Marcy wasn't very happy with me."

"What? You want me to put in a good word for you with the boss?"

"No!" he said sharply. In a lower voice, he added, "I don't think the assistant DA needs to know I was sleeping with her best friend."

She still wasn't following, but she did catch his use of past tense, as in *was sleeping*.

Damn. A good man was hard to find, and vice versa.

"I get it," she said, letting him off the hook easy. "One of those office-politics, conflict-of-interest things."

"I really can't talk about it right now. I'll call you."

The phone went dead. Gwen shook her head in bemusement and dialed the number again. Jeff reprised his spiel.

"Marcy?" she requested.

"Oh. Sorry. I'll put you through."

Marcy answered her phone in the same brisk tone her assistant had used.

"Not much news on the investigation yet," Gwen said. "I'm just calling to see how you're doing."

"No news," Marcy said slowly. "But you have no reason to think they might be . . ."

"None," Gwen assured her. "But I've got to tell you, Kyle's luck with women went straight downhill after you showed him the door."

"You know, that should brighten my mood considerably. The fact that it doesn't worries me a little."

"No shit. What's going on?"

Marcy sighed. "Kyle's not the only one who's having problems at home. Trudy has been . . . I'm not sure how to put this."

A human leech? An insecure little bitch? A spoiled, moody daddy's girl? A contender for the Jewish-American Princess crown? Hell, Gwen could take that ball and run with it in any number of directions.

"Take a stab at it," she suggested.

"She seems distracted, and more than a little disconnected. She's more jealous, sometimes to the point of paranoia."

This sounded fairly serious. Until this moment, Gwen had had no intention of telling Marcy about her encounter with Trudy. But if there was a pattern happening, it might be an important piece of information.

"I guess I should tell you that Trudy took a swing at me the other day."

"Seriously?"

"As serious as a bitch slap is ever going to get. One of these days you should let me show you two how to throw a decent punch."

She could almost hear Marcy's shudder over the phone. "Oh yeah—that's exactly what Trudy needs right now. But we all have our moods," she added hastily. "This will pass."

"Okay," Gwen agreed. "Moving on?"

"Please. And may I say, you showed remarkable restraint."

"I thought so. About Kyle—has he contacted you recently?"

"No. Why do you ask?"

The wary sound in Marcy's voice suggested that this hadn't been an unfamiliar question of late. "Just so you know, I'm going to be taking a close look at your ex. It seems his wife was fooling around. A lot. There's some question of paternity."

"Kyle knows this?"

"Yeah. He said he just found out yesterday, but with Erin and Patrick gone, the timing doesn't look good."

Marcy blew out a long breath. "Kyle's not stupid enough to do a Scott Peterson imitation. A wife and child are not easily discarded."

"It's not a question of stupidity; it's a question of arrogance."

"Is there really much difference?"

"Good point. Listen, I just wanted to let you know how this might go."

"Thanks. Keep me posted, okay?"

Gwen clicked off her phone and started to look toward the clock. She caught herself in time and turned toward the office window, instead. If she was going to do this "cycles of nature" thing, she'd better start paying attention to what was going on.

Daylight was fading, and the velvety green shadows that gathered under the old trees were venturing out to welcome the coming night. The moon would soon be rising. The scene was very pretty and possibly even poetic, but it didn't do a damn thing for her.

She gave up and looked at the clock. It was a quarter of seven. So much for being at one with the rising moon.

Gwen shut down her computer and headed for the garden.

Ian Forest was waiting for her under the old maple. One of these days, she'd have to ask him how he got around.

He greeted her with a smile that did interesting things to her heart rate. "Can you tell me where the moon will rise tonight?"

She shook her head. "I have no idea when and where the moon plans to rise, or what phase it's in. I don't feel a damn thing. But I can tell you the names of the astronauts who landed on it, if that's any help."

A frown flickered across his face. "I suppose a certain lack of awareness is to be expected. Until just recently, you haven't been among others of your kind."

"That makes a difference?"

"Of course. Qualities get stronger in proximity to others."

Gwen thought about that. "Then why are some of us left among humans as changelings? You'd think kids would grow up stronger if they were with their families, or at least with other people like them."

"You've just answered your own question. Not all Qualities are desirable in and of themselves, and some combinations can be dangerous. That's why we pay careful attention to genealogy."

"Except when you don't," Gwen said, suddenly understanding where this was going.

"Except when we don't," Ian agreed. "Sometimes we get . . . careless, and children are born of incompatible bloodlines. These children are put into fosterage with humans until their gifts begin to emerge. At that time, a determination is made."

"And then what?"

"It would depend, of course. Most often the young ones are brought in, taught what they are, and given a place among us."

"What about the rare exception? And what happens to the human babies?"

He hesitated. "Each case is decided separately."

"Yeah? Who decides?"

"That's not something of immediate concern to you. It's more important for you to concentrate on learning and controlling your abilities."

There was a strange note in his voice, and Gwen didn't think it was remorse over those lost young lives. "You're worried about this third Quality, the starlight thing."

"These gifts usually begin to manifest in adolescence. Yes, I'm concerned that you have shown only two of the three." He gave her a slow, devastating smile. "Perhaps if we spend more personal time together, this gift will emerge."

"Nice try," she said dryly. "But if this works on a the-more-the-merrier basis, I know this guy who used to work for Edmonson. Adrian Archer. Maybe we should call him over, join hands, sing 'Kumbaya.'"

Ian reacted like a clap of thunder.

"There's another?" he demanded, seizing her arm. "Here in Providence? Describe him."

"Jesus, dial it down a notch or two, would you? He looks sort of like a young Brad Pitt, minus the stubble. Taller, thinner, blonder. What's the problem?"

He dropped her arm and began to pace. "I don't know this Adrian Archer. To the best of my knowledge, I was the only one of our kind in Edmonson's . . . employ. What were the circumstances of your meeting?"

"Meetings. Plural."

She described the theft in the lab out in Lincoln, the recent drug meet on the East Side, the recent meeting at the Extreme, and the strange result of the drug testing of one of the dancers.

Ian nodded thoughtfully. "Of course I knew that drugs were available at Underhill and the other clubs, but it was my understanding that the humans—Tiger Leone, the Jamisons, and a few like them—handled that end of the business."

"Does it make a difference?"

"It might. It would certainly explain the results of the tests conducted on that dancer, and might also explain why your Captain Walsh was involved with Edmonson."

"They're selling something new, something law enforcement hasn't seen before."

"Not for several hundred years, certainly. Our people have long made potions from rare herbs, things that can have a rather profound effect on humans and none at all on us."

"What's the effect?"

"It would depend on the herb, and also its preparation. A mild infusion can be soothing. In stronger doses, these herbs usually act as some sort of stimulant."

"A mild infusion, you said," Gwen murmured. "Like a tea."

"Yes, that's right."

She considered the soothing herbal brew Alice Powers offered them at The Green Man. It did seem to have an effect on the woman—she calmed down as quickly as someone who'd popped a Valium. It had had a somewhat different effect on Jason, but then, he'd had about four cups of the stuff. And Jeff . . .

Suddenly the explanation for their two-person orgy became abundantly clear. Ditto his reserve on the phone. People coming off Ecstasy had one hell of a drop. Since Jeff was sufficiently hung-over the next morning to miss work, he probably thought she'd slipped him something.

Which, in effect, she had.

"How could you make sure this drug is what you think it is?"

"I'd need a sample."

"I'm pretty sure I've got some."

A peculiar expression flitted over his face. "Have you tried it?"

"Yeah, when I thought it was some kind of herbal tea. It didn't do a thing for me, but a friend of mine had some. A lot of it, actually. It definitely had an effect on him."

"Is he still alive?"

She laughed shortly. "Yeah. It wasn't quite *that* good."

"I'm not sure I'm following you."

"This friend was over at my place. He mixed some concentrated tea with juice. He should have added water, but he didn't, and he drank a lot of it. It made him really frisky."

Ian's eyebrows rose. "The tea acted as an aphrodisiac?"

"That's right. The effect was fairly similar to how someone might act after a hit of X. The weird thing is, a normal cup of tea seems to have a calming effect."

"I know this herb," Ian said. "In different doses and manner of preparation, it mirrors the effect of popular street drugs: marijuana, amphetamines, and, as you have observed, Esctasy. Like marijuana, it is a completely natural substance, but the intoxicants it contains are quite different from any of the known illegal substances."

"So if this stuff was tested, it would look like herb tea."

"Or a capsule of powdered herbs, or even a small tablet," Ian concluded.

"So in any form, it's virtually undetectable," Gwen mused. "Is there a lot of this stuff around?"

"That seems unlikely."

"Then I can see why Edmonson wanted Walsh in on this. If one of his people got picked up for distribution, Walsh could arrange a switch. The tea leaves look and act like weed. I'm guessing the pills and capsules are made to look like street drugs."

"I would assume so, yes."

"So the dealer's lawyer has the stuff tested, and it looks like the only thing his client is guilty of is scamming a bunch of party people."

"Yes."

Gwen shook her head. "It's a lot of trouble to go through just to avoid a routine bust for weed and speed."

"That would depend. Most low-level dealers are expendable. Few are sufficiently well informed to implicate their suppliers. The police can arrest as many street dealers as they like, and no one sheds tears over the death of a Tiger Leone. But what of the people who use the drugs? For some, the penalties can be inconvenient."

"A sting, then? Extortion?" She turned the possibilities over in her mind. "Edmonson's people could sell the herbal drugs to rich college kids, professionals, politicians—anyone who'll pay to avoid a drug conviction. If they're picked up, arrange the switch with Walsh, resell the original drugs, pocket the cash. A lot of people would pay good money for that kind of service. If they had enough chutzpah, they might even threaten the arresting officers with a lawsuit for false arrest. Edmonson would profit from that, too—he had his own law firm."

"All of this sounds plausible."

"Of course, you couldn't go to that well too often. If the ability to switch the drugs depends upon Walsh, the department couldn't screw up too often or he'd lose his job."

"Unless he was seen as a crusading, incorruptible police chief because he weeded out tainted members of the force."

"Like me," she said bitterly. "Son of a bitch."

Rage rose in her like black mist, dimming her vision. A moment passed before she realized that the dwindling clouds had reformed into a dense blackness that blocked out the stars. In the back of her mind, a small traitorous voice suggested that Gwen was responsible for this, as well.

She turned her back on Ian and drew a long, shuddering breath.

"We can do nothing more tonight," he said quietly. "Whatever the starlight holds for you is blocked by your anger."

Gwen whirled back toward him. "Then unblock it. Let's put all the cards on the table."

"Can you dance?"

For a long moment she stared at him. "Jesus Christ on stilts. You're *serious*."

"Of course."

"C'mon! Dancing in the starlight? How Tolkien is that?"

"Mind and body are closely related. Movement frees the flow of power. You can probably accept that humans can treat depression through exercise, that yoga and tai chi make their practitioners more centered and connected, that martial arts develop the ki. Given your background, you may believe that prayer is more powerful when focused by the movement of rosary beads through the fingers of a penitent. If these things are plausible, why is it so difficult to believe that dance, particularly in the company of others of our kind, strengthens our Qualities?"

"You make it sound almost reasonable," she grumbled.

"It is reasonable. Moreover, it works. Come." He extended a hand to her.

Gwen shook her head. "They didn't exactly have cotillions where I grew up. I can shake my stuff, but I don't think that's what you've got in mind. Is there another option?"

He lifted one eyebrow. "Now that you mention it." He pulled her to him and claimed her lips before she realized his intention.

The kiss was different than those she'd recently shared with Jeff. Her senses filled with the scent of woodsmoke and green forests, and the lure of darker, unknown places. Any thought of resistance faded.

They sank together to the grass. Gwen stripped off her shirt, hungry to feel his skin on hers. But in her building sexual excitement was another note—something dark and fierce, alien yet disturbingly familiar. She got the impression that every nightmare she couldn't quite remember was trying to push through a wall in her mind.

If this was the Quality, she wanted no part of it.

Gwen pulled away, chilled in a way that had nothing to do with the evening breeze on her skin. She rolled up into a sitting position and wrapped her arms around her knees. If she hugged herself hard enough, she could almost control the shaking.

Ian rolled to one side and propped his head up on one elbow. A casual pose, but Gwen detected a hint of worry in his eyes.

"Something was happening. Tell me about it."

"It wasn't good, but it was big."

"Perhaps a bit too much for a first manifestation. Our Qualities tend to manifest more powerfully around others of our kind. That's one of the reasons why we're rather widely scattered."

"Put too many in the same room, we reach critical mass and blow up?"

"Not as such. But yes, it can be dangerous. That's why some of the young whose bloodlines are in questions are placed among humans."

Gwen's phone rang. Ian shook his head in resignation and got to his feet.

"I know," he said. "You've got to take this."

He picked up his discarded coat and shirt when did that come off, anyway?—and melted into the shadows beneath the old tree.

Gwen snapped her gaze away from Ian and clicked on the phone. "Talk."

"It's Tamar. That picture you sent to me rang a bell. Can you meet someone tonight? Right away?"

She reached for her tee shirt and rose to her feet.

"Just tell me where, and I'm on my way."

Sixteen

Gwen sashayed into the pool hall down by the river and presented her GiGi Silver ID at the door. The bouncer glanced at it and gave a skeptical grunt—most people thought twenty-one was a bit of a stretch for her—but he handed back the card and waved her into the room.

There was only one man in the room wearing a bright yellow shirt. He was a big guy, Latino. According to Tamar, he was on the same kind of hunt as Gwen. Two young cousins had disappeared and he'd followed their trail from Mexico to California, and from there to Providence.

The man gave Gwen an appreciative once-over as she strode over to his table, but his jaw dropped when she mentioned her name.

"You are she the holy sister sends?"

"That's right. You got a problem with that?"

He spread both hands, palms up, in an almost courtly gesture. "Forgive me, *chica,* but I was not expecting . . ."

His eyes slid over her, taking in her gel-spiked hair, her heavily made-up eyes and her crimson mouth, the snug black top and the even tighter black jeans (not to mention the wide strip of skin in between), the garnet stud on her belly-button ring, the stiletto-heeled ankle boots.

"Me," Gwen summed up.

"Truly. The sister spoke of an . . . *ángel que se venga?*"

An avenging angel? That was a little dramatic, even for Sister Tamar.

"My wings are at the cleaners. Sorry about that," Gwen said dryly. "And if I come as a shock, you're lucky the 'holy sister' isn't riding shotgun tonight."

His dark brows met in a frown of puzzlement. Idiom overload was Gwen's guess.

Since he seemed a little uncomfortable with English, Gwen dropped into the street Spanish she'd picked up from the girls in juvenile. "Sister Tamar said you recognized the man in the sketch. Tell me where I can find the motherless fuck."

"*Mierda!* This is how the Spanish is taught in American schools?"

"Depends on where you went to school. This guy, did he have any girls with him? Two of them, blond. Probably Russian girls, and about the age of the kids you're looking for."

"If I found any girlchild in the possession of such a man, would I leave her with him?" he demanded.

Gwen shrugged. "Some would."

His offended expression melted into something very much like sorrow. "That is truth. You don't know me, so how else could you answer such a question?"

"Glad we cleared that up. Where can I find this guy?"

"Do you know Atwell Avenue?"

Gwen nodded, and he gave concise directions from that main road to one of the less savory neighborhoods on the west side of I-95. When he finished, he gave her an uncertain stare.

"This man is a wolf who preys upon young girls. You will not go to him alone?"

"I'm thinking he'll be more likely to open the door to a client."

He nodded, clearly relieved by what he thought she was saying. "I would go with you, but this man, he knows my face."

Gwen saw no reason to point out that *she* could pose as a client as well as any man. A guy who sold sex—especially someone who wasn't peddling his own ass—usually wasn't too picky about whom he sold to.

"Thanks for the offer. I hope you find the girls you're looking for."

"And you as well, *chica*." He gave her a quick smile, little more than a baring of teeth. *"Buena caza."*

Good hunting.

Their eyes met, and a moment of perfect understanding passed between them. The city was full of predators, but tonight, some of them would take a step or two down on the food chain. And neither of them saw a damn thing wrong with that.

Gwen got to the pimp's house about five minutes too late. As she killed the lights on her Toyota, she noticed a skinny, furtive man climb the front stairs. The front door swung open and the Latino she'd seen in her vision ushered the client inside.

The next half hour passed in frustration and fury as Gwen waited for the man to complete his purchase. As soon as he sauntered out, she was out of the car and heading for the front door.

The pimp stared at her, first in surprise, then calculation. "What do you want?"

Gwen tossed her head in the direction the John had taken. "Same thing he wanted."

A leer spread across the man's face, and he cupped his groin with one hand. "I can help you with that."

"Chicks, not dicks," she said succinctly. "Are you selling, or aren't you?"

"A little girl like you is buying?" he said, eyeing her skeptically.

"It depends. Do you have a girl who does hard tricks?"

His eyes widened. "How hard?"

"No bruises, no blood." Gwen shrugged. "Or very little."

"No problem. For that, two hundred for an hour."

She pulled several fifties from her leather bra. When he reached for it, she snatched it away. "An hour," she said coldly. "In an hour's time, I'm coming down the stairs and walking out of this house. If I don't, some very bad boys will be coming in to get me."

His eyes lifted over her shoulder, scanned the street. No watchers were in evidence, but then, they wouldn't be.

"An hour," he agreed, and reached for the money. This time, Gwen let him take it.

She walked up the stairs and into the door on the left. A pale-haired waif sat on the edge of the bed, looking at Gwen without surprise. Without emotion of any kind. But when their eyes met, Gwen got a vivid mental image: The blond girl down in the basement of this house, tears streaming down her cheeks as she struggled to dig a grave in the hard-packed earth.

Gwen looked around for something to write on. There was no paper anywhere, but a big oval mirror was strategically positioned by the bed.

Sick bastards.

She took her lipstick from her purse and drew a simple picture of a nun—just a smiley face surrounded by the folds of an old-fashioned wimple, shoulders, and a necklace with a cross. She sent a questioning look at the girl. After a moment, she nodded.

Gwen drew three small stick figures with skirts. She pointed to one of the figures, then to the girl, signaling *This is you.*

Again the girl nodded, and interest began to replace the dull, dead look in her eyes.

Using a corner of the sheet, Gwen erased the second stick figure. She drew it again, close to the smiley-face nun, then drew a circle around them both. She added a pair of vertical lines coming down from the circle, and connected them with a curved base. The drawing was crude, but it was recognizable as a tower. A safe place.

Gwen tapped the stick figure who'd found safety with the nun. "Irena."

A smile burst over the girl's face like a sunrise, and she said something in Russian that sounded like a brief, fervent prayer of thanksgiving. She touched her heart, then reached for the stick figure that represented her.

"I am Marina," she said carefully.

"Hello, Marina. My name is Gwen. How much English can you speak?"

The girl considered. "Some of it."

"Fair enough. Listen, I'm going to take you to Irena. Somewhere you'll both be safe."

Marina tapped her ear and shrugged helplessly.

"Great," Gwen muttered. She regarded her lipstick. It was getting low—definitely long past time to wind up this conversation.

She drew an arrow from the Marina figure to the tower, then stood and held out her hand.

The girl rose slowly and took the lipstick from Gwen's hand. She smeared the third figure, added a pair of triangles to represent angel wings, and turned mournful eyes to Gwen.

"I know," she said softly. She erased the picture with the sheet, then held out her hand again. "Let's go."

Marina's small fingers curled around hers, and she followed Gwen down the stairs.

The man met them at the foot of the stairs, his face twisted in a scowl. "You rented the little bitch, that's it. You thinking about buying, I'm gonna need to see a lot more money than you put down."

Without letting go of Marina's hand, Gwen leaned to one side and snapped off two quick kicks—the first into the pimp's face, the second catching him in the solar plexus. He folded, clutching his gut and wheezing.

A cry burst from Marina—a banshee howl of rage and pain. Suddenly she was on him like a small fury, pounding him with her fists. Gwen let her get in a few satisfying shots, then stepped in and delivered a roundhouse punch to the side of his jaw. He went down and showed no sign of getting up anytime soon.

Gwen crouched beside him and took out his wallet. It held several hundred, including Gwen's fifties. She took out the wad and handed it to Marina.

"For you and Irena."

The girl was still trembling with wrath. It took a moment for her to focus on the money, and on Gwen's meaning. Her face hardened, and she shook her head adamantly.

Gwen could respect that. Come to think of it, she wouldn't have taken it either. She pocketed her two hundred and put the rest back.

She led Marina to the front door and pointed to the battered Toyota. "You go ahead. Lock the door. You'll be safe, and I'll be there in just a minute."

Maybe the girl understood, maybe she was only too happy to

leave her captor. She ran out to Gwen's car and flung herself into the backseat.

Gwen looked around for something resembling a rope. The room on her right was a sitting room, furnished decades ago with a cheap pair of chintz-covered chairs and a sagging sofa. Faded drapes framed each of the two windows, tied back with a triple tier of satin ropes ending in unraveling tassels.

Gwen yanked off the satin ropes and dragged the pimp over to the banister. She propped him in a sitting position and tied him securely in place.

That accomplished, she slapped his cheeks until his eyes fluttered open. When they focused, Gwen rose and stepped away from him.

And *Remembered*.

She brought to mind Marina's last memories of Anya, and willed them to fill the room.

A shadow moved at the top of the stairs. Gwen looked up and smiled.

Something in her face brought a look of alarm to the pimp's eyes, and he craned his head toward the source of that malevolent satisfaction.

And started screaming.

Anya's ghostly body tumbled down the stairs in eerie silence. She landed at the pimp's feet, one limp, translucent arm flung out wide in such a manner that it seemed to go *through* him.

He kept screaming even after the vision faded away, and his eyes were wild as they tracked something moving about the room. Something only he could see.

For just a moment, fear shimmered an icy path down Gwen's spine. Maybe memories this painful and powerful left more than a psychic echo. Perhaps there really was something else in the room.

She shrugged away that thought and left the man alone with his ghosts or his guilt. It didn't particularly matter to her which.

Once outside, she pulled her phone from her pocket and dialed Damian's number. After all, she'd cheated him out of a drug bust, so she owed him. This ought to pay off the debt with interest.

Gwen dropped off Marina at Sister Tamar's safe house and called Adrian from her car. He agreed to meet her in the park where Damian had set up the drug bust.

He was waiting when she got there. Instead of speaking, Gwen held up the picture of Erin.

"I know this girl," he readily admitted. "She is one of us."

"Tell me."

"We met years ago. When we became intimate, her powers started manifesting. Two years ago, I brought her to the earl. She agreed to work for him in distribution."

"That herbal store down in Tiverton. The Green Man."

"Yes."

"But that's not your only means of distribution."

"Of course not. We offer something for everyone. The drugs were sold in all of Tiger's clubs. We have people working the schools. And, of course, street deals."

"Do you have some on you?"

He handed her a capsule. She pulled it apart and spilled the finely ground powder into her hand. An image of a rocky, almost lunar landscape flashed into mind.

"What is this stuff?"

"A very rare plant. It was found in a place in western Ireland called the Burren."

"It grows there?"

He hesitated. "It was *found* there. The Burren is one of the strangest ecosystems on earth. There are many plants among all those rocks that have no business being there: alpine plants, plants from the Mediterranean coast."

"Where is this one from?"

"That is hard to say," he replied carefully. "But it's being grown here, locally."

"Show me."

Moonlight sifted through the purposefully stunted limbs of apple trees, glinting on the tiny green globes that promised future fruit. Gwen walked down a row of trees, but saw no other fields beyond. As far as she could tell, this place looked like any other farm in rural Smithfield.

"Okay, where is it?"

Adrian pointed to a low-growing meadow flower in the grasses, a dainty blue flower growing above fernlike foliage.

"That's *it?*" Gwen marveled. "You're growing organic Ecstasy in a freaking apple orchard?"

"Yes. This is the only place in the world where it is grown."

"Who owns this place?"

His smile was faintly mocking, and his eyes searched her face as if greedy for her reaction. "It would appear that you do."

Seventeen

"I own hell's happy acres?" she demanded. "Is there any sleazy real estate in Rhode Island that Edmonson *didn't* own?"

Archer's smile broadened. "Actually, this farm belonged to your parents."

Gwen waited for some emotional response to this. Something was there, right under the surface, but she just couldn't get to it. Or perhaps she didn't want to.

"Is that the reason Edmonson killed them? To get control of this drug?"

"In truth, I don't think Edmonson wanted them dead. He wanted to know where the plants were originally found."

"But they died in the car crash."

Adrian's only response was an eloquent shrug.

"Why would he admit to killing them?"

"Because he was ultimately responsible. He started a course of action that could only result in their deaths. By our laws, there is only a slight difference between responsibility and murder. How could it be otherwise, when you're talking about a people who can influence others to do their bidding?"

Like Ian Forest. Despite everything he'd done, Gwen still felt the man's magnetic pull.

Gwen scanned the rows of trees. "So how does this work?"

"The herb is picked in midsummer. Bunches are hung in that barn over there. Once they are dry, they are sent away for packaging or processing."

"Where?"

"No one particular place. The scope of this business is still fairly small, and it's operated as a cottage industry. This is a precaution, as well as a practicality."

"I'll need the addresses of those cottages."

"Of course."

She turned a narrow-eyed gaze toward him. "You're being very helpful."

"Of course," he said again. "After all, you have my oath."

"Sure, but that doesn't mean you have to be so happy about it. You really don't seem to mind selling out your boss."

"Technically, I'm not selling him out. You are, after all, the earl's only heir."

Gwen nodded as if she actually bought that. For the time being, it was better to let this lunatic think she was ready to climb onboard.

"Is there anything in the barn?"

"No. Last year's crop has been processed. There is still some of the product in distribution channels, but the new harvest is only weeks away."

"Is this profitable?"

"Not particularly. It will be in time, perhaps."

"Then why are you doing this?"

He smiled faintly. "Why not? Haven't you ever used your Qualities to toy with the humans?"

She was about to say no when the image of the pimp's chalk-white face and quite literally haunted eyes came to mind.

"Only in a good cause," she said grudgingly.

"You don't consider simple entertainment sufficient reason?"

"That's sick," she said flatly.

"I don't see why."

"Because they're *people*?"

"They are vermin," he hissed. His face darkened, and suddenly he no longer looked like a cute blond singer from a particularly vapid boy band.

"The humans breed like rabbits. They control the planet's resources and destroy the environment in the process. Every year more species disappear, squeezed out by 'human progress.' There is a very real possibility that we, the Elder Races, might join them. What harm is there in indulging those few small pleasures that remain to us?"

"Like fucking with the humans."

Her sarcasm found no foothold in Adrian's worldview. In fact, he looked pleased that she'd grasped the concept so readily. "In a word, yes."

Gwen took a deep breath. "How many of us are left?"

He waved aside this question. "Our diminishing strength has less to do with our numbers than with our Qualities. The Old Gifts are disappearing or changing. Our birthrates are down, and acceptable powers seldom manifest with real strength."

"Okay, but what does selling drugs to humans have to do with any of this?"

"It proves that they are weak," Adrian said flatly. "They are driven by their appetites, eager for any chance to shrug off personal responsibility. They find the mildest chemicals and herbs debilitating."

He stooped and plugged a spring of lacy foliage. "You and I

could eat a large bowl of this herb with sliced tomatoes and Italian dressing, and feel no ill effects whatsoever."

"Unless there was a lot of salt in that dressing," Gwen retorted.

Adrian rocked back on his heels, looking as if she'd struck him across the face.

"It is hardly the same thing," he said stiffly.

Gwen let the point go. "So you get your jollies from watching people make fools of themselves."

"By exploiting their weakness," he emphasized. "Those of us who are strong suffer no ill effects. Those who are weak sink ever deeper into their pitiful little swamps."

"I don't like it. In fact, I want this stopped," she said, sweeping one arm wide to indicate the field.

His smile was cold. "That may not be your decision to make."

"Why not? I thought you said I owned this place."

"True, but I also said the earl's property would fall to you *if you met the terms of inheritance*. Have all three of your Qualities manifested?"

Gwen shrugged. "Ian Forest is working on that."

One corner of Adrian's mouth twitched into a sneer. "In that case, I wouldn't plan to collect your inheritance anytime soon."

Gwen parked Sylvia's black Mercedes beside the road, around the corner from The Green Man and beyond sight from the parking lot. Her landlady didn't mind if Gwen used the car from time to time. Not many people would associate the elegant vehicle with Gwen, but you never knew who might stop by for a cuppa and wonder why she was skulking around the shop.

She found a fairly comfortable spot among the trees to the west of the shop and settled in, lying on her stomach to keep out of view. It was a little damp, but she'd been on worse stakeouts.

Alice Powers drove up shortly before ten. The lights flickered on in the shop, and the tearoom lights quickly followed. Had to have that morning hit, Gwen thought. Most likely the shop owner was thoroughly hooked on her own products.

Within moments, a white Lexus pulled up in front of the shop. Gwen sat bolt upright, startled by the familiar vehicle. She quickly caught herself and dropped down out of sight.

A small, slim woman got out of the car and tucked a strand of her crimped red hair behind her ears.

"Trudy Wasserman," murmured Gwen. "Why am I not surprised?"

What she *was* was pissed. What with one thing and another, Gwen had enough to deal with without tripping over Trudy.

She waited until the redheaded woman returned to her car and pulled away. She marched into the store and grabbed two boxes of the Green Man tea. Alice Power's face darkened with dread when she took in the grim look on Gwen's face.

"Have you found Erin?"

"Not yet. Sorry, but I don't have time to chat," Gwen said, throwing a twenty on the counter. She left without waiting for her change and ran to the Mercedes.

Fortunately, there weren't too many ways to get from Tiverton to Providence. Gwen followed at a distance until she ascertained that Trudy was going to take highways: Route 24 north to I-195, then west to Providence. All the better. It was easy to tail someone in a crowd.

Trudy drove straight home. Gwen parked beside the Lexus in

the lot across from the condo. She jogged over to the building and rang the bell a couple of times before Trudy responded.

"Hey. It's Gwen. I've got something for you."

"What is it?" Even through the intercom, Trudy's voice sounded suspicious.

"There's one way to find out."

The buzzer sounded, and Gwen yanked the door opened and took the stairs two at a time. She pushed past Trudy and shut the door behind her, then tossed the box of Green Man tea at the woman.

Trudy instinctively caught the box, bobbled it for a moment. When she realized what she held, her eyes widened into limpid pools of guilt.

"Don't bother trying to sell me on coincidence," Gwen advised her.

The redhead tossed back her head and faced Gwen down. "All right, then, I admit it: I've been watching Erin Westland for some time now."

"Why?"

"She's married to Kyle," Trudy said, her tone suggesting that this should be self-evident.

"Again, *why*? Not why Erin married Kyle," she clarified, "although that's definitely a question to ponder another day, but why are you so interested in all the details of your girlfriend's ex?"

"Marcy was married to Kyle Radcliff for years. They have a history, and that can be a powerful thing. You saw how she came running to you with his problems."

"So you decide to start following the second wife? That

sounds dangerously like obsession to me. How long has this been going on?"

"A few weeks," she admitted.

Gwen raised one eyebrow.

"Okay, maybe a few months. Four or five."

"So how does this work? You follow Erin Westland down to her place of business, and decide to become a regular customer so you can keep an eye on the new missus?"

Trudy sighed heavily. "You're not going to believe this."

"That's probably true, but tell me anyway."

"I went down to The Green Man the first time not knowing Erin worked there. A friend of mine gave me a box of this herb tea. I really liked it, and asked her where I could buy it. She sent me down to Tiverton. It's the only place that sells it."

"What's your friend's name?"

"Sally. Sally Lyons."

That name sounded familiar, but Gwen couldn't quite place it. "Describe her."

"Well, she's about my age—late thirties—and about my height and build, although she's slimmer, I'm sorry to report. She has long brown hair, lovely hands. She's a very pretty woman. Very feminine."

That could describe a lot of people Gwen had seen around. "Do you have a number for her?"

Trudy went off for her phone book, and came back from the bedroom with a slip of paper in her hand. "Here's her home phone, though frankly, I don't know what you expect to learn from her. Just because she buys tea at Erin Westland's shop, it doesn't follow that she'd know something about the woman's disappearance."

"Couldn't hurt to ask. Can I give you a word of advice?"

Trudy nodded cautiously.

"Stop drinking that stuff. It doesn't exactly bring out the best in you."

Eighteen

Gwen spent a good chunk of Tuesday at the station, going over her statement about Kate Myers. She got to the church five minutes after her self-defense class was supposed to start.

Damian and Jason were already there, avidly discussing the merits of Jason's two-seater. The Miata and Damian's wreck were the only vehicles in the parking lot.

"I called it right last week," Damian told her. "Looks like you scared them all off."

"Looks like," she agreed. "Wait a minute—looks like we've got a couple of takers."

A blue SUV pulled into the lot, and two women got out. One was the blond political aide, and the other was the woman who had been so disturbed by last week's demonstration.

Gwen herded everyone into the basement and pulled the attendance list out of her file. As she went down it to check off the names of the women who showed up, she noticed the name of one who hadn't: Sally Lyons.

That was the name Trudy had given her—the friend who'd turned her on to the funny herbals.

Gwen got the two women started practicing the holds and escapes they'd learned last week. Then she stepped into the stairwell and shut the door. She called Sally Lyons's number and got a recording.

As soon as the voice message was finished playing, she dialed Kyle Radcliff.

"Have you got a recording of Erin's voice?"

"I don't think so," he said hesitantly. "She never liked video cameras, and my voice is on our phone machine at home."

"Figures. What about the shop?"

He thought about that. "I'm pretty sure Alice left the voice message. But come to think of it, Erin probably left her own message on her cell phone."

"I'm not in my office and don't have her file handy. Give me the number."

He recited the number. Gwen hung up on him and dialed it. Sure enough, a young female voice invited her to leave a message. She hung up and dialed Sally Lyons's number again.

The voices were the same.

First thing the next morning, Gwen was at the address given on Sally Lyons's class-registration form.

A little boy was in the front yard, absently kicking at a Spider-Man backpack. He was definitely the kid in the photo Kyle had given her.

"Hey, Patrick," she called, feeling a stab of guilt over using one of an abductor's favorite ploys. Call a kid by name, chances are he'll assume he should know you. Why parents insisted on displaying their kids' names on their shirts and hats and backpacks was a mystery to Gwen.

He looked up and waved at her. "Hi!"

"Is your mom home?"

"Yeah, but she's making faces today."

"Making faces," she repeated.

"Uh-huh. She's coming right out. You'll see."

At that moment Sally Lyons opened the front door, and Gwen definitely saw.

The woman with Erin Westland's child was one of the women from Gwen's self-defense class, the suburban mom in pastel pink who'd been worried about hurting her workout partner.

Suddenly Sally Lyons was gone, and Erin Westland stood her in place. "Get away from my son!" she shrieked.

The woman unsheathed her claws and came at Gwen in a sudden rush, swiping a handful of manicure at Gwen's face.

Gwen leaned away from the blow and came back with a punch to the jaw. The woman staggered back three steps, then dropped straight back onto her ass.

The little boy ran to her. She put her arms around him and glared over his head at Gwen.

"I'm not going back," she insisted.

"Well, that proves you've got some sense. I don't plan to take you and Patrick back to Kyle."

Erin sniffed. "I'm not afraid of him."

"Then what's this about?"

The woman gently moved Patrick away from her and put a hand under his chin, turning his face to hers. "Go inside, honey. Mommy will be with you in just a minute, okay?"

The child's gaze flashed to Gwen.

"I won't hurt your mother," she said.

"You promise?"

Acting on impulse, Gwen said, "I swear it by moon and star, word and wind."

The little boy's face lit up. "Hey! Can you make faces, too?"

Gwen obliged by crossing her eyes and sticking out her tongue. Patrick giggled. "Not those kind of faces!"

"Patrick," Erin prompted in one of those no-nonsense mother tones. He turned and scampered for the house.

"What didn't you want him to hear?" Gwen asked.

"He's in danger," Erin confided. "It's the others. They found out about Patrick."

"So?"

"According to the Elders, he can't exist." A bitter smile twisted Erin's face. "My son is a half-breed."

"Nice try. I know about your pregnancy. It lasted close to four years. Patrick isn't Kyle's son."

"My relationship with Kyle goes back several years. I started seeing him when he was still married to your friend Marcy."

"Wouldn't surprise me. But what about the other men?"

"What other men?" Erin demanded.

"Kyle had quite a photo album."

"Oh, that. Do you have any idea how easy it is to alter photos? Anyone who worked for Edmonson had access to a lot of pornography. It wasn't hard to find a photographer who could shoot me in similar positions and impose my face on some other woman's body."

"Kyle was pretty pissed off."

"That was the whole idea," she retorted. "I didn't want him looking for me. The man has an ego the size of Texas. If he thought

I was fooling around, he wouldn't want me. If he thought Patrick wasn't his, he wouldn't waste another moment on him."

That also rang true with what Gwen knew of Kyle. "And what about Trudy Wasserman?"

Erin huffed. "What *about* her? I was tripping over her every time I turned around, so I decided to give her another hobby."

"An addiction."

The woman shrugged.

"You're deliberately getting people hooked on this stuff. And not just Trudy."

"I need the money," Erin stated. "I've stretched my local identities to the breaking point. It's time to start over, somewhere far away. The Green Man was giving me a chance to build up a nest egg."

"So why aren't you gone?"

"I can't get at the money without giving myself away," Erin said. "That's where you come in."

Gwen lifted one eyebrow. "You're looking to hire me?"

"I figured Kyle might end up coming to you when I left. So I signed up for your self-defense course to see what you had. I figured, if you could find me, you were probably good enough to help me disappear."

"Glad to know I passed your little test," Gwen said dryly. "As much as I hate to admit it, I'm being shadowed fairly closely by one sneaky pointy-eared son of a bitch. If I can find you, chances are he can, too."

Erin's face fell. "I hadn't thought of that."

"I know where you can go. A friend of mine runs a safe house. There's excellent security, police protection. They won't bother you there—keeping a low profile is a high priority to these people."

"*Our* people," Erin corrected. She conceded with a shrug. "Very well. I'll go to this safe house."

"You're welcome."

She shrugged again and started toward the house. Gwen fell into step. "I hope it won't come as a shock to hear that I don't exactly trust you."

Erin darted a surprised glance in her direction. "Why should you?"

"Just so you know, I'm going to be very unhappy if anyone at Sister Tamar's place is hurt because of you."

"I'll keep a low profile." Erin smiled sweetly. "Like you said, that's what we do best."

Much to his dismay, Ian found himself obliged to pay a call on the man who called himself Jason Cross. An unannounced visit, of course. Unfortunately, Jason wasn't even slightly startled by the sudden appearance.

The man leaned against the kitchen counter in his "father's" bungalow and crossed his arms. "So. To what do I owe the honor of this intrusion?"

"You haven't contacted me with your findings on Gwen."

"What findings? If you told me what you were looking for, I'd have a better chance of noticing it."

"Selective observation? No, thank you. Tell me what you have managed to discover."

Jason gave a concise report of her online activities, as well as those of people who did her more complicated Internet work for her.

"Anything she knows, I know," he concluded. "She's working on a number of things. Some background checks, a missing woman."

"Tell me about them."

"Aren't we supposed to be following a drug connection and erasing ties to this Captain Walsh?"

"We must know everything she's working on." Ian gave him a keen look. "It could be particularly uncomfortable if she starts looking too closely into Frank Cross's death."

The man returned his stare. "Yes, I can see how that would be a problem for you."

Doubt flickered in Ian's mind. He was certain that this man had killed Frank Cross, but he couldn't pick up any inkling of guilt from the young man. Perhaps he was a sociopath who knew no such emotions?

"Tell me about this missing woman."

"Her name's Erin Westland, aka Helene Tremaine. She's married to Kyle Radcliff, the ex-husband of Gwen's friend Marcy Bartlett. She has a son. They're both gone."

Ian's heart seemed to leap into his throat, then thud painfully back into place. This was a most disturbing development. Especially now that Jason Cross was involved.

"What progress has Gwen made?"

"We've visited the woman's shop. An herb shop down in Tiverton called The Green Man."

This, too, was disturbing news.

Shaken, Ian left the little house and hurried to his car.

He drove to Erin Westland's shop and bought a box of the store's tea.

As soon as he got back to his car, he spilled some of the dried herbs into his hand. He sniffed them, then touched a pinch to his tongue. The taste was unmistakable.

It was true, then. These herbs, banished for centuries, must have blown into the Burren from a gate that led into the Hidden land. And that could mean only one thing:

James Avalon, Gwen's father, had figured a way in.

Nineteen

Gwen decided to take Sylvia's car to East Greenwich. In Kyle Radcliff's neighborhood, a black Mercedes was the next best thing to camouflage. And unlike her aging economy car, the Mercedes could exceed the speed limit. She drove with grim concentration, weaving around slower vehicles and pushing the sedan to its limits. The sooner she got to Kyle's place, the sooner the coming confrontation could be done and over.

She'd never seen his house in East Greenwich. The home he'd shared with Marcy in Providence had been pretty spiffy, but this place was obscenely huge. A sprawling French colonial, all steeply peaked rooflines and small gables, was set in at least an acre of manicured lawn and carefully landscaped beds. The circular drive curved around a sea of late tulips, and azaleas bloomed amid the foundation plantings. A fenced area behind the house suggested an in-ground pool. Erin Westland was escaping a very posh cage.

Gwen pulled up at the front and rang the bell. No answer. She tried a couple of times before deciding that Kyle had missed their appointment, probably just to be a pain in the ass.

She was turning to leave when a fluttering curtain caught her eye. The movement drew her gaze to the open window—and the grim scene beyond.

A tall, fair-haired male lay faceup on the carpet, his arms flung out wide. Gwen went over to the window for a closer look.

It was definitely Kyle. His cable-knit sweater, once a natural sheep-colored beige, was dark with blood. His face was unmarked, and his cold gray eyes were open and staring.

Gwen reached for her phone to call it in. On impulse, she stopped, stuck the phone back into her pocket, and climbed through the open window.

The room was remarkably tidy and very, very beige. The carpets, walls, and furniture were all shades that could be found in a bowl of oatmeal. The only color in the room was the pool of blood seeping into the carpet around Kyle Radcliff's body.

As far as Gwen could tell, there was only one wound, but it had done the job. Someone with remarkable aim had gotten him right in the heart. Judging from the angle of the body, he'd been facing the open window and had fallen straight back.

Gwen crouched beside the body. Her brow furrowed as she studied the wound. The placement was perfect, but it was like no gunshot wound she'd ever seen. Both his clothes and the flesh beneath had been torn, as if he'd been stabbed with some sharp but strangely shaped object.

A glance at his hands discouraged that theory. Kyle lay with his arms flung out wide and his palms turned up. There were no defensive wounds on his hands. There probably would have been, if someone had come at him with a knife.

She picked up one hand and turned it to study the nails. They were neatly trimmed and buffed, so her eyes went at once to the single imperfection: caught under one nail was a single wavy, bright auburn hair.

Trudy's hair.

Gwen sat back on her heels, stunned into immobility. True, the woman was ridiculously jealous. Marcy had said Trudy had been acting strangely, and yes, she'd taken a swing at Gwen, but murder? It didn't seem possible.

She rose and walked over to the window. The angle was too perfect. Whatever had hit Kyle had come through the open window. And the red hair? It was Trudy's, Gwen had little doubt of that, but that didn't necessarily mean that Marcy's lover had been in this room. Someone was manipulating the scene.

Gwen pulled out her phone and dialed Sister Tamar's private line. "Is Erin still there?" she demanded.

The nun sniffed. "Yes, and she's quite the princess. Why? What's happening?"

"Her husband's dead. There's a chance that whoever killed him might come after Erin. Lock the place down. Don't let anyone come or go."

"Done," Tamar said. "Do you know who did this?"

"Not yet. I've got to go."

She went to work on the body, searching for more telltale hairs. There were three, two on the sleeves of Kyle's sweater and one entangled in his hair. None were on the blood-soaked torso, which, to Gwen's way of thinking, argued strongly for their placement after Kyle's death.

Her next stop was the kitchen, where she denuded a roll of paper towels. She set to work wiping clean every surface in the room, including the windowsill and the doorknobs, inside and out.

When she was reasonably satisfied that she'd obliterated every false trace of Trudy's presence, she picked up her phone to call it in. She started to dial Quaid's number before she remembered he was on leave, pending investigation in Kate's murder. After a moment's thought, she dialed the station and asked to be patched through to Ben Cerulo.

"It's Gellman," she told him. "I'm working on a missing-persons, and I just got to a client's house for a meeting. Instead of a client, I have a body."

"I'll be right there," he said without hesitation. "Give me the address."

"Well, that could be a problem. It's in East Greenwich."

He huffed in exasperation. "Why are you calling me instead of the townies?"

"He has an estranged wife. She's not a suspect—she's been in Sister Tamar's safe house since this morning. But she might be in danger. Can you get someone over there? Preferably plainclothes?"

"You got it. Do you have any idea who might have killed your guy?"

Gwen's eyes slipped to the telltale red hairs she'd placed in a Ziploc sandwich bag. "I'll leave that to the East Greenwich people. Thanks."

On her way out, she left a fresh set of prints on the windowsill, the front doorknob, and the doorbell. The town cops would know there'd been a housekeeping, and her prints would suggest that it had happened before her arrival.

Before she called the townies, she did a circle of the property, looking for weapons conveniently stashed in the landscaping. When she was confident there was nothing to find, she sank down on the front step and dialed 911.

After the East Greenwich police were finished with her, Gwen drove straight to Marcy's condo. Her friend's little sil-ver BMW was not in the parking lot, but Trudy's Lexus was.

Gwen entered the building by following two male tenants and took the stairs up to the third floor. She knocked on the door for a while before Trudy swung it open.

The redhead was dressed—barely—in a sea-green teddy and a matching short robe. She looked rumpled and sexy, as if she'd been called from her bed, but not from sleep.

Trudy regarded Gwen with a beatific smile. "Hello gorgeous," she said in a cheerfully awful imitation of Barbra Streisand imitating Fanny Brice.

Gwen cast her eyes toward the ceiling. "Forget it," she advised. "You don't have the nose for it."

The woman actually giggled. "I did, once," she confided. "I had it bobbed. See?" She presented her profile.

"Yeah, whatever. Where were you this afternoon?"

"Oh, who cares?" Trudy swayed closer and draped her arms around Gwen's neck. "Hold still, will you?"

"I'm not moving," Gwen pointed out as she tried to disentangle herself. It wasn't easy—the woman looked as boneless as a lap cat and twice as blissful, but she clung to Gwen with surprising strength and rapidly increasing passion. "Jesus, how much of that stuff did you drink?"

"What the hell is going on in here?" demanded Marcy.

Gwen glanced over her shoulder. Her friend stood in the open door, looking as if she'd just been whacked between the eyes with a two-by-four.

"Don't just stand there," she snapped. "Help me get Trudy into bed."

"Why? It looks to me like you're doing just fine on your own."

Just then Trudy managed to plant a wet one squarely on Gwen's mouth. Gwen seized two handfuls of wavy red hair and held her off. "A little help? She's higher than a weather satellite."

"Impossible," Marcy stated flatly. "Trudy doesn't take drugs."

Gwen raised an eyebrow.

"Okay, she'll smoke some weed once in a while, but other than that she is extremely health conscious. Annoyingly so."

Trudy started to sag as euphoria gave way to stupor. Gwen staggered under the sudden deadweight. "Give me a hand, would you?"

Finally convinced, Marcy kicked off her heels and came over to help. Between the two of them, they got Trudy into bed. She promptly rolled over to her side, curled up, and started snoring.

They slipped out of the bedroom. Marcy closed the door and walked over to the liquor cabinet. She poured herself a glass of wine with shaking hands.

"Has she been acting like this a lot recently?"

Marcy slumped into a chair. "If you mean has she been dry-humping my friends and associates, no. But she's been having mood swings. She has definitely been more insecure and possessive."

"The weaknesses grow stronger," Gwen murmured, remembering Adrian's screed in the orchard.

"What is she taking? Do you have any idea?"

"An herbal blend. Something new. It's powerful stuff, but it hasn't found its way onto the list of illegals yet."

Marcy shook her head in sorrow and astonishment. "How long has this been going on?"

"The best I can figure, four or five months."

She was silent for a long time. "So it's gotten to be an addiction."

"I'd say so, yes."

She set down her glass and covered her face with both hands. "I don't know what to do with this." Her voice sounded muffled and shaken, as close to tears as Gwen had ever seen her.

"Take your time. This has got to be a shock."

Marcy took a long breath and lowered her hands, folding them in her lap. "If this isn't a recognized substance, can she go into rehab?"

"It probably wouldn't be covered by major medical, but I don't see why not."

Marcy waved that obstacle away. "I can afford to pay for treatment. The thing is, what happens after? I don't know if I'm up to dealing with this. You know about my father."

Gwen nodded. Marcy had been raised by her maternal grandmother because her father was usually too drunk to pay much attention to his kids. The experience had left Marcy with an extreme aversion to any kind of overindulgence. That was one reason superhealthy, squeaky-clean Kyle had appealed to her. It was one of the reasons she'd gravitated toward health-conscious Trudy. There was something ironic in the fact that Trudy was probably an addict before she discovered the herb. The fact that she was addicted to a *person* just made it harder to recognize.

"Would it help to know that she didn't realize what the herb was when she started taking it?"

Marcy nodded slowly. "I hate to admit it, but yeah, that does help."

"Good, because you've got a lot of hard decisions ahead of you. I hate to dump this on you right now, but it won't wait. Marcy, Kyle is dead."

"*What?* When? How?"

"He was stabbed or shot once, right through the heart. I found him at his house."

"How awful." Marcy reached for her hand. "I'm so sorry you had to deal with that."

Gwen squeezed her friend's hand and released it. "There's more."

She took the little plastic bag containing Trudy's hairs from her pocket and tossed it onto the table beside Marcy's chair. The woman glanced at it and looked up, her face ashen.

"Where did you find these?"

"I think you know."

Marcy exploded to her feet and began to pace like a caged panther. "Damn it, Gwen, please tell me you didn't tamper with a crime scene!"

"Would you rather I left evidence incriminating Trudy?"

"Yes!" She whirled away, and her shoulders slumped. "No. But it doesn't matter what I think. If Trudy killed Kyle, you've just made both of us accessories after the fact."

"Do you honestly think Trudy is capable of stabbing a guy through the heart?"

"No, but I never expected to come home and find her trying to drag you into bed, either. She can't stand you."

"That's the cross I have to bear," Gwen murmured. "For what it's worth, I don't think Trudy killed Kyle."

"I don't either, but I trust the system to prove her innocence. You did, too, once upon a time."

"As in, before I was framed and pushed off the force?"

Marcy came back over and sat down across from her. "Gwen, I'm sorry as hell about what happened to you, and I won't argue that the justice system is infallible, but I can't ignore all the rules just because someone I care about is involved."

"And that's the problem: I'm involved. Walsh is gunning for

me. If he finds any connection at all between me and Trudy, you'd better believe the evidence will turn against her."

Marcy studied her face. "Walsh would do that? You're sure?"

"Very. He's involved with the people who held Tiger Leone's leash. They have something on Walsh—what, I haven't been able to find out. But I'm pretty sure he ordered the call that turned Tiger Leone onto Tom Yoland and Carmine Moniz the night Winston's was busted. Just last week, someone in vice set up a couple more cops who were looking into that mess. That didn't work. Now one of those cops is trying to work his way out of a murder frame-up."

"Can you prove any of this?"

"It may take a while. Until then, I'd like to keep Trudy out of the line of fire."

For a long moment, Gwen watched the struggle on Marcy's face. She felt as guilty as hell about dumping this on her friend, but she didn't see a better way to play it.

"What if Trudy . . ."

"One way or another, I'll find out who killed Kyle," Gwen said. "You have my word on that, by moon and star, wind and word."

Marcy looked puzzled. "What's all that about?"

"It means," Gwen said quietly, "that you can be extremely fucking certain the truth will come out."

Twenty

Gwen's phone rang as she emerged from the building.

"There's a problem at the safe house," Tamar announced.

The nun sounded more rattled than Gwen had ever heard her. "What happened?"

"It's Oscar, our English sheepdog. He was killed last night."

An unexpected wave of nausea roiled through Gwen even before Tamar's memories hit her. She swallowed bile and tried to blink away the image of a gutted sheepdog, his long fur matted with blood. She hadn't quite believed the tale the midwife told—at least, not until this moment.

"You're sure Erin didn't leave last night?"

"Absolutely. What does that have to do with Oscar?"

"Did anyone else leave?"

"Yes," Tamar said slowly. "We have another young mother here. Rita. She left earlier that evening, before you called. But she doesn't look anything like Erin—she's blond and a little plump."

"What about her kid?"

"A little girl, about four years old."

"Did the kid walk out with her mom?"

"No. She was sleeping and wrapped in a blanket. Rita carried her out. Where is this going?"

"Go check on Erin and call me back."

Gwen reached for the electronic gate opener clipped to her car's sun visor and pulled into Sylvia's drive. A green Civic followed her in. She recognized Jeff's car and groaned. The last thing she needed right now was a confrontation with an irate fuck buddy.

He came out of the car like a well-groomed thunderstorm and followed her into her office. "We need to talk."

The phone in Gwen's hand sounded, and she held up a finger to indicate Jeff should wait.

"Erin's here," announced Sister Tamar.

Her voice didn't sound any steadier than it had during her last call. "You're sure?"

"Yes! Why do you keep asking that?"

"What about the blond woman and her kid?"

"That's where things get strange. Rita came in shortly after you last called, only she didn't have her daughter with her."

"Was this before or after you checked on Erin?"

A long silence greeted her question. "Someday you're going to tell me what's going on."

"*Before* or *after?*"

"Shortly before."

Whatever Tamar said next was drowned out by a woman's scream, shortly followed by the sound of angry voices raised in accusation and protest.

"I've got to check on that," Tamar said.

"Call me back."

Gwen clicked off the phone and turned to Jeff. The cool-off time seemed to have done him some good. The expression on his face had dialed down from furious to merely agitated.

"You were saying?" she said resignedly.

Jeff pointed to the photo of Erin on Gwen's desk. "Who is that?"

She picked it up and handed it to him. "Someone I was hired to find. You know her?"

"No, but I've seen her around. A lot."

"Tell me."

Jeff put the picture down. "I saw her several times around the courthouse, near the office. Once or twice when I went out to lunch with Marcy, she'd be in the restaurant. I saw her once in the health club where Marcy and I worked out."

"Did you ever point this out to Marcy?"

His face turned red. Gwen caught on, and suppressed a smile. "You thought she was following you."

Jeff shrugged.

"Hey, it was a logical assumption, especially if she'd seen you in your racquetball shorts."

His grin was faintly sheepish. "Thanks. I guess. So she was following Marcy?"

"Well, since she was living with Marcy's ex-husband, that seems like a reasonable assumption. When did all this happen?"

"Not for a while. Four or five months ago. I haven't seen her since."

Gwen could understand why. If Erin was planning Kyle's death and needed someone to pin it on, she'd probably decided that Trudy was a better candidate than Marcy. Erin certainly wouldn't be the first among the Elder Folk to recognize and exploit a human weakness.

And they didn't stop with humans. Obviously Erin had made a point of learning about Marcy's friends. She knew enough about Gwen to sign up for her self-defense class. Quite likely, she knew a

few things about Gwen's friends—including Sister Tamar. All that
bullshit about protecting her half-breed son was a way to get into
Tamar's safe house. That gave her an airtight alibi for the time of
Kyle's death.

Gwen's phone rang again. "Put Erin on the line," she said by
way of greeting.

"I don't think that's a good idea," Tamar said. "She's extremely
upset."

"Let me guess: She woke up and went to check on her kid, and
found out that Rita's blond daughter was in the bed. Patrick is
nowhere to be found, but Rita denies leaving the safe house, much
less absconding with Patrick."

"How the hell did you know that?"

"Lucky guess. Put her on."

A ragged snuffle announced that the grieving mother was on the
line. "Nice touch with the dog," Gwen said softly. "You just had to
rub my nose in it, didn't you?"

"She took Patrick!" Erin wailed. "My baby's gone!"

"Go ahead—work the room. But listen carefully, bitch: You're
fucking my friends, and that's not allowed."

"What can you do about it?" Erin said tearfully.

"Don't worry. You'll be finding out soon."

She clicked off and dialed Damian's number. She'd called him
on the way to confront Trudy and asked him to help watch over
Tamar and her girls. There were other cops around, but Gwen
wasn't convinced she could trust any of them.

"Go," he said—his usual greeting.

"Erin Westland is about to leave the safe house. How soon can
you get there?"

"Can she do that?"

"Sister Tamar can't hold anyone against her will. Erin is about my size and age. Big blue eyes, long brown hair. Or she might look about thirty-five, with brown eyes. Hell, she could look like damn near anything."

"So I follow whoever leaves the safe house, and hope it's the right person. Is that the plan?"

"I wish I had a better one."

Jeff set the picture down on the desk. "You seem busy. I should let you get back to work."

"Thanks." When he didn't move, she raised an eyebrow. "And yet you're still here."

"What was in that stuff I mixed with the juice?"

She shoved both hands through her hair. "It's an herbal mix. Nothing chemical, no lasting harm. But it can be a strong aphrodisiac. You can believe me or not, but I didn't know what it was at the time."

He shook his head. "I don't know what to think. But I was out of it until nearly noon. How did you get up early to go to work?"

"I never went to sleep. After you conked out, I took a shower and left early."

"How is that possible?" he demanded. "That stuff affected you as much as it did me."

"Afraid not. Different metabolism. Listen, I don't have time to explain it right now." Since he didn't seem inclined to leave, Gwen headed for the door. He grabbed her arm and swung her back to face him.

"Make time."

The petulant, demanding expression on his face was all too familiar. Maybe the herbal tea made people act like possessive assholes, maybe it just fanned embers that had been banked and hidden. Gwen didn't know, but at the moment more pressing matters were demanding her attention.

"You were affected by the tea. I wasn't."

"That's impossible, you were a wild woman."

"That was all me that night. I usually dial it down with you."

"Oh."

He released her arm, and the stricken look on his face confirmed beyond question his ex-fuck-buddy status.

"Sorry about the hangover," she said. "I guess I'll see you around."

He mumbled something and left the office. Gwen dialed Marcy's home number on the way to her car.

"How is she?"

"Sleeping like the dead," Marcy said. "How long is that likely to last?"

"Until midmorning, at least. Call me as soon as she wakes up."

"Why? So the three of us can get our stories straight?"

Gwen let the sting fade a bit before responding. "I guess I had that coming."

The phone rang again almost as soon as she ended the call.

"Gwen, this is Shawna O'Riley. I'm at Providence Hospital. It's Damian."

"What happened?"

"They're not sure. He was hit in the chest with enough force to break two ribs. Fortunately he was wearing Kevlar."

"Smart man. How's he doing?"

"He's alive, and we're all grateful for that. Whatever hit him stopped his heart, but a good Samaritan gave him CPR and called an ambulance. He's in a lot of pain, but he's asking for you. Can you come down?"

"I'm on the way."

She made the drive to the hospital in a record eighteen minutes. A nurse directed her to the waiting room where the O'Riley clan gathered. There were at least a dozen of them, and they all looked up when she entered the room. The collective force of all those brown eyes set her back a step.

For the first time she understood what Ian meant when he said the Elder Folk gained strength in numbers. She wondered, briefly, what it would have meant to grow up with this kind of support.

Shawna rose and came over to her. "You won't be able to stay long. The doctor's only letting you in because he figures it's the only way Damian will behave."

Gwen smiled faintly and followed her down the corridor. Damian was propped up in bed, looking strangely pale for a Black man.

"Thanks, sis," he said. He winced, as if even that much talking was painful.

"Don't be long," Shawna warned. She backed out and shut the door softly.

Gwen leaned against the door and folded her arms. "Do you have any idea what hit you?"

"Could be wrong about this, but I think it was a motherfucking *arrow*. What's next? Twin motherfucking scimitars?"

"Take it easy. Did you see who shot you?"

"No. Judging from the angle, the dude was in the *trees*. I hear this *whoosh* and something long was coming down at me. Next thing I knew, that Forest guy from the sports bar was pouring something nasty down my throat."

So Ian was shadowing her friends now?

"Next time I see him, I'll kick him in the balls for you."

"Appreciate that. Though you should probably also thank him for saving my life."

"I'll be sure to pass along your regards. After I kick him."

"He left pretty fast. Probably took off after whoever shot me."

"That'd be my guess. Where was Erin Westland in all this?"

"Damned if I know. One minute I was watching the bitch, the next I was flat on my ass."

The door behind Gwen started to open. She moved away, and a middle-aged nurse came into the room. Her hair was seriously red—a color that was too bright to be anything but a home dye job, but she had the pale, freckled skin to lend credence to the basic color scheme.

"That's long enough," she told Gwen as she bustled over to the bed. "Officer O'Riley needs to rest."

"Don't you be coming over here with that needle," he warned the nurse.

"It'll help you sleep," she said soothingly.

"I sleep just fine. Back off, Freckles."

The nurse's face firmed in disapproval. "You promised to rest after you talked to your partner."

"You lose. She's not my partner."

"True story," Gwen confirmed. "You want Quaid down here?"

"Hell, no. What I want is for everyone to go home and get some sleep. Pass that along to the family, will you?"

"For what good it will do."

He glanced at the nurse. "Tell you what, Red. Go check on the family. Anyone who looks too wide awake, you feel free to go ahead and stick 'em."

The nurse huffed and sailed out of the room. Gwen grinned. "She likes you. I can always tell these things."

"Uh-huh. Why don't you use your powers for good, and go get me a couple bags of fries?"

Gwen glared at him. "Now that was just plain mean."

"Hey, when you're the one with your ass hanging out the back of a hospital gown, you get to take a few free shots."

His voice slurred a bit toward the end. Gwen crossed the room and dropped a kiss on the top of his head.

"Yeah, yeah. Go tell the rest of the family to go home," he mumbled.

Something opened in Gwen's heart, something that felt like a tight, empty fist relaxing its grip.

The rest of the family.

He might not remember it, but he'd said it. Better yet, Gwen was pretty certain that he meant it.

She quietly left the room and went to relay Damian's message to the O'Rileys. But the best part of it, she fully intended to keep for herself.

Twenty-one

By eleven o'clock the next morning, Gwen was back at Marcy's condo.

Trudy was awake, mostly sober, and very, very worried.

"So tell me what happened," Gwen said.

Trudy glanced at Marcy. She nodded.

"I don't remember going to Kyle's house," she began. "To be honest, I don't know exactly where it is."

"You've been stalking his wife for several months, and you never went to the house?"

"It's true," she insisted. "I know it's in East Greenwich, but I've never been there."

"How do you explain the hairs on Kyle's sweater?"

Trudy shook her head helplessly. "I wish I could."

"So tell me what you do remember."

"After my last class, I went shopping. I always go to the whole-food store, the one on Waterman?"

"I don't care. What then?"

"I ran into one of my students. We started talking. He offered to buy me a cup of tea."

Again with the tea, Gwen thought. "What's his name?"

"You know, I really should know that. But the new term just started, and I'm still putting names with faces."

"Okay, so what does this guy look like?"

"He'd be easy to pick out of a crowd. Very blond, very pretty."

Gwen began to get a very bad feeling. "And after the tea party?"

"I can't remember. I wasn't feeling well. I think he drove me home."

"Eventually," Gwen muttered. "Tell me this: Did you two talk about Marcy?"

Trudy nodded, looking thoroughly miserable. "He mentioned he'd seen her the other day with a man who matched Kyle's description."

"And how would this student recognize me, much less Kyle?" Marcy demanded.

"He saw the two of us together the night we went to the string quartet concert at Brown, and he remembered you," Trudy said miserably. "All he said about it was, 'I ran into a friend of yours the other day.'"

"I see," Marcy said coolly. "He made a casual remark, only you couldn't let it go. You kept at him until he coughed up a description you recognized as Kyle. For the record, I haven't seen him since the night I brought him over to talk to Gwen."

"I believe you," Trudy whispered.

"How very gratifying. Late, but gratifying nonetheless."

"Hold that thought," Gwen interjected. "Preferably until after I'm gone. Now, back to last night. What time did you and this guy meet up?"

Trudy thought about it. "The class was over at four, and I finished my shopping in about an hour. We went down to Angell Street afterward—"

"Who drove?"

"I did. My groceries were in the car. We got a cup of tea and chatted for a while."

"And in all this time, you never asked his name?"

Trudy massaged her temples with both hands. "I must have. It must have come up. I have no idea why I can't remember."

Gwen had a pretty good idea. Probably Adrian had some sort of hypnotic ability. What had he said in the apple orchard the other night? The Elder Folk had the ability to influence minds and behavior.

Come to think of it, maybe that wasn't one of Adrian's Qualities. Maybe it was something *all* the Elder Folk could learn to do. The idea was intriguing, and far too appealing for Gwen's peace of mind.

Fuck that. She didn't want that sort of power over people.

Why, then, did she immediately think about what had started when she'd been lip-locked with Ian Forest in Sylvia's garden? There was a darkness inside her, a disturbing energy that rippled just under the surface. When that third Quality came out, what would she become?

It occurred to her the questioning had gone on without her. With difficulty she tuned in on what Marcy was saying.

". . . and you said your groceries were in the car when you had tea with this student, who afterward drove you home."

"Yes," Trudy said hesitantly.

"So did someone bring the groceries up, or are they still in your car?"

Trudy shrugged helplessly.

"I don't pay that much attention to what's in the fridge, so I didn't notice a difference," Marcy said. "Where are your keys? I'll go down and check the car."

"Why does it matter?"

"It matters," Marcy told her grimly, "because it tells us whether or not he was in this apartment."

She rose and began to pace. "I know how you feel about the police department right now, Gwen, but it's time to bring someone in. If this man had something to do with Kyle's death, if he was at Kyle's house, he might have left prints. His fingerprints here could go a long way toward clearing Trudy."

"They won't find prints at Kyle's house," Gwen said.

Marcy stopped abruptly and turned to Gwen. "You didn't."

"I wanted to make sure things wouldn't get messy for Trudy."

"By destroying evidence that could lead to the real killer?" She dug both hands into her thick blond hair and gripped her head for a moment with an intensity that suggested it might otherwise explode.

She collected herself and turned cool gray eyes toward Gwen. "You used to cross lines from time to time, but you were all about finding answers and solving problems. If anyone suggested that you'd try to manipulate the situation, you would have ripped them a new one. What has happened to you?"

That was a fair question if Gwen ever heard one.

"I'm still looking for answers," she said slowly, "but I have good reason not to trust the conventional channels."

Marcy flopped into a chair and rubbed her eyes. "Do I want to know what you mean by 'unconventional channels'?"

"Probably not."

The attorney rose and walked to the door, picking up her purse on the walk. Without turning around she said, "I'm going to need some time to think about all this. And right now, I really need to be alone."

The door closed quietly behind her. A long moment of silence passed before Gwen glanced at Trudy and observed, "I never thought I'd see you and me on the same shit list."

That earned a sickly smile. "A shit-list sisterhood."

"Don't get carried away," Gwen cautioned. "I need your car keys."

Trudy made an impatient gesture. "I don't care about the groceries."

"Neither do I, but I need to check out the car. There's a chance I can find out something about this guy, and—"

Inspiration came suddenly, striking her dumb in midsentence. Gwen dug the keys to her Toyota out of the pocket of her leather jacket and tossed them on the coffee table.

"In fact, I need to take your car for a while. Here're my keys in case you need to go anywhere. But I'd recommend that you stay close to home."

"I've seen your car," Trudy grumbled. "How far could I go, anyway?"

Gwen paused at the door. "One more thing: that herbal tea you got from The Green Man? Throw it out."

"Why?"

"If I'm right, it's part of an elaborate setup. There's some serious shit in that tea, and you've been drinking it long enough to be hooked on it."

Indignation firmed the redhead's lips into a straight line. "That's ridiculous."

"Really? Have you had a cup yet this morning?"

"No . . ."

"And how are you feeling?"

She grimaced. "I could tell you precisely how I feel, but my mother raised me not to use those words."

"What were you thinking of doing as soon as I left?"

Trudy shrugged, conceding Gwen's point and dismissing it in one gesture. "So what? You always start your morning with coffee."

"Sure, but it doesn't affect my behavior. Look back over the past four or five months. You've changed. I've noticed it, and Marcy sure as hell has noticed."

"What did she say to you?"

"Knowing Marcy, a lot less than she said to you. I'll tell you what I've observed. You've gotten clingy, dependent, and paranoid. Not to mention edgy and moody and bitchy."

Trudy's shoulders slumped, and she looked down at her hands. "I haven't felt like myself," she admitted. "But I've been drinking the herbal tea and taking the supplements because that makes me feel better."

"Duh. Do you think people get turned on to addictive substances because they enjoy feeling like shit? But after a while you start needing it to feel normal, and needing a lot more to feel good."

"You make it sound like I'm some sort of junky," Trudy protested.

"Same shit, different tea bag."

Since it was apparent that Trudy wasn't completely convinced, Gwen went to the kitchen and started opening cupboards. She found the telltale boxes and poured the leaves into the garbage disposal, let the water and the disposal run until every last fleck was washed away. When she glanced up, the stricken look on Trudy's face proved that this instinct had been sound.

"What are you thinking?" Gwen asked. "Don't filter it."

Trudy shook her head in denial. "What you did right now—it doesn't really matter. It *shouldn't* matter."

"Then why do you look like your world just went down the drain along with that tea?"

Silent tears began to run down Trudy's pale cheeks. "What do I do?"

"The same thing any addict does. You acknowledge there's a problem—and I think you just did that—and you do what's necessary to beat it. We'll make sure you get through this."

"We? Are you so sure Marcy will come back?"

In all honesty, Gwen couldn't give the answer Trudy wanted. She crossed the room and crouched down in front of the woman's chair so that they were eye to eye.

"I'm going to introduce you to a friend of mine. Sister Tamar is very good at helping people find their way. You'll get through this. I'll be there with you, whether you want me or not. Although," she added, lifting one eyebrow, "judging by the other night, I think we've covered that pretty thoroughly."

Trudy flushed and covered her face with her hands. "I'm sorry, I'm sorry."

She dropped her hands suddenly, anger pushing aside embarrassment. "You're teasing me. I don't believe this. How can you joke about this? What kind of heartless bitch are you?"

Gwen rose, suppressing a grin. "Hey! I thought your mother taught you not to use words like that."

"My mother," Trudy said grimly, "never met you."

———

Trudy's white Lexus was parked in the lot across the street. Fancy car, with too many whistles and bells for Gwen's taste. It even had a navigation computer to show you how to get where you're going. She turned the key, and the engine responded with a welcoming purr.

As she suspected, the last destination was still on the navigation screen.

Adrian hadn't forgotten to erase the screen. He wasn't stupid, and neither was Erin. They were together now, and they wanted Gwen to find them.

Once again, Gwen was being manipulated in someone's deadly little game. It made her mad as hell, but she figured she might as well get used to it.

Because one thing was becoming abundantly clear: the Elder Folk—Gwen was starting to think of them as Effers, for more reasons than one—toyed with humans like malevolent cats playing with cornered mice, and they weren't all that different when it came to dealing with one another.

Twenty-two

Gwen followed the map on the navigation screen to an old brick warehouse in Pawtucket. She parked Trudy's car and walked around the building, checking for the best way in.

A narrow lot behind the building was empty but for a few discarded crates and a large elm tree. Remembering Damian's observation about the direction of the arrow that'd hit him, Gwen jumped up and caught the lowest branch. She swung herself onto the limb and began to climb.

The roof of the warehouse was oddly shaped—a long series of sawed-toothed triangles, each fronted by a pane of glass to let in light. She walked along the roof's edge until she found the broken pane.

She dropped to her stomach and peered in. Sure enough, the system of pipes and venting ducts provided enough handholds to take her across the ceiling to the narrow walkway that lined one side of the open room. From there, she could take stairs down to the main floor.

Gwen reached for the first pipe and gave it a tug to test its strength. It held, so she swung herself into the opening and began to move hand over hand toward the walk.

The room was eerily silent. The only sound was the faint creak of ancient pipes, and the skittering of tiny clawed feet as rats went about their business in unseen corners.

She dropped lightly onto the walkway. Her boots hit the scarred wooden planks with a ringing thud—a small sound, under most circumstances.

"Down here," called a familiar voice.

Gwen made her way cautiously down to the main floor. Behind a stack of crates she found Adrian Archer.

He sat on the floor, his face as pale as the visage of the dead woman in his arms. One trembling hand stroked her brown hair, over and over, as if to imprint this last tactile memory of her on his heart.

For a long moment Gwen studied the grim tableau. This was not at all what she'd expected to find. Erin wore a pale blue sweater, a color similar to that she'd worn in the photo Kyle had carried. It was now soaked with blood. There was a single hole in the sweater, directly over Erin's heart—a precise, killing stroke.

The same death wound Gwen had found on Kyle Radcliff. The same spot as the shot that had nearly killed Damian.

"Where is Patrick Radcliff?" she asked.

Adrian shook his head. "I have no idea. Erin must have made some arrangements for him, but she never told me what they were."

"I'm curious—did she know Patrick wasn't her son?"

He glanced up sharply. "What are you saying?"

"Erin raised a human baby. Her son was taken from her at birth. He's a changeling, just like his mother, and he's out there somewhere."

Grief flooded Adrian's face, removing any lingering doubts Gwen had about Patrick's paternity.

She crouched down on the floor and nodded toward the dead woman. "Why?"

Adrian tangled a strand of silky brown hair around his fingers. "Our Qualities vary greatly, both in type and power. Hers was a very special gift."

"The glamour."

"That's right. When that began to manifest during her adolescence, she was brought in. Willingly she came, glad to be among people like herself. She was relocated quite some distance away. After a time, she disappeared. I was sent to find her. We didn't expect her to return to the same area she'd known during her early life. By the time I found her, she had already made contact with others."

"Wallace Earl Edmonson."

"That's correct. He was intrigued by her gift and offered her a place in his business. By the time I arrived, she had already started to use her own products."

"So? I thought that didn't affect Elder Folk."

"It doesn't. It shouldn't," he corrected grimly. "But Erin became addicted to the herbs she sold, and she knew what that meant."

"Tell me."

"The Elders are very concerned about keeping the bloodlines pure. If someone starts displaying human traits or weaknesses, he disappears. Erin knew this. For some time, she has been getting ready to disappear on her own terms."

"Her husband has a record of violence. She hoped her disappearance would be blamed on him. And she had him killed to make that trail harder to follow."

Adrian responded with a grim smile. "She was right. No one will find Kyle Radcliff's true murderer."

"I think I just did."

"It doesn't matter," he murmured.

"Oh, I think it does. A friend of mine was set up to take the fall, and that's not going to happen."

He shrugged as if that, too, didn't matter, and turned his attention back to Erin's still face. "She was so lovely, and so very clever. I couldn't bear to see that oaf lay a hand on her. She knew that. She provoked him into striking her, knowing that I would see, knowing how I would respond."

Gwen watched as he stroked her hair. "She manipulated you into killing for her. You don't seem too upset about that."

"Why should I be? The man's death means nothing to me."

She had no idea what to say to that. After a moment, she told him, "I'm going to take you in."

Adrian looked up sharply. "You're talking as if you're still a member of the police force."

"Ever hear of a citizen's arrest?"

"You can't do that, either. I've explained why. My death will be yours, as well."

She rose to her feet and pulled her gun. "I'll take my chances."

The blond man carefully laid Erin Westland aside, his movements slow and tender. He was on his feet almost faster than Gwen's eyes could follow.

She fired, point-blank.

The pain in her ears was immediate and excruciating. The sound of the gunfire echoed back to her in short, sharp stabs, as if she'd fired in a bank vault.

Then Adrian plowed into her, knocking her flat onto her back. She fired again, but her arms were flung out wide and the shot rang harmlessly off into the empty warehouse.

He seized both of her hands and dragged them up over her head. He slammed her gun hand against the floor with numbing force. Gwen felt the crack of small bones, and nothing else. She tried to flex her fingers around her weapon but had no idea whether they were closing on steel or empty air.

She'd be willing to bet on the latter.

"How are you still alive?" she demanded.

Her question must have been spoken aloud, because Adrian sent her an arrogant smile. His lips moved for several seconds, but lip-reading wasn't among her skills, and all she could make out was the word "Qualities."

It wasn't possible that Adrian could stop a bullet. Was it? She knew that some people, some humans, had a stronger energy field than others. Frank Cross had never been able to wear a wristwatch—the damn things always stopped whenever he put them on. Was it possible that Adrian could generate an energy field with a stopping power that was greater than Kevlar? She wouldn't have thought so, but for two things: the man pinning her to the floor should be dead, and a high-pitched ringing in her head was starting to take the place of stunned silence. She wouldn't have been deafened by the sound of a bullet plowing into a vest.

Gwen gathered her thoughts and focused all of her energy into a single move, twisting her body under his. He winced as her shoulder slammed into his chest, but he didn't loosen his grip on her wrists.

He pushed her back down on the floor and shifted his weight, pressing his knees between hers and forcing her legs apart. In another too-quick-to-follow move, he lifted himself into a kneeling position and slammed one knee up between her legs.

White-hot pain seared though Gwen's lower body, as she knew it would. Any woman who thought only men could be hurt by a shot to the groin had never taken a direct hit. Back in juvenile hall, she'd taken a couple of shots and given back a few of her own. She knew only too well what it could do.

So did Adrian. He moved off her, confident that she would be out of the fight for a while.

Gwen curled up on her left side, breathing in shallow puffs and willing the pain to subside enough for her to finish this.

As Adrian kicked her gun well out of the way, she inched her hand into the pocket of her jeans and drew out Trudy's keys. There were three on the ring: car, house, and probably mailbox. She worked them in her palm so that a key protruded from between each of the fingers of her left hand. That was a slight problem. Naturally ambidextrous as a young child, she'd been pushed into favoring her right hand. It would probably be a good long while before she'd be able to pick up anything with her gun hand, but her left hand would have to do.

Andrian reached down and seized the wrist of her right hand and dragged her to her feet.

Gwen came up swinging.

Her roundhouse punch connected with his cheekbone with enough force to snap his head to one side. The three keys raked across his face, carving deep, bloody furrows. As the Lexus key slid over his eye, there was a wet, sickening release. The key punched deep into the eye socket.

Adrian screamed and fell from her, clutching at his bleeding face.

Gwen willed herself to deliver a kick that would end the fight. But the room spun around her, and she was none too steady on her too-high heels.

She dropped to her knees, which in her opinion was better than falling on her face, and punched straight out from her left shoulder.

Again the makeshift weapon sank deep into flesh, and again her opponent shrieked in agony. Gwen rolled to one side to avoid his falling body.

She came up in a crouch, ready to throw herself back into the fight. But Adrian was finished.

Gwen waited until a soft groan announced his return to consciousness.

"You killed Erin," she said quietly.

He carefully pushed himself up into a sitting position, grimaced with pain at every move. "I've known for a long time that I would have to."

"But you were putting it off. Why?"

"Because I loved her," he replied simply. "And because she was the mother of my child."

"You didn't know that Patrick wasn't yours? That your son is out there somewhere, a changeling growing up with humans?"

"No. I had no idea." His eyes held hers imploringly. "Find him. You have to find him."

"Oh, I plan on it."

"Swear it to me that you will restore him to our people. Swear it by the most powerful oath known to you."

"Forget it," Gwen said flatly. "I'm not promising anything until I have a better idea what I'd be getting the kid into."

"Surely he'd be better off among his own kind than among the human rabble!"

"Yeah? Was Erin? Would her adoptive parents have sent a hit man after her if someone decided she wasn't quite talented enough?"

"It is more complicated than you're trying to make it."

"I'll bet it is. If you guys get all Master-Race anal about these fucking Qualities, how do you deal with physical imperfection?"

Adrian sent her a hate-filled glare. "You have not quite unmanned me. I will heal."

"I'm not talking about you, asshole. Erin's son was born with an extra toe. Bet the big boys aren't going to be too happy about that shit."

Horror and revulsion filled his eyes. "You're saying the child was imperfect?"

"That's what I'm saying, all right. Still want me to find him?"

"There's no need," he said dully.

"Why?" she persisted. "Because you don't want to acknowledge a son with a minor birth defect? Or because you know that kids like him wouldn't be allowed to grow up?"

His glare sent a wave of ice shivering down her spine and raised goose bumps on her arms. It was quite simply the purest embodiment of evil Gwen had ever seen.

"You are the most damnably curious thing I have ever encountered that didn't meow and chase mice," he hissed. "It gives me some small measure of satisfaction to know that you will go to your death tormented by a hundred unanswered questions."

Gwen glanced around pointedly. "It's just you and me, pal, and I don't think you're up to dealing death at the moment."

"You're still determined to turn me in to the human authorities?"

"Damn straight."

"Then your intention has sealed your death. The rest is simply a matter of time."

Gwen gestured to Erin Westland's body. "Why are so you worried about being arrested? You've already bought yourself a certain death by killing her."

"Not if you're a Black Arrow."

Something flashed in his eyes, something dark and shining with malice. Gwen understood the impulse that prompted that look—understood it far better than she wanted to. Adrian Archer knew that he was dead, and he was going to inflict as much pain on her as he could while he was still alive.

Conflicting impulses raged through her. On one hand, she burned to end this, to silence his taunts. But as he'd pointed out, there was so much she needed to know.

"I'll bite. What's a Black Arrow?"

"An assassin, sanctioned by the Elder Council to mete out punishments duly approved by the royal court."

Gwen's head swam with the implications. The Elder Folk had a royal house? With their own branch of assassins? What the hell *were* these people?

His smirk celebrated her dismay, and his eyes shone with eagerness to deliver the next blow.

"Let's hear it," she said.

"Your parents were not killed in the car crash. Oh, they were definitely in bad shape when I found them, but they were still very much alive. I killed them both, as I was ordered to do. I killed the baby, too, even though that wasn't part of my assignment. And why not? It was pleasurable at the time, and all the more so now, having met you. Would you like to know precisely how the *real* Gwenevere Gellman died?"

Gwen leaped at him in a sudden rush that sent them both rolling to the floor. She straddled his body and gripped his throat with both hands. Pain seared up her right forearm. Gwen ignored it and tightened her grip, then shook him hard enough to thump his head painfully against the floor.

"Who gave that order? And why? What did my parents do?"

"So curious," he said with malevolent satisfaction. "So many unanswered questions."

Something in his smile changed, something in his eyes telegraphed his intention. Gwen caught the glint of metal in her peripheral vision and dived to one side.

A thick ripping sound followed her as her ancient leather jacket took one final scar. Fire seared across her lower back as she kept rolling, leaving a trail of blood on the warehouse floor.

She scrambled to her feet. Incredibly, Adrian did the same. He came at her in a rush, knife held high.

Gwen dashed toward him and seized his wrist with both hands before he could begin the downward slash. She pushed his hand higher and slammed her body into his. He grunted in pain from the impact.

She twisted hard, putting her back to him while still holding onto his wrist, and continued the motion to bend sharply at the waist.

Adrian flew over her and landed hard on his back. Air wheezed out of his lungs in a powerful, painful gust.

Gwen let go of his wrist and danced out of reach. But he kicked out hard, deftly hooking one of her booted feet.

She went down, and suddenly Adrian was on top of her. He lifted the knife high.

Again she seized his wrist. They struggled and rolled, fighting for ascendancy.

Suddenly Adrian went limp, leaving Gwen atop him, their hands entangled around the hilt of the knife.

"I know who killed Frank Cross," he said. Then he tugged down hard, pulling the knife into his heart.

Gwen rose and stood over the bodies for a long time, wondering what the hell to do with them. If she called the police, she was as good as dead. On this matter, if no other, she believed Adrian told the truth.

She could call Ian Forest. He was very, very good at making bodies disappear. But how would he react if she told him she had two Effing bodies ready for disposal? Ian had been pretty gung-ho about getting rid of Edmonson for killing Elder Folk, and it was possible he would take the same view here. Sure, he seemed very interested in getting into her pants, and he seemed to take his role as mentor seriously, but what did that mean? Hell, Adrian had loved Erin Westland, but that didn't stop him from putting an arrow through her heart.

Who, then?

An echo of Jason Cross's words, so unexpected at the time and so deeply felt, came to her mind: *I can live with that.*

She pulled her cell phone out of the pocket of her coat and dialed his number.

Twenty-three

Gwen and Jason stood on a hill overlooking the farm in Smithfield. A waning moon shone overhead, but whatever power it held over Gwen was lost in the welter of emotions that stormed through her.

"I still can't believe you agreed to help me do this," she murmured.

Jason turned his calm brown eyes to her. "Like the old saying says, 'A good friend will help you move; a *great* friend will help you move a body.'"

A reluctant smile tugged at the corners of her lips. "Who said that? Mark Twain or Oscar Wilde?"

He smiled, remembering the reference to an early conversation. "It's usually one or the other."

She reached for his hand, and their fingers entwined. "Seriously, why are you doing this?"

"Those visions of yours were pretty convincing. You showed me enough to make me glad the two people we buried under those trees are no longer among the living."

"Is it really that simple for you?"

A bleak expression flickered across his face. "Nothing is simple,

Gwen. I believe what I saw because I know a few things about visions. You know that my mother was part Narragansett?"

"Sure. Frank mentioned that."

"I've always been deeply interested in that part of my heritage, and I've studied some of the old ways. I know holy men and women who seek visions through meditation aided by drumming or dancing."

"Or mushrooms?"

"Different tradition," he said. "But I've seen people in a vision state, and I've had a few of my own. Yours are different from any I've experienced. I don't know anyone else who is powerful enough to share a vision with another."

"So you believe what I told you."

"Yes. And I believe what you did was right."

"Don't you want to know why I have visions like that?"

He sent her a faint smile. "I figure that you and I are truly related. We probably have a common ancestor a few generations back."

"That's a nice thought," Gwen said.

"You've heard of a sport? I'm not talking about a physical activity like baseball and football, but a genetic throwback. Perhaps you're a sport of some powerful shamanic line."

"It's something to think about," she said.

He gave her hand a squeeze, then released it. "Are you ready to do this?"

She nodded and reached into the pocket of her new leather jacket for a book of matches.

The first spark flared into the night. Gwen stooped and touched it to the straw they'd carefully scattered among the trees—straw that had been soaked in highly flammable insecticide.

They watched in silence as fire snaked out through the orchard, branching out in every direction like rows of flaming dominoes. Gwen's throat clenched as the flames crept up into the apple trees. The hiss and groan the moist branches made as they burned sounded like the death cries of living beings.

In moments, the entire orchard was engulfed. And with it, the sole crop of the herb—the cruel toy that had caused so much misery.

"We need to go now," Jason said.

Gwen followed him down the hill and into a nearby wooded area. They'd hidden two bicycles there near a narrow dirt trail. No one would see a vehicle leave the area, and they would be on the other side of the woods before anyone responded to the fire. From there, it was a short walk to the small motel where they'd rented a room earlier that evening.

It wasn't a bad plan, but Gwen felt no great satisfaction over the work they'd done. She couldn't wait to collapse on the motel bed, and to seize a few hours of respite from the questions that had come to dominate her every waking hour.

Ian Forest slipped from his hidden place among the trees, escaping a single heartbeat before the apple tree caught fire.

He moved away from the rapidly spreading flames, keeping just beyond the light of the fire. And at the edge of the orchard, he watched as the traitorous Jason Cross linked hands with the elf girl who could either save or destroy her exiled people.

Ian was certain that he would hear nothing of this night's events from the human agent. Obviously Jason Cross was not so committed to Edmonson and his successors as Salvadore Anselm seemed to think.

Or was he?

It was no secret that Ian had resented his service to Edmonson and disagreed with the earl's mode of doing business. But the fact that he had been returned to Edmonson's service seemed to indicate that he had been forgiven his old indiscretion:

Sylvia Black.

A lovely woman with an almost elflike capacity for passion, she was one of those rare humans who possessed a quality that drew Elder Folk to her. The old stories of elves and humans falling in love had some basis in truth. Ian had come very close to losing his heart. He had come closer still to losing his Qualities.

Oh yes, he had reason to know the dangers of ties that bound the Elder Folk too tightly to their human companions. He was determined to keep Gwen from following the same dangerous path. If Jason Cross wished to destroy Gwen, this was one way to do so.

Her sexual adventures meant nothing. There were many ways to toy with humans. But Gwen was capable of deep loyalties, and her ties to the humans were strong.

She not only had friends—she had family.

The young magus had accepted Gwen's true identity almost without question. That alone would have raised concern, but Damian O'Riley had entrusted his family problems to Gwen, and had come to treat her almost like a sister. And Sylvia Black had all but adopted her.

With such chains holding her back, how would her starlight Quality emerge?

And if they did not, what would become of her?

Of all of them?

———

Jason waited until Gwen's soft, steady breathing assured him that she was deeply asleep. He picked up his backpack and slipped from the room, taking the route through the bathroom window they'd used twice before that night.

He made his way into the woods, moving away from the path they'd taken earlier and in the opposite direction of the orchard he had helped to destroy. And with every step, his heart grew heavier.

He came to a small clearing, a circle of bare earth deeply sheltered by vine-covered trees. A scattering of stones in the center obscured the fire he had built the last time he came to this place.

Jason dropped his backpack to the ground and arranged the stones in a circle. He placed some dry wood inside and lit the fire. When it was burning steadily, he settled down beside it and started unpacking.

Under the clothes he'd packed for tomorrow was a small wooden drum. He tightened the hide and began to tap a soft, rhythmic pattern.

His hands repeated the pattern over and over, until it became a soft sea of rhythm that carried him away on its rise and fall. He was barely aware when the pattern began to change, adding new rhythms that carried him deeper into hidden places within his own heart.

Much later, Jason emerged slowly from his trance, like a swimmer coming up from great depths. He was not surprised to see that the small fire had long ago burned itself out, or to note that his limbs were cold and stiff from long inactivity.

It was no easy thing, this strengthening of his shields against the elven magics.

He had told Gwen nothing but the truth—if not quite all of the truth. He had been raised by a shaman, a wisewoman who came from a long line who guarded the knowledge that elves existed. For all his life, he had known it was his task to walk among them. To learn their ways, and undo their plans.

And, ultimately, to find a way to destroy them all.

Shortly before dawn, Ian Forest stepped out of the shadows of a stand of birch trees near an old blue farmhouse. He took a moment to regard his surroundings. Small, neat fields were tucked among rows of fruit trees, the rich soil heaped into long mounds over newly planted seeds. A greenhouse held rows of seedlings that would soon be ready to plant outside. The pretty farm was framed by a majestic sweep of mountains, the tallest of which was still crowned with snow.

Spring had come late to Vermont this year.

The barn held quite a fine assortment of equipment. The delivery truck was nearly new, as was the small car parked beside it. And best of all, there was a long ladder that would be perfect for his purposes.

Ian circled around behind the farmhouse and easily dispatched the lock on the back door. He slipped inside, making his way through the bottom floor and up a narrow flight of stairs. The house was furnished with very nice antiques, and bowls of fresh flowers scented every room he passed.

The elves had paid this particular agent very well.

He found the woman's bedroom and walked soundlessly in. He seized the collar of her nightgown with both hands and dragged her up into a sitting position.

She awoke with a sound that was part gasp, part shriek. Her eyes focused on Ian's face, and surprise chilled into terror.

He released her and stepped away, sending her a faint smile. "If I had wanted you dead, why would I have bothered to awaken you?"

"For sport," she hissed at him.

"Well, yes, there is that," he said agreeably. "But I assure you, this visit is entirely about business."

The woman shook her head emphatically. "I'm out of that business," she told him. "You told me the Morgan baby would be my last job."

"So I did." Ian hooked his thumbs in his pockets and leaned back against the dresser. "Of course, I have been known to lie when the occasion demands."

"What do you want?"

"I understand you received an interesting phone call recently."

Fear edged into her eyes. "I didn't tell her anything."

"In truth, I believe you told her entirely too much. And I don't believe I can trust you with the information about our changelings' whereabouts."

"I'd never tell that! Can you imagine the trouble I'd be in if I admitted to switching babies?"

"Can you imagine the trouble you are already in?"

He waited until that idea took hold, until the knowledge of her coming death blazed in her eyes.

The force of his blow snapped her head sharply to one side. Bone gave way with a brittle crack, and the changeling midwife slumped lifeless to the bed.

Ian opened the dresser drawers and removed the sort of clothing one might expect a woman to wear as she went about the business of running a farm and household. Dressing her was an unpleasant necessity, but the local authorities would hardly believe that she fell off a ladder in her nightgown.

When the agent's body was ready, Ian slung her over his shoulder and carried her out behind the house. He dropped her to the ground and went back to the garage for the ladder. This he placed against the house, near the tallest window. He tossed a pail of soapy water and a kitchen rag to the ground to complete the deception.

The task completed, Ian returned to the circle of birch trees and stepped into the shadows. If he hurried, he could check on his youngest changeling before the sun crested the Vermont foothills.

Epilogue

Ian Forest stood with Salvadore Anselm on the edge of the sea cliff, admiring the view—and pondering the temptation. The man he'd joined forces with to oust Edmonson had not proved to be much of an improvement.

But at least they were in agreement on two things. They believed they were better off without the potent herb, and they were furious that the council had seen fit to send a Black Arrow assassin into their territory.

"Dominance and control," Anselm summarized. "That is why we traffic in such human vices as sex and drugs. Edmonson lost sight of the central purpose, and Erin Westland was a pathetic weakling. Distribution, much less use, is beneath us. We don't *become* Tiger Leones, we *use* them."

"For that matter, what purpose is there in controlling the weak? Better to concentrate on those in positions of power, tools with a purpose."

Anselm smirked. "No doubt this is your segue to the Captain Walsh report?"

"In a manner of speaking. Would it interest you to know that Jason Cross did not eliminate a single link between Edmonson and Walsh?"

"He killed the doctor, did he not?"

Ian shook his head. "Gwen's visions are growing in power. She visited Kate Myers's home a second time and learned the truth of what happened there. Adrian Archer tormented the woman, like a wicked child pulling wings off flies, but he did not kill her. Walsh did."

"Ah. And now that we know this, and assuming we can convince him of this knowledge, there is little chance that Walsh will betray our interests."

"That is my reasoning, yes."

"Well done." Anselm toed a stone loose and watched it fall into the surf below. "A shame your methods were not quite so successful where our changeling is concerned. We have less hold over her than the humans do. Her 'family' is thriving."

"How so? Her mentor is dead, her young protégé is in the hospital, her most recent partner will be tried for Kate Myers's murder. Even Erin Westland's bungling attempts to shift the blame for her husband's murder have borne fruit. Gwen alienated Marcy Bartlett, her closest friend, when she tampered with a crime scene to protect Marcy's lover. Thanks to her emerging Qualities, she has alienated two casual lovers in as many weeks. Other than an aging, foul-mouthed nun, where can Gwen turn?"

"To Jason Cross," Anselm said gloomily. He shot a resentful look in Ian's direction. "I will admit that your judgment concerning the man was sound. We may have a problem in Jason."

The smile that crossed Ian's face was that of an angel contemplating paradise. "A problem," he said softly, "that can easily be resolved."